A MURDEROUS MIND

Recent Titles by Jane A. Adams from Severn House

The Naomi Blake Mysteries

MOURNING THE LITTLE DEAD
TOUCHING THE DARK
HEATWAVE
KILLING A STRANGER
LEGACY OF LIES
SECRETS
GREGORY'S GAME
PAYING THE FERRYMAN
A MURDEROUS MIND

The Rina Martin Mysteries

A REASON TO KILL
FRAGILE LIVES
THE POWER OF ONE
RESOLUTIONS
THE DEAD OF WINTER
CAUSE OF DEATH
FORGOTTEN VOICES

A MURDEROUS MIND

A Naomi Blake Novel

Jane A. Adams

This first world edition published 2015
in Great Britain and 2016 in the USA by
SEVERN HOUSE PUBLISHERS LTD of
19 Cedar Road, Sutton, Surrey, England, SM2 5DA.
Trade paperback edition first published
in Great Britain and the USA 2016 by
SEVERN HOUSE PUBLISHERS LTD

British Library Cataloguing in Publication Data

Adams, Jane, 1960- author.
  A murderous mind. – (A Naomi Blake mystery)
  1. Blake, Naomi (Fictitious character)–Fiction.
  2. Ex-police officers–Fiction. 3. Blind women–Fiction.
  4. Murder–Investigation–Fiction. 5. Cold cases
  (Criminal investigation)–Fiction. 6. Detective and
  mystery stories.
  I. Title II. Series
  823.9'2-dc23

ISBN-13: 978-0-7278-8563-0 (cased)
ISBN-13: 978-1-84751-672-5 (trade paper)
ISBN-13: 978-1-78010-728-8 (e-book)

All Severn House titles are printed on acid-free paper.

Severn House Publishers support the Forest Stewardship Council™ [FSC™],
the leading international forest certification organisation.
All our titles that are printed on FSC certified paper carry the FSC logo.

Typeset by Palimpsest Book Production Ltd.,
Falkirk, Stirlingshire, Scotland.
Printed and bound in Great Britain by
TJ International, Padstow, Cornwall.

PROLOGUE

Outside of his professional life, he mostly slipped through the world unobserved. Unless he chose to be noticed, it was usual for people either to ignore him or, if he did impinge upon their consciousness, to forget him almost immediately. 'Ordinary' most would have said had anyone asked. 'Just an ordinary man'. Not tall, not especially short. Dark hair, maybe? Perhaps greying? Eyes of an indeterminate colour – unless he decided to wear his contact lenses, of course, then they might be blue or brown or, on the odd occasion, even green. In his professional life, of course, there existed a very different state of affairs. He was regarded as an authority on his subject and engaging, even charismatic in his presentation.

This odd duality served his purpose admirably. To spend so much of his life in near invisibility and the rest valued and feted. From time to time, however, in that outside, ordinary world someone did take note of him. He *registered* on their consciousness in a way that somehow puzzled, frightened or intrigued them.

He was always fascinated by these few. By those who *really* noticed him, who recognized him – no, that wasn't quite right; who seemingly recognized what he really *was*.

They always regretted it, of course. The old woman down in Colchester, who'd looked up from her tea and cakes and gossiping friends and had stared so hard at him. Looked him inside and out – just as he had later, turning her dead body out on to her bedroom carpet.

The man who had bumped into him in the supermarket car park. Any other time and a quick apology would have swept the incident aside. But this one hurried on only to turn and look and then look again and in his gaze there had been recognition and a degree of fear. The man had understood that he had just encountered a predator and that had been enough to bring vengeance down upon his head.

Then there had been the girl. She'd been one of the early ones. He held the memory of her in his mind, folded like a treasure in the soft sheets of a little, pink bed. Fresh washed, the sheets had been, the scent of powder and softener still clinging to them, filling his nose as he laid her down. He had turned her over, pressed her face hard into the pillow so her last breath would be sweet and fragrant, imbued with the scent of artificial flowers and soft soap. Her death earned by the chance act of her asking if he could change a fiver so she had money for the phone. In the days before everyone and their dog carried a mobile. She needed coins to feed the bright red box so she could call her mother and ask for a lift, the town being dark and the last bus gone and her friends off with the new boys they had just picked up in the bar.

She had *noticed* him. That was the thing. Of all the people she might conceivably have asked, she had chosen him and once she had chosen him she had been frightened by her own judgement. Had started to apologize, to back away and say that it didn't matter. That her friends were waiting for her inside the club – despite the fact that he'd seen her exit with them only minutes before and she had waved them a reluctant goodbye. She had noticed him, selected him and he in turn had selected her.

There had been others, of course, both before and since and of course there had been those that chance or circumstance had denied him. And it was a rule of his; if the fates intervened, then he left well alone. He never rode his luck the way some did.

Most recently there had been the boy. Now he wasn't exactly one that got away so much as one that from the start would be denied. The boy had spotted him one day as he walked through town. Had noticed him again when he'd followed the object of his curiosity into a local café. The boy had looked at him again with those puzzled, analytical eyes and there had been no fear, this time, only knowledge. Recognition. And he had been so sorely tempted. Such a one as this would be a precious treasure indeed.

But he had resisted, not because of any sense of self-restraint but because he knew that this one had already been chosen. He was protected. He was already owned. And there were some people that you did not cross. Some that *he,* in his turn did not want to be noticed by.

But the experience had not been wasted. The boy had led him to his new interest. A new girl as fresh and blonde and neat as the first one he had taken from this little town all those years before. As appealing as the girl who had needed coins so she could use the phone. This new girl had come into the café with a group of others and they had seated themselves close beside the boy who interested him so much. It was clear that these were not close friends, that their meeting had more to do with necessity than real choosing. Books were produced and laid out on the little round tables, notes taken and exchanged and, as he moved to a closer table so he could listen in, he had realized that this little group was arranging some group project or other. An assignment that required cooperation and division of labour. He was amused by the good-natured arguments over who should go to the library and who should take pictures of the bridge over the main road. The boy said little, seemingly content for the others to assign tasks and taking what was left.

The blonde girl suddenly got up and to his surprise, she approached the table where he sat nursing his cup of coffee.

'Mind if I take some sugar?' she asked. 'There's none left on our table.'

He nodded and pushed the little brushed steel pot towards her. She took three packs.

'Thanks,' she said, then turned away with a bright smile.

He held his breath. Waited. Had that been an end to it he would have kept to his rules, left well alone, deselected her. But as she sat back down she glanced at him again. A swift but appraising look, another automatic smile, a gaze that lingered too long and with too much, almost flirtatious, interest but it sealed her fate. She had noticed him. She would remember. She was now his chosen one.

ONE

When the New Year dawned uneventfully, Naomi dared to hope that it would be a peaceful one – if only in comparison to the one just passed. Frankly, she was glad to see the back of the previous year.

Alec seemed more settled now and had even enrolled in a couple of evening classes. He was still no nearer deciding what he wanted to do with his life post police force, but he was at least doing something and for that, Naomi was deeply grateful even if she wasn't convinced that his choice of evening activity – creative writing on a Tuesday and pottery on a Thursday would hold his attention for very long. Her old friend Harry just suggested she let him be and don't fuss.

'Find something you'd like to do too,' he suggested. 'Get yourself out. You've spent the last six months cooped up and worried. It's time you had some fun.'

He was right, Naomi conceded. Both she and Alec had a lot to put behind them. The death of friends, the threat of violence, the car crash that had nearly taken Alec's life. It was a lot to come to terms with. And Harry was probably right about allowing Alec some slack; she'd fussed enough for a lifetime, never mind a twelvemonth and it really was time to let go and focus her fussing elsewhere. But what did she actually want to do? Neither of Alec's choices really appealed; she considered the writing option impossible, unless she took someone along with her to take notes, or she took her laptop with the voice input software. And pottery just seemed too messy. It had been Patrick, Harry's eighteen-year-old son who finally came up with an alternative.

'He's always wanted to learn to dance,' Patrick said. 'Why don't the pair of you find a class? Really, Naomi, he could do with the exercise and losing a bit of weight.'

Naomi laughed at the idea. 'Great, Patrick. Just one small thing. I can't see what the dance teacher shows us. Small matter of being blind, remember.'

She couldn't actually see his shrug, but she could hear it in his voice. 'If you get a good teacher, I'm sure you can get around that. Dad said you did some when you were younger anyway, so I'm sure you'll pick it up again.'

Naomi smelled a set-up. 'You and Harry have already talked about this?'

'Yeah, well just a bit. I mean I can hardly go along with him, can I?'

Much against her better judgement Naomi had agreed to give it a try, on condition that they found the right teacher, only to discover that Patrick and Harry had already made some enquiries.

'She says it's not something she's done before,' Patrick said. 'But she and her partner are willing to give it a go if you are. Soo . . .'

Naomi gave in. Secretly, she was always buoyed up by the way Patrick and Harry just seemed to assume she could do anything if she put her mind to it. And, she thought, it might be fun. She had taken up Latin dance in her teens and learnt it for about three years. She'd never been brilliant, but it had been good exercise and, as Patrick suggested, she could remember a bit of what she'd done.

Patrick and Harry's rather cavalier attitude to what others saw only as her disability put her in mind of another she had come to call friend and who had a very similar – maybe even more extreme – disregard for things she couldn't do. Gregory had been in touch over the Christmas period, sending a card and a small gift and phoning them on New Year's Eve to wish them the blessings of the season. Occasional texts and a post-card from Aberdeen had followed. Naomi found she thought of him often and of the younger man that Gregory currently had charge over, having nursed Nathan back to health after he had taken two bullets and almost been lost to them. Naomi didn't know Nathan so well but circumstances had conspired to bring strangers together and now those strangers were part of what Naomi considered extended family – though maybe the kind that no one talked about, or at best discussed in hushed whispers when the children or the more respectable members couldn't overhear.

Harry and Naomi had their first dance lesson on the first Tuesday in the New Year, roughly at the same time Alec went to learn to wrangle words. Ninety minutes later and Naomi was hooked. She had held her own in a class of both beginners and those who had started to learn back in the autumn term and despite the difficulties – Harry having to interpret what the teacher was showing them – and sore toes, there had been moments when Naomi had remembered how to perform basic steps. Brief instances where she had even been able to direct Harry and one very precious minute where the teacher had called upon her class to 'look at what Naomi's doing. That's what you're aiming for.'

She had practically floated up the stairs to her flat when Harry dropped her home after that first class and dancing had now become a weekly pleasure. Tonight had been no exception. She'd struggled a bit with some new steps, but so had the rest of the class and the resultant almost childish giggling had lifted her spirits.

Alec, as usual, turned up about twenty minutes later.

'You look happy,' he said. 'You had a good time?'

'Wonderful,' she said. 'You?'

'Yes, I think so. I read out that poem I'd been working on and got some good feedback. I think I might look for something different next term, but it's been an interesting experience. There's a conversational Italian starting in the same slot. Thought that I might give that a go.'

Naomi laughed. 'Does that mean we ought to plan a holiday? You know, try it out?'

'It's not a bad idea,' Alec said. He bent to fuss Napoleon, Naomi's large black guide dog. 'Did you get to watch, old man? How did she do, then?'

'He wouldn't know,' Naomi said. 'He went to sleep. I could hear him snoring.'

Alec laughed. 'Very sensible,' he said. 'I don't mind admitting, I'm tired. I've got out of the habit of using my brain. I'm hungry too.'

They ordered takeaway and settled in front of the television waiting for it to arrive. It's going to be all right, Naomi dared to whisper to herself as Alec went to answer the door. She could hear him chatting to the delivery man and he sounded so much more like his old self. We're going to get through this.

All they needed now, she thought, was a bit of peace and quiet, time to work out what they both wanted from what she was starting to think of as their new lives. Their old ones – the police, responsibilities, anxiety, shed like so much dead skin. Now it was time to start over.

Naomi closed her eyes, her sighted habits still surfacing when she was stressed or even just remembering past worry. Please let everything be OK now, Naomi whispered, not really praying but putting the thought out there for anyone that might conceivably be listening.

Alec bustled through. She heard him in the kitchen, rattling plates and dishing up their supper, chatting to Napoleon who thought that as his people were getting an extra meal maybe he should be entitled as well. She found her thoughts turning to Gregory and wondered where he was right now. How he was. What this year might bring for him.

Alec set her tray on her knee and told her where everything was. 'There's a late film on,' he said. 'Or do you just want to eat and then go to bed?'

Something in his voice hinted that he might not just be thinking of sleep.

TWO

Patrick Jones had driven over to Bob Taylor's place early as he always did on a Tuesday morning. He worked for a morning before returning to the university for the afternoon lectures. Had Patrick had his way then he would not still be on his uni course; he enjoyed his time working with the artist far more than his studies, but both his father, Harry, and Bob had told him that he should not throw away this time. That he should enjoy broadening his knowledge base and meeting other people following Patrick's general path.

Patrick had hated University in the first term, but his dad and

Bob had been right and he'd not only got used to it but he had made some good friends – though he still thought he was learning far more from Bob Taylor than from his degree course.

As Patrick arrived a courier van was turning out of Bob's gate and a wooden crate sat on one of the tables in the studio when Patrick went through.

'Do you like a puzzle?' Bob asked.

Patrick frowned. 'What kind of puzzle?'

'Mysteries. Nothing dangerous, nothing life or death,' he reassured. He and Patrick had met because of a situation that really had been life or death and both were acutely aware of that. And not keen to repeat the experience.

'Just abstract sort of puzzles. Like who painted what, or who might just be saying they did.'

'Forgeries?'

Bob shrugged. 'It's not always that simple,' he said. 'Forgery implies intent. Sometimes that intent is there, sometimes mistakes are made, sometimes artists allow their students to use their name and their influence. Sometimes copies are made and at the time everyone knows they are copies. Then time passes, memories are lost or a new owner sets out to deceive. You have to peel back the layers, find the objective truth, the forensic truth if you will, and then you get to the other minutiae. The subjective truth, the opinions. The mystery and the deceit. It's fascinating stuff, Patrick.'

Patrick looked speculatively at Bob Taylor. 'And is that what the courier brought this morning? A mystery?'

'Yes and no. I've been asked to look at a painting and make a judgement as to its authenticity. As a matter of fact, I'm pretty sure it's a fake. I'm even pretty sure I know who made it. What I'm not so sure about is what I'm going to say.' He winked at his wife, Annie, who laughed.

'You'll do the right thing,' she said. 'You always do.'

'Maybe I don't know what that is this time?'

'Maybe the right thing isn't what other people might think,' Annie parried.

Patrick got the feeling he'd walked in on an ongoing conversation. 'Why might you not?' he asked. 'Why would you like to tell a lie?'

'Because,' Bob Taylor said, taking up a scalpel and gently easing a layer of tape away from the edge of the box, 'because some people don't deserve to own anything beautiful. Because all they want to know is what it might be worth and it would amuse me to let them think they may have something really valuable, in monetary terms anyway, just for a while before I let them down.'

He pulled the tape free and then started on the second edge. Patrick moved in closer, aware that Annie had been unable to resist and had come to stand beside him.

'And because if they think this is genuine then they'll either try to sell or they'll shove it into a bank vault somewhere just so it can get even more valuable. If they think it's a fake then they'll make sure it's destroyed and that hurts me, Patrick. That hurts me very much. No one should be permitted to destroy a thing of beauty, just because it isn't worth as much as they hoped.'

He continued to remove the tape to reveal the wooden frame of a box, the sort Patrick had become familiar with in the studio because Bob packed his own work for shipment in something similar. Bob removed the tape and pins holding the top of the box in place and lifted it aside. Patrick and Annie both craned in for a first look.

'It's beautiful,' Annie said.

Patrick almost held his breath as Bob eased the picture from its box and laid it out on his worktable. Beautiful, he thought, didn't even begin to describe it. The picture glowed in the weak winter sunlight. It was small, maybe thirty centimetres by twenty, he guessed and enclosed in an ornately carved wooden frame with a flat, inner border. Areas of gold leaf on the inner mount gleamed softly, the gilded gesso worked with punches to add texture; more surfaces to catch the light. The subject was traditional. A Madonna and child with an older woman, he guessed, probably St Anne. Patrick, having now spent several months as assistant and general part-time factotum for Bob Taylor, was getting his head around medieval iconography. They sat at rest in a landscape of trees and rocks, the grass beneath the virgin's feet scattered with delicate flowers. Both women leaned in towards the toddling child, protective arms ready to catch him, should he fall. The colours were fresh and clear as only egg tempera could be after all this time, he thought. Then reminded himself that it might not be 'all that time'.

'The Bevi Madonna,' Bob said softly. 'A masterpiece in any language. Any except the language of hard cash.'

Patrick looked up at him. 'Surely, no one would want to destroy this?' he argued. 'Even if it wasn't an original. It's still . . .' he sought the words. How could you describe something that glowed from within, the expression on the women's faces so intent and so loving, the embroidery on their robes so detailed and delicately wrought that a skilled needleworker could have recreated the pattern of it. Now he looked more closely he realized that this was actually a transitional painting, the artist breaking free from the technical and traditional stricture of pure tempera. There were areas of transparent glaze, colours finely and thinly applied over the tempera underpainting, effects that could only have been achieved by using oils in conjunction with the tempera. The result was one of restrained . . . joy. It was the only word Patrick could come up with. The artist had poured love and skill and a sense of awe into this picture and the result was something that lit up the room. It was jewel-like and uniquely lovely and Patrick could not countenance even the possibility that anyone could wish it harm.

'Who is supposed to have painted it?' Annie asked.

'It's attributed to a student of Giovanni Bellini.' He tipped the painting forward to show a selection of imprints on the wooden support. 'As you can see there is a selection of collector's marks, all impossible to verify, of course. Two of the collections do actually mention a Madonna and St Anne in their catalogues, but as there are no details . . . Bevi was an art finder; bought for a number of collectors, that mark there—' he pointed to a triangle inside of which was some kind of stylized, plump bird – 'purports to be his.' Bob shrugged.

'And who do you think actually did paint it?'

Patrick found he was holding his breath again. He wanted to believe there was no doubt. That this beautiful little object was under no threat.

'I think it's one of Freddy's,' Bob said.

'Freddy?' Patrick asked.

Bob turned to him with a sad smile. 'Frederick Albert Jones,' he said. 'One of the greatest artists never to be recognized by the establishment. He died a couple of weeks ago, which is why the sudden doubt about the authenticity of this piece. Trouble was, when Freddy died, there was another Bevi Madonna sitting on his easel.'

THREE

Ginny tapped on her friend's door and then knocked harder. 'Come on, time to rejoin the living. We've got a lecture in half an hour, remember.'

Still no response, not even the usual sleepy grunt that would have told Ginny that she had at least been heard. She tried the door. Leanne rarely bothered to lock it and Ginny often got the job of shaking her friend into full consciousness. Leanne was not a morning person.

Finding it unlocked she pushed it wide, her nose wrinkling at the strange, unpleasant smell that suddenly issued from the now open room. The curtains were still drawn and the room twilight dark. Ginny could make out the bed and the heaped bedclothes that she assumed still concealed her sleeping friend.

'Leanne? You OK? It's time to be up.'

She sniffed again, wondering at the smell. It was more familiar now and even more unpleasant for the recognition. Some combination of butcher's shop and the bathroom after Sam had used it.

Ginny made to take a step forward and then paused. The small sense of wrongness that Leanne was still not awake and had not answered her call now grew into a massive certainty of wrongness that held her, frozen in the doorway.

'She not up yet?' Sam asked from across the kitchen. He dumped his bag on the floor and reached into the cupboard for his jacket.

'No,' Ginny said. 'Sam, I think . . . I think there's something wrong.'

'Like what?' he asked. He came over and stood beside Ginny in the doorway. 'Christ, what's that smell?'

Ginny reached around the door frame and switched on the main light.

'Oh my God,' Sam whispered, his voice suddenly failing him as though his breath was forced from his lungs.

Ginny didn't even manage that. I should be screaming, she thought. But I don't know how. Instead she stared and stared, disbelief fighting what her eyes knew to be true. What was left of their friend lay on the bed and the whole room was red with her blood.

FOUR

Patrick had driven Bob over to the auction house. Annie was coming into town later and said she would pick him up. These past months Patrick had worked with him, gaining valuable practical experience alongside his university studies and Bob had taken his role as mentor and employer very seriously, introducing Patrick to new techniques, to artwork in the hands of private collectors that Bob knew and, as with the purpose of this auction house visit, to the more esoteric aspects of his profession.

Bob Taylor was an internationally renowned artist but he had always shifted pretty much for himself, never taking on assistants or feeling the need for an entourage of young interns. Until Patrick had been catapulted into his life the autumn before.

Bob's wife, Annie Raven – she had kept her own name after they had married – had a friend that she regarded as a brother. She and Nathan Crow had grown up together, shared a life that Bob still only partly understood, but it was a past that had brought danger right into Bob's own house. If it hadn't been for Nathan, Bob thought, then the man with a gun would not have arrived in his studio, but if it hadn't been for Gregory, then Bob would certainly have died there.

Patrick had, somewhat unexpectedly, come as part of this

package of unlikely friendships. Bob had extended a friendly hand to the young artist, recognizing his developing skills and his utter determination, and what had begun as a favour to the man who had saved his life had developed into a role that was part teacher and pupil, part fellow artists – despite their difference in age and experience.

'What are we looking for?' Patrick asked. Bob was obviously well known at the auction room. He'd been greeted by name and led over to a table piled high with old prints and loose drawings.

'Anything like this,' Bob said. 'But also old books. They don't have to be in good condition, in fact, the tattier the better, but look at the age. Anything nineteenth century or earlier. By the early eighteen hundreds, we're really getting into commercially produced, machine-made paper, but it's still usable for some projects.'

He could see Patrick's puzzled look. 'The end papers,' Bob explained. 'They are usually blank. I can clean them up and use them.'

'That means taking the book apart,' Patrick objected. Somehow, that didn't seem right.

'Which is why we're looking for tatty ones.' Bob smiled at Patrick's consternation. 'If you feel bad about it, Patrick, we'll take what we need and I'll teach you to rebind the rest. I've got all the kit back at the studio.'

Patrick nodded and relaxed. Most people would have laughed at him, he knew, but Bob usually 'got him' and his odd tendency to empathize with inanimate objects.

'Go and take a look around, see if you can turn up anything useful and I'll go through this lot. When you come back I'll show you what I've found and why I want it.'

Patrick nodded again and wandered off back towards where he'd spotted a pile of books on the way in. He'd never been to an auction house before. They'd come on the viewing day and the massive, high-ceilinged space was quiet. People wandered purposefully, catalogues in hand, perusing items for potential bids and no one paid him much attention. The auction house was situated in an old chapel, the offices back where the vestry would have been and Patrick found himself listening to the place. The quiet footsteps, the thick dustiness that seemed to deaden sound. The occasional cough or scrape or slide as people inspected the stock. Naomi would like this, he thought. She was acutely aware of how places sounded. He supposed it was mostly because she could no longer see, but he was also pretty sure that even in her sighted days she would have listened to a place just as much as she'd have looked at it. Close association with her since his fifteenth year had taught Patrick to do the same and now, at eighteen, it had become ingrained habit.

'You're with Bob, right?'

Patrick turned to look at the speaker, a middle-aged woman in jeans and a tweed jacket. She had glasses on a string around her neck.

'Yes,' Patrick said.

'Then he'd probably want a look at these,' she said. She led Patrick over to a stack of boxes set back in the corner of the chapel. 'They're catalogued as three boxed lots at the moment, no one's really been through them properly, but it's typical Bob Taylor junk.' She smiled and Patrick realized there was no malice in her words.

'Thanks,' he said. 'I'll take a look.'

She nodded. 'So you're Bob's assistant,' she said, regarding Patrick with discomforting interest.

'Um, yes. Part-time, I'm still at uni.'

Someone was calling to her from the back office and Patrick was relieved when the woman, apparently named Mitzi, left him to it. He was never good at explaining himself. An old oak table stood next to the stack and he took the first box and set it down on the table top. 'Old,' Patrick muttered. 'Old stuff. The older the better.' How did he tell?

He glanced across the chapel to where Bob was still sorting and chatting to another man. The two obviously knew one another well. Between Bob and Patrick, the browsers moved, examining, marking notes in catalogues, making judgements. They did so, Patrick noted, in isolation, shuffling around one another almost without acknowledgement, intent on their tasks. Bob and his friend were the only real animation in the room. Patrick turned his attention to the first box of books, setting them out on the table and then returning to the box anything that was obviously twentieth century. He discarded the paperbacks and the children's books, setting aside anything that looked as though it might warrant further investigation. He recalled that his father, Harry, who liked to browse in secondhand bookshops, usually looked for printing dates and edition numbers. Harry didn't really collect first editions, just books he liked and wanted to read, but Patrick knew he was always pleased when he found an early one.

Methodically, Patrick started his investigation.

Whoever had owned this collection, Patrick thought, had an odd and eclectic taste. A book entitled *Froggy's Little Brother* sat on top of William Blake's collected poems. Many were beautifully bound and Patrick felt his chest constrict at the thought that Bob might want to take them apart. He supposed it might be possible to carefully slice out the end papers and leave little trace but as Patrick ran his fingers across the embossed cover of *Le Morte d'Arthur* he knew he'd find it hard to countenance even that level of vandalism – and even if it was his friend Bob doing the damage. He comforted himself with the thought that the book was probably not old enough to interest the artist, the paper was very obviously machine-made, he could see the lines from the rollers lightly impressed across the surface and whatever project Bob had in mind, Patrick reckoned he'd be looking for something that at least appeared to be earlier.

He'd sorted out a half dozen possible paper sources when Bob Taylor came over.

'Found some nice tatty ones, I see.' He grinned at Patrick and then picked up the volume he'd been admiring earlier. 'I love these bindings,' he said caressing the tooled leather and smooth cloth as Patrick had done earlier. 'I've got a stack of books like this in the back bedroom. If I ever get around to getting the book shelves, I thought I'd turn it into a library.'

'I thought these might be OK,' Patrick said, indicating the small stack of extremely tatty Victorian volumes. 'But they're all obviously machine-made paper, so . . .'

'No, they'll be fine for you to practise with,' Bob said. 'I can teach you to clean the muck off without going too far and bleaching all the tone out of it. And we can practise getting rid of the foxing, that sort of thing. If it all goes wrong it's no great loss. But if I'm eventually going to trust you with the seventeenth century stuff, you're going to have to know what you're doing.' He smiled at Patrick. 'Part of your apprenticeship,' he said. 'Being a decent restorer will help keep you in work. Think of it as a safety net. Right, I'll go and have a word with Mitzi about these, see if we can strike a deal now or at least get her to list them as a separate lot and then I'll show you what I've found over there.' He jerked his head back towards the stack of prints he had been looking through earlier.

Patrick nodded and watched Bob disappear into the office. His eyes gleamed with excitement. Every day with Bob Taylor he was learning new things. Bob knew stuff and not only was he willing to share that knowledge, but he seemed to be enjoying the process just as much as Patrick.

FIVE

DI Tess Fuller stood in the kitchen doorway and looked. Beside her, Vin Dattani, her sergeant, remained silent, waiting for her lead. Both were dressed in pale blue coveralls and bootees ready to face what Vin, with typical restraint, had told her was a messy scene. His presence, Tess thought, was always satisfyingly solid and quiet; he understood that she needed to stop and think – and prepare – before facing yet another body.

Shared kitchen, Tess thought, but very different from her own student days when she'd lived in a tatty communal house with six others. This was fresh and new, the old office block having been recently converted into yet more student accommodation. Sometimes, she thought, the town was set just to become one big campus.

Breakfast pots on the table – or maybe left from the night before, she reassessed. The remnants of takeaway pizza lay on the kitchen counter. But the room was untidy rather than dirty and a stack of washed crockery beside the sink attested to at least sporadic attempts at housekeeping.

Away from the kitchen area was a communal living space with a television and a selection of uncomfortable-looking chairs with padded seats and backs and wooden arms. This part of the space looked less used than the kitchen, the odd magazine on the floor, a set of headphones and an MP3 player on the arm of a chair.

'What's in this cupboard?' Vin asked.

Distracted, Tess glanced sideways at the large wooden door. She pulled it open and found a vacuum cleaner, sweeping brush and a few occupied coat hooks. Then she turned her attention back to the kitchen and the doors that led off the communal area.

There were four heavy doors with self-closing hinges, each emblazoned with stickers that announced them to be fire doors that must be kept shut and a number on each that, as they were in the mid three hundreds, she guessed must be a continuation of a system used throughout the student flats in the rest of the building. One door stood open, propped by a rubber wedge and Tess could see the blue-clad figures of the two CSI moving inside.

'What do we know?' Tess asked.

Vin consulted his notes on the tablet he held. 'The victim's name is Leanne Bolter. She was eighteen years old, a first year foundation arts student. She came to the uni from Manchester, her parents, apparently, thought she'd be safer and cope better on a smaller campus. First time away from home,' he added.

Tess nodded. 'Do we have a photo?'

Vin scrolled through the images on the tablet and showed Tess. A smiling, blonde haired teen looked back at her. She was pretty, Tess thought, not exceptionally beautiful but attractive in that generalized, youthful way that teenage girls were somehow meant to be. She nodded, consciously committing the image to memory in preparation for what she knew she was going to see. She had learnt very early in her career that it was better to have a positive image to take to bed with you than just the picture of what was left at the crime scene. True, it was a strategy that didn't always work, but she still figured it was better than nothing.

'And they found her when and who – and how?'

Vin had been first on the scene, Tess joining him after she left court that morning – following another adjournment due to non-appearance. He'd done the preliminary witness interviews. 'Found by her flatmates, Ginny Reed and Samual Ford. He calls himself Sam,' Vin added. 'Leanne wasn't awake and they'd got a lecture so Ginny knocked on the door and then opened it when she didn't reply. Apparently it wasn't unusual for Leanne to sleep late, so they'd not been worried before.'

'And they didn't notice anything wrong? You can smell the blood and shit when you come up the stairs.'

'All these doors are fire resistant,' Vin pointed out. 'They're thick and they're designed to seal to keep the smoke out. And the heating in the victim's room had been turned off. It would all mitigate against them suspecting anything.'

Tess frowned, but accepted the logic. 'And she was killed, when?'

'Best guess, given all the possible factors, is between two thirty a.m. and maybe six.'

'So the others in the flat. They were all in bed?'

'Ginny and Sam came in at about one. Leanne was still up and they all shared pizza. She turned in just before two and the others soon after. The other housemate had stayed at her boyfriend's last night.' He pointed back across the kitchen at the other doors. 'Three one five is Sam's, the next one over is Ginny's and the one next to Leanne's room belongs to Tina Sanders, she wasn't here.'

'And we've checked up on that?'

'We spoke to a flatmate of the boyfriend. Tina had already left. She had a class at nine and he doesn't know where she'd be after that. The boyfriend had gone to work so we've got someone heading over there.'

Tess nodded. She knew she could have asked him this afterwards, that she was putting off the moment of confrontation. Once she stepped into that room and the CSI moved aside so she could get a proper look at the crime scene, that would be it. The image of the smiling young girl in the photograph on Vin's tablet would be finally and irrevocably tainted.

Times like this she wondered if she was in the wrong job or at least in the wrong branch of her chosen profession.

'OK,' she said and stepped across the threshold into the room.

Plates had been laid to create a path across the carpet. 'Stop there, please,' the crime scene manager requested. 'You can see everything from there, but after that you're into the blood and we're still processing.'

Instinctively, Tess looked down at the carpet. It was a coarse grey cord, presumably designed to be hard-wearing, but just beyond where she stood the colour had been changed; stained and darkened and Tess realized with shock that it was soaked in the girl's blood.'

'It's even on the frigging ceiling.' Vin sounded awed and Tess looked upward at the spray that reached halfway across the room.'

'Arterial blood?' she managed to ask, though her mouth was so dry her lips stuck to her teeth as she tried to speak.

'Looks that way,' the CSI said. 'But frankly it's not easy to get a handle on things just yet.'

Tess tried to swallow but her mouth was too dry. Her nostrils filled with the stink of blood and faecal matter and body fluids. She gripped her hands into tight fists, the nails digging into her palms. The two CSI stepped out of her way and she saw the body properly for the first time. It took a moment for her brain to interpret what she was actually seeing.

Leanne Bolter lay on her bed, slit open from throat to pubic bone, her intestines spilling out on to the floor, lungs stripped out from beneath shattered ribs.

'Oh my god,' Tess whispered. Defensively, she tried to look away, her gaze falling on the girl's face, oddly, though the rest of her body had been utterly desecrated, her face appeared to be untouched and her eyes were closed. Beside her, Tess felt Vinod move, a sudden jerk as though something shocked him.

'Her hair,' Vin whispered. 'He combed her hair?'

'Looks that way,' the crime scene manager said.

Tess stared. Somehow that one tiny bit of order in amongst all of this brutal chaos was even more shocking, though she could not have said why. She guessed from Vin's reaction that he thought so too. She had seen enough.

'Thanks,' she managed. 'I'll let you get on.'

She was halfway down the stairs before Vin caught her. 'Best take that off,' he said, pointing to the coverall.

'Right. Yes, of course.' She paused and began to strip the blue garment away, balling that and the bloody shoe covers in her hand before stuffing them into the bag that Vin held out to her.

'I stink,' she said. 'I can't do the interviews until I've changed my clothes. I—'

'OK, go home, I'll carry on here.'

She glared at him, looking for disapproval in his tone but found none. 'You probably stink too,' she said.

He shrugged. 'Hard to tell,' he said. 'My nose refuses to tell me anything. All I can smell is her . . . I think it'll take more than a shower and a change of clothes to get the smell out of my nose and lungs. Tess—'

She nodded, understanding what he was feeling and what they both felt unable to say. 'Looks like the bastard thought he was channelling Jack the Ripper,' she said. 'And her friends never heard a thing. How didn't they hear anything?'

'The doors are heavy, designed to keep smoke out and probably noise too. And the friend who would normally have been in the next room wasn't there. I suppose he got lucky. I suppose . . . hopefully it means she died quickly, that there was no noise. Nothing for them to hear.'

He paused, 'So what do you want to do,' he asked. 'Go home or get straight on with the flatmates?'

She turned away, knowing she had to cool off and calm down before she could make any kind of decision. Did this make her a bad copper, she wondered. This utter horror she felt at crime scenes. She knew officers who seemed utterly unmoved by the sight of blood and violence.

And she knew she didn't believe them.

And she knew, if they were telling the truth about that, she didn't want to be one of them.

Together they stood outside the building, gulping in the fresh air. Vin found some mints in the depth of a pocket and they shared half a pack. The wind cut down the narrow road, chilling Tess to the bone. She welcomed it. She was alive enough to feel the chill; to shiver, to draw up her coat collar and feel the frigid air biting at her fingers. Leanne would never do that. Leanne would never feel anything again. And the last thing Leanne Bolter ever got to feel was utter terror and excruciating pain.

SIX

P atrick arrived back on campus just before lunchtime, ready to grab a quick bite to eat before his one o'clock lecture. He made his way to the student union café to meet up with friends. He could see something was wrong even from across the crowded restaurant. Emmie had been crying and Maeve was doing her best to comfort her. Hank just looked bemused and uncomfortable – but then, that was normal for Hank. Daniel was pale, even for him.

'What's up?' Patrick sat down and dumped his bag on the floor, then rooted in his pocket for some cash. He nodded towards the counter. 'Anyone want anything while I'm over there?'

'You've not heard?' Maeve said.

'Heard what. I've been at the auction house with Bob Taylor. He just dropped me off.'

'There's been a murder,' Maeve announced. She sounded awed, excited and just a little scared. Emmie wailed and turned on the waterworks again.

'Who? Where?' Patrick demanded.

'Student flats on Curzon Street. Penfold House, I think. There's a police cordon up.'

'Could be just a burglary,' Patrick suggested.

Hank shook his head. 'It said on the news a student had been attacked and killed. We just don't know who.'

Patrick wasn't sure what to say.

'But Ginny and Leanne weren't in the lecture this morning. Neither was Sam. He never skips lectures.'

Patrick frowned. 'A lot of people live in that block. They

might just be . . . I don't know, maybe the police are talking to everyone.'

Hank shrugged. Emmie wailed again and Maeve looked anxious. Daniel didn't say anything, but then, Patrick thought, Daniel generally spoke less than even Patrick on a bad day. He talked to Patrick, though. Mostly.

Patrick stood up and began to head towards the counter.

'How can you think about food?' Maggie demanded.

'I'm hungry,' he said simply. 'I can't think when I don't eat.'

Daniel followed him over to the counter. 'I walked past Penfold House this morning,' Daniel said. 'There were three police cars and a van and a forensic team. They were all in those blue overalls. It looked bad, Patrick.'

That was quite a presence, Patrick thought. 'Anyone tried texting them?' he asked, then thought, of course they have. That would be the first thing his friends would do. He didn't know Ginny and Leanne particularly well; they shared some classes, but that was all and this term they'd been allocated the same assignment, which meant working as a loose team to put a presentation together. Sam was someone he knew a little better as they were in the same seminar groups.

'No one's answering their phones,' Daniel said. 'Susanne Marks said the whole block had been evacuated and the police have said they may not be able to go back today.'

That really was bad, Patrick thought. It meant something really serious had gone on. He selected a sandwich and ordered coffee at the hot drinks counter. 'What did the news say?'

Daniel asked for a coffee too, then glanced back at the table where they'd left their friends as though embarrassed to be thinking about refreshments at a time like this. 'It said a student had been attacked at the halls of residence on Curzon Street. It didn't say which one. It said they had died from their injuries and police were treating it as murder. The radio said it was breaking news and that police would be issuing a statement later.'

'Right,' Patrick said. He knew it was an inadequate response, but was unsure of what else he could possibly say.

'Emmie's convinced herself it's Ginny or Leanne. She says she can sense these things.'

'Let's hope she's wrong. Let's hope the news got it wrong.'

'Not likely, is it,' Daniel said.

Patrick shook his head.

They headed back to the table and Patrick glanced at his watch. Half past twelve.

'Are we going to the lecture?' Maeve asked. 'Will it still be happening?'

'We should go,' Patrick said. 'There might be an announcement or something.'

Maeve nodded. 'Right,' she said. She hugged Emmie. 'He's right, hun. We might be able to find out more. It might not be them. Like Patrick said, there are a lot of people in that block.'

Emmie sniffled miserably. Patrick ate his sandwich in silence. Whoever it was, he thought, someone had died. He wasn't sure it mattered who it was. Patrick, who had experienced more than the average in terms of loss in his short life, knew what ripples spread outward from such violent acts and knew that, however you looked at it, this was still a very bad thing.

SEVEN

Leanne Bolter's flatmates had been taken to a conference room at the university together with a nurse from the medical centre and a police liaison officer. Their parents had been summoned and were on their way. Ginny's had further to come than Sam's; his, Tess was informed, would arrive within the hour.

She and Vin had walked across from the student flats, through crowds of young people just released from lectures and others heading to. Their chatter, laughter and music so much at odds with what she had just seen. Most of them, she noted, seemed to be half plugged in to MP3 players. One earbud in, one hanging loose, conversations with friends continuing against the backdrop. The rules of social interaction seemed to change with every generation, Tess mused. Her parents would never have condoned anything less than complete attention when someone spoke to them.

Technically, the two young people she was going to interview were adults and she didn't need a parent or other appropriate adult to be present, but Vin asked the question she was mulling over as they walked up the stairs towards the conference room.

'Are we going to wait for the parents to get here? God knows what state they'll be in.'

'I'd rather not,' she said. 'I want them to talk as soon as possible, while all the first impressions are uppermost. Once they start getting babied, they might well clam up.'

'That's a bit harsh,' Vin argued. 'They're only kids.'

'And their friend is a dead kid. We don't have time to be sentimental.'

She pushed open the conference room door and they both slipped inside. At the far end of the room a little group clustered. The two flatmates, the liaison officer and a young woman Tess guessed must be the nurse sent over from the medical centre. She got up as they entered and switched the electric kettle back on. It stood on a sideboard together with tea and coffee and biscuits. Tess guessed it had been much used this past hour.

Tess introduced herself and Vin and they drew up chairs close to the young people. 'I know this is hard,' Tess said quietly, 'but I need to know everything. What you did, what you saw, if you were aware of anything odd happening last night or any strangers hanging around. Any small thing might be vital. You understand that?'

Sam nodded and, after a slight hesitation, so did Ginny.

'So, start with last night. What time did you come home and did you see Leanne.'

She already knew they had, but it seemed better to start with something familiar, something easy.

'We got back about one,' Ginny said. 'She looked at Sam for confirmation and he nodded. 'We'd brought pizza and Leanne was still up so she ate some too.'

'And how did she seem? Happy, worried?'

'No, she was fine. She'd been finishing an essay. We chatted for a bit and then we all went to bed.'

'And the other girl who lives with you? Tina Sanders?'

'She was staying over at her boyfriend's place. He had the place to himself last night so she'd gone over there about eight.'

Tess nodded. 'And you saw or heard nothing unusual. There was no one in the street when you came in?'

Ginny shook her head. 'No one. The doors were shut like always and we used the key code to get in and then the key code for our floor. I mean, you'd need both of those codes to get anywhere near our flat, so how—'

'You could see someone enter the one to the building,' Sam said. 'If you stood and watched, you might be able to see that, but . . . the one on our floor?'

Tess wondered how often the key codes were changed. The university building used identity cards to open doors to staff areas and post rooms but so far as she could ascertain, all the student residences relied on key pad entry and physical security guards who patrolled and in some cases actually had control posts within the larger blocks. Penfold House was relatively small and shared security with three others on the same street, but there was no one on duty at that time of the morning. By then overall control had passed to the campus security night shift and they were based a half mile away in one of the main buildings.

'And this morning,' Tess asked gently. 'What happened this morning?'

Ginny's hands tightened around the mug she held. It was almost empty, but she clutched it like a lifeline and her hands still shook. 'We'd got an eleven o'clock lecture. Leanne was always late getting up but this morning she was really late. I'd knocked twice and then when she didn't answer me or anything when I knocked again, I thought I'd better go in and wake her up.'

'Did you have to do that often?'

Ginny nodded. 'Sometimes, yeah. She wasn't usually as late as this, though. I mean . . .'

'So you knocked,' Tess prompted.

'And then I opened the door. She didn't usually bother locking it. We none of us did unless, you know, we really didn't want to be disturbed.'

'And you went inside?'

Ginny shook her head. 'No, it was like . . . there was this awful smell. It hit me as soon as I'd opened the door and then

I realized that I like, caught a whiff of it earlier, but it wasn't strong enough that I'd taken much notice. But when I opened the door, it was . . . it was just horrible. Like a butcher's shop, but worse. And I called out to her, but I didn't go in and then Sam came into the kitchen and I told him, something was wrong.'

'And then?' Tess switched her attention to Sam.

He shrugged. 'I went over. The room was kind of dark, but not totally dark. We could see the bed and a heap of something on the bed. I thought it was her duvet.' He swallowed nervously. 'And then Ginny switched on the light and we could see her.'

Two bright spots of colour burned on Ginny's cheeks as she tried hard not to start crying again. By contrast, Sam was white, the blood drained so even his lips were faintly blue.

'I was scared,' he said. 'I wanted to get out. We went on to the landing and I closed the door and called the police and Ginny ran downstairs to see if we could get some help. We didn't want to be on our own.'

'I tried the caretaker's office,' Ginny said, 'but he wasn't there and then I ran down the road towards where the security people have their office, and then I saw that police woman. The community . . . community—'

'Support officer,' Tess said.

Ginny nodded. 'We used to always say hi to her when we went to our eleven o'clock. She was usually about then, with the other one. Lizzy. She was on her own today though.'

'And what did you tell her?' Tess asked.

Ginny looked away from her. 'That Leanne was dead,' she replied. 'And that there was blood everywhere.'

A few minutes later they were interrupted by a member of campus security. He had a young woman with him; Tina Sanders, the final housemate. Her boyfriend had texted her but not before she'd already returned home to find the police outside and a crowd gathered. Now she knew what had happened and was utterly distraught. A security officer had volunteered to escort her to her friends.

Tess made a mental note to reprimand whoever was in charge of the crime scene. The girl should have been taken by a police officer not a civilian – however well meaning. Tina rushed to Ginny and the two girls hugged and wept, while Sam looked on and Tess could see that he'd have liked to have been included in the hugging and the weeping but didn't quite know how to ask and then the door opened again, this time to admit a uniformed officer and two people that, when Sam scrambled across the room to get to them, Tess realized must be his mum and dad.

She drew Vin aside. 'I'm going to head back to the office,' she said. 'You finish up here, see if there's anything else to be learnt and wait on the other parents.'

Vin nodded. Sam's parents had now drawn the two girls into their little circle and the hugs and comfort were being spread around. Tess spoke to the liaison officer and then slipped quietly away, leaving things in Vin's capable hands.

The lecturer took up her position behind the computer console and set down her notes. She waited until the tiers of students had quietened down and all eyes fixed on her.

'You'll have heard rumours,' she said 'and seen the police cars and I'm so sorry to tell you that the rumours are essentially true. A young woman, a student at this university was found dead by her housemates this morning.'

A ripple of gasps and horrified whispers travelled across the room and she waited for stillness before she continued. 'I can't give you names. For one thing, I don't have them and even if I did, the police would not want anything made public until the family has been informed. All I can tell you is that the police presence will continue on campus for the next few days, at least. That this is a serious, terrible incident and I'm sure all your sympathies go to the family and friends of the student involved.'

'This was on Curzon Street. Penfold House?' Someone urgently wanted confirmation. Patrick looked to see who it was but the speaker was a girl he only knew by sight and not from any of his seminar groups.

'Curzon Street, yes. Hence the police cordon. One more thing I have been asked to tell you is that the police are looking for any witnesses who might have been in the area between midnight last night and six this morning. Anyone you might have noticed, anything unusual. They have also asked if any of you have noticed people hanging around the student accommodation on campus. People you've not recognized or who looked out of place . . .'

Like a killer would make certain they looked out of place, Patrick thought. Murderers didn't wear a badge. They didn't stand out.

'Anything unusual, however small or insignificant. I have a number you can call. Or if you feel awkward about speaking directly to the police, then go to your tutor or a member of staff you feel comfortable with. There will also be counsellors on hand for anyone that wants to talk. I know this is going to be a difficult time for everyone, but we are here for you. We will get through this. Together.'

'Like fuck we will,' someone muttered.

Patrick looked down at his notebook. He could hear someone had started to cry. A soft, despairing sound and the uneasy murmur of voices from further down the row of seats. 'I'm going home,' someone whispered. 'I don't want to stay here.'

Daniel nudged him and Patrick turned to look at his friend. Daniel just shook his head; now he had Patrick's attention he couldn't think what to say.

The lecturer was trying to reclaim their attention, directing them towards the image now projected on the electronic white-board but Patrick doubted anyone would remember anything she said.

They all struggled on for the next half hour, some actually taking notes, most staring at the screen or whispering to one another until even the lecturer gave up and dismissed the class with ten minutes of lecture time to go.

Patrick shrugged into his coat and headed for the ground floor, the rear entrance closest to Curzon Street.

'Are we going to look?' Daniel asked. Patrick had barely registered that he had followed.

'I just need . . .' Patrick couldn't quite explain. Daniel just nodded.

They stood at the end of the road close to the cordon, gathered together with a little group of fellow students. The shocked, the concerned, the few detached enough to be just a little thrilled by it all – thrilled and more than slightly scared.

Patrick watched the blue-clad CSI move from van to entrance and disappear inside again. There were two Scientific Support vans on site and a couple of police cars. Several officers at each cordon, others in the street. Patrick saw no one he recognized as friends or acquaintances of Naomi or Alec.

'I think I might go home,' Daniel said. 'You bothering with the seminar?'

'I think so,' Patrick said. His father would still be out at work and Patrick didn't fancy going back to an empty house.

Daniel seemed to guess this. 'You can come back to mine,' he said.

Patrick thought about it for a moment, then shook his head. 'We'd best go to the seminar,' he said. 'We're supposed to be seeing the rest of our group. I told Sam I'd give him those pictures of the bridge. Anyway, someone might know something.'

Daniel shrugged. 'OK,' he said and the two of them made their way back to the applied arts building.

A small group had already gathered before they got there and Patrick and Daniel settled at their usual table to wait for the rest of their study group to turn up. The tutor arrived, his face grave. Hank took his place at their table. But no Sam, no Leanne, no Ginny. Patrick realized that all three of them were watching the door, that the tutor, looking at his register, looked uneasy and concerned. It was Hank who voiced what they had all begun to think.

'It's one of them, isn't it?' Hank said. 'They all live in the same block, on the same floor. They share the kitchen, they . . .'

His face was pale and his eyes wide with shock and Patrick just knew that Hank was right. One of their friends from the study group was the victim. Sam or Leanne or Ginny was gone.

Another member of staff, Paul Metcalf, who was Hank's tutor, came in and spoke to the seminar leader and then came over to Patrick and his friends and gestured for them to follow.

'Who is it?' Patrick demanded. 'Sam or Leanne or Ginny. They're not here and they live . . .'

'I've been asked to come and find you all,' the tutor interrupted. 'You need to have a quick word with one of the police officers, tell them when you last saw . . .'

He broke off, gave up on the official and controlled display. Patrick could see that Paul was also close to tears. 'It's Leanne Bolter,' he blurted the words out, 'I'm so sorry. Ginny found her dead this morning.'

EIGHT

'Excuse me, Inspector, could I have a word?'

Tess looked up from the computer and smiled at Sergeant Briggs. 'Sit down. What can I do for you?'

Alfie Briggs had been around for as long as Tess could remember. He'd joined up long before she had and, she recalled, was only about a year off retirement. Most of his career that had been spent in uniform with occasional spells on secondment to CID. A good deal of his working life had been spent as a community officer. He was good at it, calm, efficient and with a genuine interest in the people he served and an absolutely encyclopaedic knowledge of both the petty and the monumental when it came to misdemeanour.

'You know I've been based at Conning Street this past year?'

Tess nodded. Conning Street was on the university campus. The uni helped to fund the small office out of which Briggs and a couple of constables operated, sharing premises with the university security team. It was an arrangement which had grown out of a cost-cutting exercise, but one which seemed to have worked out surprisingly well.

'When the girl was found this morning, I went to the flat, with two colleagues from campus security.'

Tess grimaced. 'I didn't realize you were FOA,' she said.

'Well, strictly speaking I wasn't the first officer in attendance. The girl who found Leanne Bolter, Ginny, she'd rushed out to try and get help while her friend called the police. She'd spotted one of our Community Support officers. I think she knew they patrolled that time of the morning because she'd have seen them on the way to lectures. Anyway, Linda, that's the CSO, realized this was a bit above her pay grade and didn't get any further than the kitchen, for which I think she'll be eternally grateful.

'Anyway, she got the two young people out of the way, took them downstairs to the caretaker's office and she made sure the scene was secured. She'd got the keys off Ginny and locked the main flat door. We arrived a couple of minutes later and went inside.' He paused. 'I went ahead and when I saw what we were walking into I ordered the two campus security out.'

'Good,' Tess approved. The less people who had to live with what she had seen that morning the better.

Briggs smiled. 'They didn't take much persuading,' he told her. 'Anyway . . .'

'Go on.'

Now that he'd reached the important point, he seemed very reluctant to go on.

'Anyway,' he repeated. 'Inspector, the fact is I'm sure I've seen something like that before. Fact is I'm certain of it.'

Tess felt her belly start to cramp. 'What do you mean?' she asked cautiously. 'Briggs, I've heard of nothing like this. Certainly not around here.'

He was shaking his head. 'No, you wouldn't have. You weren't even out of school then. I'm talking, what fifteen, sixteen years ago, maybe a bit more than that. But you ask your friend Alec Friedman. He was either on his probationary year or just finished it. Either way, he was green and I suspect it gave him a few second thoughts about staying in the force. It was a murder that caused a stir at the time, but a lot of the details were kept out of the media. It was reported, publicly, as a stabbing and it's still an open case, so far as I know.'

'Still open?' Tess frowned.

He nodded. 'Unsolved, just gone cold. But the thing was, it was part of a group of killings, all unresolved, all, they thought, down to the same man or possibly same group of men. There was trace evidence of two others at a couple of the scenes, I think, but I don't know that any conclusion was reached as to whether these were accomplices or not, or if it was just trace carried by the killer.'

Tess stared at him. Are you sure? She wanted to ask, but she only had to look at Brigg's face to know the answer to that. You're talking about a serial killer, she thought, but somehow saying the words out loud was beyond her.

'Can you dig up the reports,' she said, 'and Alfie, who was the lead on that other murder?'

He looked uncomfortable. 'Well that's the thing. It complicates matters even more I suppose. The lead was Inspector Joe Jackson and we all know what happened to him.'

NINE

P atrick and his friends were taken into one of the empty classrooms on the next floor up. A young woman in uniform smiled at them and invited them to sit. A second officer arrived a few moments later. Paul Metcalf stood close by. He looked awkward and out of place as though suddenly uncertain of his role or what he could do to help.

'If you want someone here. Parent, your personal tutors . . . I can get them,' he said.

'This isn't a formal interview of any kind,' the female officer reminded him gently. 'We're just trying to talk to friends of the victim. It's just routine.'

'It's all right,' Patrick said, not sure if he was trying to reassure himself, his friends or the tutor. 'We want to help. We're OK.'

'What happened,' Daniel asked.

'And you are?'

'Daniel. Danny Goldman. This is Hank Miller and Patrick. Patrick Jones.'

Their names, it seemed, were already on her list and she ticked them off. 'This must be very hard for you all,' she said gently. 'We'll be asking the same questions of all . . . all of you.'

'You mean all friends of Leanne's,' Patrick said.

Paul Metcalf looked embarrassed and the policewoman frowned at him. 'Mr Metcalf—'

'We'd guessed, sort of,' Patrick said. 'It wasn't his fault. Ginny, Sam and Leanne are all in our seminar group. They all live in the same student flat. None of them turned up to class and none of them have been answering texts or calls. It had to be one of them, didn't it?'

'I have to impress upon you—'

'That we don't say anything.' Hank's voice was flat. 'We won't, but we won't be the only people to have worked it out, you know. Have her parents come up yet?'

'I believe so. I understand they got here an hour ago.'

'God,' Daniel said. 'They'll be . . .' He shook his head. He didn't know how they'd be, Patrick thought. Patrick had some idea. He didn't want to think about it.

'So, what can we tell you?' he asked. 'Hank knows Sam quite well, but the rest of us, we just happen to be in the same group. We're doing an assignment together, but—'

'Has Leanne seemed her usual self in the past few days?'

They looked at one another, not sure if they'd really know what Leanne's usual self might be. 'She seemed happy enough,' Hank said at last. 'We all met up in the café on Highcross. *The Duck*,' he added. 'It used to be a pub but it changed into'-

'She was fine,' Patrick interrupted. 'She and Sam had already organized tasks and we pretty much agreed. She seemed really . . . involved with it all. I think she liked organizing things.'

'Sam said she did,' Hank agreed. 'She was good at it, I guess.'

'What was the assignment about?' the second officer asked.

Daniel and Hank looked at Patrick.

'It's about changes in architecture along a specific bit of road. What it tells us about changes in society and environment,' Patrick managed. 'Sort of contextualizing the buildings, I suppose.'

'I see.' The officer nodded and the policewoman cast him an impatient glance.

'When was this, exactly?'

They told her, guessing how long their meeting had lasted.

'And was that the last time you saw her?'

'No, she had a class with me, three o'clock yesterday. Sam and Ginny would have been there too,' Hank said. 'Then Sam and Ginny went out with a crowd of us last night. Leanne had an essay to finish so she stayed home. Ginny and Sam took pizza back with them. They got extra for her; Sam said she was bound to be up.'

'Did you all go out?'

Daniel and Patrick shook their heads. 'I had work this morning. I had to be there early,' Patrick said.

'I just went home,' Daniel told her.

'Are you all local?'

'I'm not,' Hank said. 'I'm from Canterbury. I live in the next block to Ginny and . . . and Sam.'

And Leanne, Patrick thought. But she didn't live anywhere any more.

'I need your details,' the policewoman said. 'And, Hank, if you could write a brief account of where you all went last night?'

'But Leanne wasn't with us?'

'I know, it's just routine.'

Hank looked uncomfortable. He pulled a notebook from his bag and pulled off a sheet, began to write while his friends added their addresses and phone numbers to the list of names the police officer had.

'You two can go if you want to,' she said.

'We'll wait for Hank,' Patrick told her.

They waited in silence for Hank to finish scribbling his account and when he'd handed it over the officer reminded them that they should say nothing about Leanne Bolter. That there would be a formal announcement later that afternoon.

Paul Metcalf followed them out into the corridor. 'You all OK?' he asked. He looks anything but, Patrick thought.

They nodded.

'What was all that about,' Hank said. 'Why did she want a statement about last night? Leanne wasn't even there?'

'I think they're just gathering information,' Paul Metcalf said. 'I just get the impression they don't know which bits they need to gather yet so they're just scooping up everything.'

'So, what now,' Daniel asked.

'Well, the seminar will have finished, I should get off home,' Paul told them. 'You've nothing more today, have you?'

He departed soon after and Hank took out his phone and texted Maeve and Emmie. It turned out they'd had a similar interview just a little earlier. Emmie wanted to meet.

'*The Duck*?' Hank asked the other two.

Daniel nodded. Patrick shrugged. 'OK, just for a bit.' He was suddenly, painfully conscious, that none of them wanted to be alone.

TEN

Patrick was not an avid watcher of the evening news, but that evening both he and Harry were in position for the start of it. The murder of a young student was big enough to have made the national programme and it seemed strange to see their familiar little town as the backdrop to the piece on camera spoken by such a high-profile reporter. They waited then for the local bulletin, to see if there was more. The identification of the dead girl had been confirmed. Leanne Bolter, eighteen years old and studying foundation arts.

'This was a brutal killing,' the police spokesman was saying.

'Is there any other kind?' Harry asked.

'And made worse because the young woman was attacked in a place where she'd have every reason to feel safe. Every right to feel protected.'

'No one is ever safe,' Harry said. 'No one is ever really protected.'

Patrick glanced across at his father and knew that he was remembering; mourning for the young girl who'd been taken from his own life. Harry's sister had been murdered when she was just thirteen years old.

'Leanne's friends have been able to provide valuable information,' the spokesman continued, 'but police are appealing for possible witnesses. To anyone who might have been in the area last night and may have seen someone or something to get in touch. It doesn't matter how trivial or how small, any information you might possess could be valuable to the enquiry. Meantime, our thoughts are with Leanne Bolter's family and friends.'

'They've got nothing, then,' Patrick said. 'They're just stock statements.'

'Probably.' Harry agreed. 'You didn't know her well?' he asked, for what Patrick estimated to be the fourth or fifth time.

'No, not well, but that doesn't matter, does it. She was one of us. Our group, our friends. Someone killed her.'

Harry got up. In passing Patrick's chair he paused and gripped his son's shoulder, silent sympathy pouring down through his fingers. Patrick heard him go through to the kitchen and fill the kettle, Harry's usual defence in times of trouble.

Patrick's phone pinged, telling him he had a text. To his surprise, it was from Daniel. *'Have you seen the news?'* it said.

'Yes, just watching it. You heard anything more?'

'Nothing. Lots of people are going home. Hank said he's calling his parents. He needs money for a ticket.'

There would be a lot of people fleeing, Patrick figured. Murder was like a contagion. It would be no use trying to persuade students or parents that the campus was probably one of the safest places to be right now, with the police presence and extra security drafted in. Murder still felt like something you could catch if you stayed in the vicinity.

'Will you be in tomorrow?'

'Yes. You?'

'Yes.'

'Good.'

Harry returned with a tea tray and set it down on the coffee table. 'I can stay home from work tomorrow if you like?'

Patrick smiled. 'I won't be here,' he said. 'I've got a nine o'clock start and lectures all day.'

'Ah, of course, it's Thursday, isn't it. You'll be going in then.'

'I want to, Dad. It doesn't seem right not to and besides, I'd like to see people, you know?'

Harry nodded. 'I know.'

Later, after he'd gone up to his room, Patrick texted Gregory and told him about Leanne. He wasn't sure why, just that it felt like the right thing to do. He didn't know that in his own bedroom, his father, rising to the self-same impulse, had done the same.

ELEVEN

Most people had already left for the day when Tess read through the case summary on the death of Rebecca Arnold. The similarities to Leanne Bolter were startling. She too had been eighteen, blonde, slim build. Though not a student. She'd left school at sixteen and worked in a department store, now long closed, on the opposite side of town from the University. She still lived with her parents and had a steady boyfriend she'd been with since school.

And she'd been killed when other people were in the house. Her parents had been in bed in the next room while their daughter died.

Unlike Leanne Bolter, Rebecca's throat had not been cut. She had been asphyxiated, smothered when her killer pressed her face hard into the pillows on her bed and then sat on her back while she fought to breathe.

Tess found herself gasping for air as she thought about it, her chest tightening as though wrapped in a steel band. She took a sip of her coffee, trying to calm her nerves and almost choked; the liquid just didn't want to go down her suddenly constricted throat. She sat with the hot coffee in her mouth, hoping no one was looking her way, until the spasm finally eased and she managed to swallow.

She pushed the cup aside.

The rest, though, the evisceration, the arrangement of the body, the time it must all have taken, all that was horrifyingly similar to what had been done to Leanne Bolter, even down to the careful combing of the hair.

Tess stared at the crime scene pictures and found that she was no longer able to tell the two girls apart. Were all the victims like this? How many and over what period of time. How was it that the media wasn't all over this? For it to be reported as a stabbing implied collusion between the parents, the press, and any number of officers who worked the case. She knew it was routine to always keep certain facts that only the killer would know out of the public domain. That was standard practice, but to downgrade what she was seeing in the photographs to something that, though still terrible, seemed almost normal in comparison; that would have taken some doing. Surely.

But then again, Tess thought, playing devil's advocate with herself. If I'd been the parent of a girl killed in such a horrific way, would I be able to cope with, to process, the full truth of it. Would I feel more . . . comfortable was the wrong word . . . comforted, maybe, by the idea that my child had died quickly and, if not cleanly, then certainly less horrifically. Asphyxiation generally took longer than most people thought. There would probably have been minutes of Rebecca fighting for breath, desperate and terrified and in pain before unconsciousness finally took her. What parent would want to be left with that image?

Tess sighed and leaned back in her chair unable to say if that train of thought made any more sense. There was so much she didn't know. So much none of them knew. She was almost resentful of Sergeant Briggs; had he not told her of the previous case then she'd have remained in blissful ignorance; have been able to fool herself that this was a one off. A terrible, horrifying killing, but an isolated incident.

Even as she allowed the thought to be formed, Tess knew it would never have been like that. The scene was too practised, too confident, too precise. Whoever did this was cocky, arrogant, knowing. First kills were clumsy and opportunistic for the most part and were usually last kills too. Tess had decided long ago that most people were potentially capable of killing another human being but few people were cut out for premeditated murder and even fewer, thankfully, had the kind of mind that could, that wanted or needed to make a habit of it.

She wondered how long it would take for her request for information to be fulfilled and how many other reports like this would land on her desk and who would take over the enquiry when it was accepted that this killer was back – if he'd ever really gone away. How many more deaths had there been between Rebecca and Leanne? Who had died before that?

And then there was the added complication, the added taint. Tess hadn't been mentored by the famous – now infamous – Joe

Jackson, but Alec had and Naomi and many others who still
served as senior officers. Most had managed to escape the fallout
from Jackson's crime; enough distance had been established
between their time with him and their subsequent careers, but
if Jackson was in any way involved with this . . . Tess didn't
want to think of the consequences. Not for anyone.

Vin came into the office and dropped down in the chair beside
her desk. He looked pretty pissed off, Tess thought.

'Tell me,' she said, though she could guess what news he brought.

'Well the slightly good news is that we're getting Chief
Inspector Field back. At least we know him.'

Tess nodded. 'And the less good news?'

'There's a team from Internal Affairs heading our way too.
They'll be shadowing the investigation.'

Tess groaned.

'We knew it would happen.'

'I know, I know. But that doesn't mean I have to like it.
How's it going to affect our team?'

'Well, those that worked most closely with Joe Jackson are
mostly retired or moved on, thankfully. There's only a couple,
like Sergeant Briggs, left around here and I don't think he's in
for any flack. It's not going to be pleasant, though.'

'No, it's not. Any news on the rest of the case files?'

'Coming with the Internal Affairs team,' Vin said. 'And you
and I have been assigned to facilitate.'

'Of course we have,' she said bitterly. What had already been
a lousy day had just promised to get ten times worse.

TWELVE

It was getting dark when Alfie arrived at Naomi and Alec's
flat. It was a while since Alfie Briggs had spoken to either
of them. He'd moved to a job twenty miles down the coast
just about the same time as Naomi had her accident and was
forced to leave and only returned the previous year. He'd run
into Alec on occasion since then and kept himself abreast of

Alec-related news. Had been shocked when he heard that Alec had quit. To his mind, Alec was a born copper, despite the slightly rocky start. He had an investigating head, Alfie Briggs had always thought; a need to know that few other jobs could satisfy.

And now, his boss DI Tess Fuller had sent him on a bit of a mission and Alfie was not at all sure how Alec and Naomi were going to take what he'd been told to say – and what he'd been told to ask.

He arrived around eight in the evening, ringing the bell and announcing himself over the intercom. When he pushed the heavy, part-glazed door open and entered the hall, Alec stood at the top of the stairs, a big black dog at his side.

'Sergeant Briggs,' Alec said laughing. 'Of all the people I didn't expect. Come along up.'

Alfie climbed the stairs and paused to fuss the dog before shaking Alec by the hand. 'It's been a while,' he said.

'Ages. Years. Come on in.'

'I'm sorry to intrude—'

'You're not. Come and have a mug of tea and a piece of cake and tell us what brings you here. I'm not going to flatter myself that this is just a social call. Not after all this time.'

'I'm afraid not,' Alfie said.

He followed Alec into the flat. Naomi came out of the kitchen, wiping her hands on a towel. 'Hello,' she said. 'It's been a while, Alfie.'

'It has indeed, my dear. You're looking well. Very well. And your old man's retired, I understand. Shame on you, Alec. A young man like you.'

'I wanted to get older,' Alec said. 'I didn't think I was going to manage that if I stayed where I was.'

'Right. No, well I've heard stories, of course. You've had an eventful couple of years.'

They were dancing around the purpose of his visit, Alfie realized. He didn't want to talk about Joe Jackson and Alec and Naomi both realized that his arrival must mean trouble. He'd never been a close enough friend or colleague that a sudden visit after what must be five years at least might just signal a sudden impulse.

He said yes thanks to tea and cake and settled himself in a chair by the window and wondered how he should begin.

'You've seen the news?' Alfie asked.

'The murder?' Naomi guessed. 'Yes, we heard it on the six o'clock. A student, isn't it?'

'Yes. Leanne Bolter. Eighteen years old.' He paused, knew they were waiting. 'Alec, you remember in either your probationary year or just after. You and I went to a scene, a young girl, killed in her bed while her mam and dad slept in the bedroom next door. I know it was a long time ago, but—'

'But a sight like that isn't one you forget,' Alec said quietly. 'I was twenty-two, not much older than the dead girl.'

'Her name was—'

'Rebecca Arnold,' Alec said. 'Whoever did it, he was never found.'

'No. Alec do you remember'-

'What he did to her? Alfie, like I said, that's not the kind of thing you forget. I couldn't understand why it was reported the way it was. Couldn't get my head around how cautious everyone was.'

'The official report said she was stabbed. But the truth was far more than that,' Alfie agreed.

'What happened?' Naomi asked and Alfie was reminded that she and Alec had not been together then. Had been only casual acquaintances, so far as he knew and that actually Naomi may not even have been a police officer at that point. She'd joined the force a year or so after Alec. 'The killer knelt on her back and pushed her face into the pillows. When she was unconscious he turned her on her back and . . . eviscerated is the word, I think. Then he combed her hair out on the pillow and left her there for her mam to find in the morning.'

Naomi winced. 'And that was all held back? Why?'

'Because the boss, DI Jackson, thought it was for the best. There was evidence this wasn't his first. The killer. That he'd done this before. No one wanted mass hysteria, that's what he said. And the higher-ups agreed with him. He was a persuasive bugger was Joe Jackson.'

He saw Naomi flinch as he said the name. Alec's face was grim. 'And what does that have to do with Leanne Bolter?'

Alfie paused, not wanting to say more. Not wanting the look of shock to deepen on Naomi's face, or the despair on Alec's. They didn't want or deserve this, he thought. 'The killer didn't suffocate her this time,' he said softly. 'He cut her throat. But the rest is the same, even down to the hair.'

'My god,' Alec said. 'But Alfie, it's been what, fifteen years. No, must be closer to sixteen. No one goes quiet for that long.'

'Unless they're locked up or something,' Alfie argued. 'Alec, Naomi, I was there. I saw the similarities, I had to speak up. They'd have been noted later down the line anyway. Internal Affairs are reopening the earlier case and they're looking back at the others. They'll want to talk to you, being as how you worked with Joe.'

'We all knew him,' Alec said. 'He was the biggest thing round here.'

'And you've come to warn us?' Naomi asked.

'Tess; DI Fuller, she wanted you both given the heads-up. She knew it would be painful. Reopening old wounds. They'll be interviewing everyone who was involved in the original case. Asking about Joe Jackson. Making certain that nothing was missed. Alec, you were only a very tiny cog in the machine, back then. I doubt they'll be much interested in you, but—'

'But I still worked the case,' he finished. 'Alfie, looks like I retired at the right time after all. At least I'm just a civilian now.'

Alfie nodded. 'There are not many of us still around,' he said. 'It's going to be unpleasant, for those that are.'

'Is Tess SIO?' Naomi asked.

'Until DCI Field arrives. He'll get up here tomorrow, along with Internal Affairs. Look, I'd best go. Thanks for the tea. I'll try to pop round just for a social call next time. It would be nice to catch up properly.'

'It would,' Naomi agreed. 'Take care of yourself, Alfie.'

Alec saw their old colleague to the door and then resumed his seat. 'Do you think Patrick knew her? Same course, isn't it? From what they said on the news.'

'Sounds like it. Give them a ring. It's odd that Harry hasn't been in touch about it.'

She listened as Alec dialled the number and waited. 'It's engaged,' he said. 'I'll try Harry's mobile . . . later.'

He sounded suddenly deflated, Naomi thought. 'You OK?' she enquired.

'Yes, of course. It's just. Well, like I said to Alfie.' He laughed uneasily. 'Not that I need to tell you. But you don't forget a scene like that. You put it to the back of your mind and carry on and try not to think about it too often or too much because you know it's still a story without a conclusion. But then someone comes along and reminds you and it's like . . . Like you're back there again. You know?'

Naomi nodded. 'And now someone's done it again, and what we don't know is if Joe Jackson and his crew screwed up the investigation first time around.'

He broke off and Naomi could almost feel the apologetic look she knew he had cast in her direction.

'Sorry,' Alec said. 'I know it hurts.'

Hurts, Naomi thought. That was putting it mildly. Joe had been her mentor and her friend and not just after she had joined the police force. Before that, after her best friend, Helen, Harry's sister had disappeared, Joe had been her support and her confidant. He had seemed perfect. Gentle, understanding, the one person able to coax Naomi out of her all-consuming grief – and then she had discovered that Joe was as guilty and as underhand as . . .

'He was a good detective,' she said quietly. 'Whatever else he was. I can't imagine him stinting on a case like that.'

'I hope you're right,' Alec said. 'I really do.'

THIRTEEN

Gregory had called. Disturbed by their texts he had gone online and read everything he could find on the murder and then he called Harry.

'It's a bit late,' Nathan said, watching him dial.

'Harry won't mind. Anyway, he texted me. So did Patrick.'

'But you're calling Harry,' Nathan observed.

Gregory paused, thinking about that, then he nodded. 'I'm trying to consider family dynamics,' he said. 'I think my mother would have preferred me to call her first in similar circumstances.'

'In similar circumstances, might you not have been calling her to confess rather than offer condolence?' Nathan queried.

'No.' Gregory shook his head emphatically. 'Believe it or not, I always did my best not to cause her more worry than I already had.'

Nathan, uncertain as he often was, if Gregory meant that as a joke, opened his mouth to speak, then thought better of it. Instead, he settled back into his armchair and stretched his feet closer to the fire. He felt the cold, lately. Getting shot put a strain on the body, Gregory had informed him. Nearly dying had a negative effect on most people.

In Nathan's case it seemed to have chilled him to the core. Something deep within him had frozen and now refused to thaw even with the passing months. Nathan had been shot at before. His work, both legitimate as a medic, and his more secretive assignments on behalf of his guardian, had taken him to most of the world's war zones but this time had been different. He had not just been shot at, the bullets had hit and Nathan had nearly died. Had it not been for Gregory carrying him away and then driving like a demon to get him to safety, Nathan would have bled out and that would have been that. Nathan was shocked, deeply shocked, at how much of an effect near death had inflicted.

Harry must have picked up on the third or fourth ring because Gregory announced himself and then sat down in the chair across from Nathan and rested his elbow on the arm, leaning into the phone pressed against his ear. Nathan listened to the one-sided conversation, to Gregory's questions of 'what happened', and 'is the boy all right'.

'Do you want us to come down?'

'If you're sure?'

Nathan let his attention drift, knowing he'd get the full briefing anyway. He liked this little room. He liked this little house, if it came to that. They'd been here for two months now and even

Gregory had started to talk about it as home. It was remote and quiet and in another phase of Nathan's life it had been used as a safe house by his guardian, Clay, a man who had made a career out of secrecy, a cold war warrior working for the British Secret Service, a career that had continued until Clay had been considered as a dinosaur by some and a grand master by others. It was a career that had also allowed Gustav Clay to create an organization of his own, initially for that work which even the SIA denied took place and later, for Clay's own benefit.

This little cottage might have come into his possession because of either or both of Clay's parallel careers. Nathan didn't know and really didn't care. It did not appear on any inventory of property the authorities would ever have seen. At the land registry the owner was a Sonia Tindle and deeds to that effect were lodged with a local solicitor. Nathan had no idea whether or not Sonia Tindle had ever existed but Clay's paper trails were generally impeccable. The house had been, Gregory reckoned, a gamekeeper's cottage for a local estate now long ago broken up. Living room, kitchen sparse but functional, bathroom and a couple of bedrooms surrounded by a garden with a veg patch and a lot of brambles . . . and a concealed basement equipped with more security cameras and surveillance equipment and weaponry than the average rogue state. Food and supplies too. Nathan figured they could retreat and withstand anything from siege to nuclear attack. Gregory loved his 'toy room' as Nathan had taken to calling it. Nathan preferred the comfort of the living room with its civilized if shabby furnishings, its warm fire and bookshelves stacked with tatty paperbacks.

'So, what did he say?'

'That the girl was a friend, but not a close friend, of Patrick's. That everyone is upset, of course, and the police are releasing few details, but Patrick tells him that her flatmates were home when she was killed. One of them found her the following morning.'

'Cool customer then.' Nathan frowned. 'How did she die?'

'That,' Gregory said, 'seems to be a bit of mystery. The news reports I read say she was stabbed but Patrick's friends seem to think there was more to it. Anyway, there's nothing we can do. Harry says there are police everywhere on campus and no, he doesn't want us to go down. I think he and Patrick just wanted to touch base, you know?'

'We being the go-to guys where violence is involved,' Nathan said, a small, sour smile curving his lips.

Gregory looked curiously at his friend. Nathan was some twenty years his junior but there were times when pain and weariness etched much deeper lines on his face than Gregory had earned. But then, Nathan felt things in ways that Gregory did not. His dark hair was wavy and he wore it longer that Gregory ever had. And he had green-grey eyes that seemed to look straight into the hearts of others.

Clay had trained this young man well. He had killed, he had broken most of the laws known to god and man, but he was not a 'killer'. Nathan had trained as a doctor, worked for relief agencies all over the world and Clay had encouraged this career choice, seeing it as perfect cover for the jobs he had instructed his young protégé to carry out. But Clay had never realized – or never wanted to understand – that Nathan actually believed in what he was doing. That he put his heart and soul into it. Gregory was not convinced that Gustav Clay had been possessed either of a heart or a soul.

Gregory got up and wandered restlessly around the cosy little room. 'You want a cup of tea or something?'

'No, I think I've had enough.'

'You fancy a walk?'

Nathan laughed. 'If I thought you actually meant a 'walk' then I might say yes. If you mean a Gregory-style yomp across the moors, then no. I don't think I'm up for that. Not tonight. You go. I'll make some calls, see if I can find out what really went on with the girl.'

Gregory nodded and, minutes later, Nathan heard the back door close.

He needs a job, Nathan thought. He needs a project. The restlessness had been growing since New Year and Nathan could tell it had now become acute. Nathan, on the other hand, still did not feel ready to rejoin the fray. He still felt . . . slow, behind the game. Nathan had been injured before, twice seriously, but this time had seemed somehow different. Gregory, sometimes strangely wise, had suggested that this was because his injuries coincided so closely with the destruction of so much of Nathan's world. The death of Clay, the undermining of the organization he had run. The exclusion of Nathan albeit by his own choice from the reconstruction of that organization; others moving to fill the vacuum on both the legitimate, legal and the decidedly not legitimate or legal side of things. Nathan had made it clear that he wanted no part in any of it and had walked away, claiming only a little of Clay's estate as his own and protected because, like Clay, his mentor and guardian, Nathan knew where all the bodies had been buried and, because of Gustav Clay's careful training, how to ensure that those secrets would not be betrayed should Nathan meet a sticky end.

Nathan, like Gregory, found himself on the outside when only a few months before he had been right at the heart.

He picked up his phone and called Annie knowing she never minded a late night conversation. Annie, married to Bob Taylor, Patrick's artist mentor, had seemed to take the changes in her stride. Slipping into her new, semi-domesticated role peacefully and gratefully relieved, Nathan thought, not to be at Clay's beck and call, not to have to leave the man she loved at a moment's notice never knowing if or when she would return. Nathan wondered if the relief would last for her, carry her through into middle-aged, and then elderly, contentment. He hoped so. Annie was probably the only person Nathan had ever truly loved.

'Hi,' she said. 'I thought you might call. You heard about Patrick's friend?'

'Yes, Harry contacted us.' Nathan laughed. 'I think Harry sees Gregory as some dark guardian angel.'

'What a thought. Gregory with big black wings. Cormorant wings, like some of the depictions of St Michael. Patrick's due to come over tomorrow to do some work for Bob, if he does I'll have a chat, see how he's doing.'

The conversation drifted to other things, to an exhibition Annie was organizing for a group of students she'd been working with, to the blossom in the orchard. Finally to Nathan.

'How are you,' Annie said.

Nathan considered. 'Better,' he said. 'But still kind of hollow, you know. Annie, I've not felt like this since . . . since I was fourteen and Clay found me. After my parents died. After . . .'

He didn't need to explain. Annie had been there. Clay had rescued her too only a day or so after he had pulled Nathan from the wreckage of his family's assassination and the two lost children had been thrown together, clung to one another, been, Nathan thought, the only point of sanity in a world gone to hell and in which Clay had been both saviour and manipulator. In the end they had loved and hated him in equal measure. In the end the hatred had won.

'It will ease,' Annie told him softly. She wasn't crass enough to tell him it would go, they both knew better than that. You made an accommodation with pain but it never fully went away.

'Goodnight, Annie. My best to Bob.'

'Goodnight, Nathan.'

He stared at the phone for a while after he'd rung off remembering the scruffy, frightened girl he had first met, with the black hair and massive violet eyes sitting on the narrow bunk opposite and wondering whether or not it was OK to cry.

Annie Raven and Nathan Crow. Clay had named them both, created an identity and, somehow it had amused him to name them both as birds.

Hair dark as a raven, Clay had said of Annie. And you, my Nathan, my storm crow.

Nathan could remember his amusement at that. Annie had taken her name and revelled in it, somehow. World renowned photographer and now wife of an internationally respected artist. Nathan had continued to be the storm crow, camouflaged against the darkness of the clouds.

FOURTEEN

The lecture theatre was strangely empty that Thursday morning. Patrick estimated that about half the students were missing. Some had gone home, some just stayed away. He had met up with Hank on the way in.

'I got a text from Ginny,' Hank said. 'She said Sam was texting you?'

Patrick nodded. 'You going?'

'Course I am.'

Ginny and Sam's parents had both been put up at the same hotel and their offspring had joined them. Now they wanted to see their friends. They wanted, Patrick sensed, something normal in the midst of all the pain and chaos. From the texts the boys had received it seemed that the police liaison officer had been against it, but the parents had intervened and overruled. Patrick and Hank were to go to the hotel after their lecture.

In the lecture theatre, other students looked their way, whispered to one another, looked anxiously in their direction. Everyone knew by now just who had died, who had found her, who their associates were.

Contagion, Patrick thought. They're scared of catching it.

He concentrated on digging out his pen and notepad and his laptop, laying them on the bench in front of him, impatient for the lecturer to arrive and the class to begin.

'Dad wanted me to stay home,' Hank said. 'Is Daniel going to the hotel? Did he say?'

'He said he'd meet us there.' Daniel didn't do the module this lecture related to. He should, if Patrick remembered right, be in a seminar just now. 'Emmie's mum is coming for her this morning. Evie is already gone.'

Hank nodded, the lecturer arrived and eyed the diminished group, glancing at her watch and then at the door to check for habitual latecomers. Patrick saw her take a deep breath and then look away from them as she arranged her notes, checked the images she wanted to use on the PC. Two other students arrived, signed the register on the front desk and then slid into their seats. The room was silent now, oddly so. The hum of conversation rarely diminished fully until she began to speak. The lecturer fiddled with her notes again and then, with a determined look, surveyed the room.

'Today,' she said, 'we will continue our examination of the Bauhaus movement and the changes that occurred when the Bauhaus moved from Weimar to Dessau in 1925.'

Patrick sighed, positioned his laptop and began to make his notes.

FIFTEEN

There had been police and reporters all over campus when they left their lecture, but the press were kept behind cordons and reduced to shouting questions at staff and students. A couple were doing pieces to camera, Patrick assumed for the lunchtime news, and he wondered what they'd find to say about a campus that was trying hard to look normal when half the students seemed to have fled. He supposed they'd say exactly that.

Once they'd left the campus the police presence thinned and the media all but disappeared. He spotted a couple of stray photographers drinking coffee in one of the local cafés, cameras on the table, other paraphernalia propped against the wall. They looked cold and bored. By the time Patrick and Hank reached the hotel where their friends and their families were holed up, there was nothing out of the ordinary.

The bar of the hotel was open in daytime for coffee and sandwiches and Patrick and Hank were soon ensconced with Ginny and Sam. Daniel had called to say he was on his way but had to hand something in first. Sam and Ginny's parents had fussed a bit and the police liaison officer, out of uniform and casually dressed so as not to draw attention, had come down and looked official and then departed, following Ginny's mum. Patrick felt for the officer; Naomi had told him that it was a really hard part of the job, dealing with families and not really being able to do anything useful or particularly helpful a lot of the time. Just being on hand, in case something happened and a familiar face was required. He supposed that her job was different in this event. Ginny and Sam had *found* their friend, but not themselves been victims. He assumed that Leanne's parents must be somewhere, maybe in another hotel, maybe still at home and that another liaison officer was keeping watch over them, dealing with their grief, fielding the practicalities that still had to be dealt with.

'Mum and Dad want me to go home,' Ginny said. 'The police said they'd rather we hang around for a bit in case . . .' she didn't seem to know in case of what. 'I think we're going in the morning. We just wanted to see people, you know?'

'Emmie and Maeve have already left,' Hank said.

'I know, Maeve keeps texting me.'

'Emmie's phone is flat. Again,' Hank said. 'She needs a new battery. I keep telling her you can get them for fuck all on eBay.'

Ginny nodded. She kept glancing over towards the doors that led into the main body of the hotel and through which she'd watched her mother depart a few minutes before. It was clear to Patrick that now they were here, despite Ginny wanting to see her friends she was now uncertain that had been the right decision. He could almost feel her wondering what they should talk about.

'We've been told not to talk about anything to do with Leanne,' Sam said. 'But.' He exchanged a glance with Ginny. 'I can't stop thinking about it. I can't stop seeing her.'

Ginny blinked back tears. 'I went into her room to wake her up and there was this smell. Like blood and . . . and stuff. Sam put the light on and we saw her.'

The door to the bar opened and Daniel slipped through and came over to the table taking his place beside Patrick.

Ginny continued. 'She was just . . . just propped up against the pillows and her hair was all spread out like someone had combed it. Like the killer had combed her hair. And he'd cut her open. All the way down. There was blood. On everything.'

She was staring into the distance and her hands were tightly clenched. Patrick guessed that she was seeing her friend, bloodied and laid open, her body torn and mutilated.

Sam put his arm around her and gave her a hug. 'We've had to go over it again and again,' he said. 'Like we're likely to have missed anything. We told them everything we saw the first time.' He sounded angry more than upset now and they all fell silent, not knowing what to say or what comfort they could possibly offer.

After a while, Ginny straightened up and released herself

from Sam's embrace. She wiped at her eyes and sniffed and then busied herself finding a tissue in her bag.

Sam was clearly looking for a distraction because he asked Daniel, 'Did you get your essay in on time?'

Daniel nodded. 'Yeah. I think it's crap, though.'

'You always say that and it never is.'

Ginny wiped her eyes. 'Did you go to the lecture?' she asked Hank.

He nodded. 'You can use my notes if you like, and she's posting a summary on Blackboard with some links. There was hardly anyone there.'

Ginny looked relieved, Patrick thought, to be talking about something ordinary. 'It was about the Bauhaus stuff again,' Hank added.

'Ah, right. I think I might do my assignment on that.'

'Really?' Patrick couldn't think of anything more tedious.

'Yeah, it's kind of straightforward. I mean there are clear theories and those theories were applied practically and there's all the historical context stuff.'

He nodded, now she put it like that it seemed like a better idea.

The conversation stumbled on for a while and Patrick could see that Ginny, at least, was feeling better for it. But they couldn't escape for long from the weight of grief and horror and, Patrick realized, the sense of responsibility.

'The police keep asking us if we saw anyone hanging about,' Sam said. 'If Leanne was worried about anyone.'

Hank laughed. 'Leanne never worried about anything,' he said. 'She would chat to anyone, she was just like that.'

Silence fell for a while and then Sam said, 'Her parents came to see us this morning. I can understand why they wanted to, but it was horrible. It was just—'

'I felt so guilty,' Ginny said. 'Like I could have *done* something. We were *there*. We should have *known*. We should have heard something. Leanne's mum couldn't understand why we hadn't *heard* anything.'

'But we didn't,' Sam said. 'We just slept through it all. Our friend was murdered and . . . and cut up and in pain and we didn't hear anything.'

'She had to have been unconscious or something,' Patrick said. 'If she'd been in pain she'd have screamed out.' He wasn't sure if that was true, but he felt he had to say something comforting, something to relieve the horror, just a little bit.

Ginny pounced on it. 'You think so? Sam, Patrick's right, she'd have screamed or shouted for help or something. Wouldn't she?'

Patrick could see that Sam didn't believe it, but he nodded anyway. It was a little shred of comfort, a small hope in amongst all of the devastation. 'I hope so,' he whispered, but Patrick knew that his friend was imagining every wound, every moment Leanne might have suffered. Every last second of pain and it was eating him up from the inside.

Ginny's parents appeared just after that and told her that her gran was on the phone and really needed 'to hear her voice'. Ginny apologized and followed them back upstairs. Sam watched her go and then looked back at his friends. 'The police say they'll be clearing all our stuff out of the flat,' he said, 'and the university has been talking about offering new accommodation. Ginny says she doesn't want to come back.'

'And what do you want to do?' Hank asked.

Sam shrugged. 'I don't want to go back home,' he said. 'I came all the way up here so I didn't have to live at home. I'm stopping. Dad's already gone back and Mum will be leaving in the morning. She wants me to go with her and we had a big row because she can't understand how I'd rather be here after what happened. She says it's stupid and . . . perverse.' He grinned suddenly. 'She likes the word perverse, uses it for anything that doesn't fit with what she thinks.'

Patrick, Hank and Daniel laughed awkwardly, and Patrick knew that Hank was probably wondering what he'd choose to do. Daniel just looked puzzled and Patrick figured he was undecided. Daniel often was, seemingly, undecided. For Patrick it would have been easy. He'd chosen this university precisely because it meant he could live at home. Patrick knew he was far from ready to leave the safe place he had with his dad and he thought, not for the first time, how lucky that made him. He and his dad got along just fine most of the time. He counted Harry as a friend. But then, they had been through such a lot together and bonds had been forged that didn't usually happen between fathers and sons.

'Where are they going to move you to?' he asked.

'Kingston House,' they said. 'Down near the canal.'

'It's nice there,' Hank said. 'Sam, you have to do what feels best. I think I'd be running for the hills. And then I'd probably feel bad about it,' he added. 'I'd feel like I was letting Leanne down.'

The bar doors opened again and Sam looked up, hoping, Patrick thought, to see Ginny return. A man came in, bundled up against the cold and damp of the day. He went over to the bar and ordered a coffee then wandered over to a seat beside the window.

Patrick frowned. There was something familiar about him.

The man glanced around as he undid his coat and dropped it on a spare chair, meeting Patrick's gaze for an instant before turning his attention to the barman who'd just come over with his drink.

Patrick filed that sense of familiarity away in the back of his brain and turned his attention back to his friends. The memory would either surface or it wouldn't.

They left soon after that. Daniel had an afternoon of lectures and Patrick was heading over to Bob's and had to pick up his car. He had surprised everyone – including himself, by passing his test the first time. The insurance had cost an arm and a leg and part of what Patrick earned from assisting Bob went towards that each month, Harry taking up the slack on the rest.

He thought about Sam and Ginny as he drove down the wet country roads towards Bob and Annie's place. How they must be feeling, how long it would take them to get over what they had witnessed and he knew that Ginny, once she had left would not return and had the feeling that she would slowly but surely break contact with them all too, hope that distance and denial might help her to recover and forget.

Patrick knew that she was wrong.

SIXTEEN

DCI Field had arrived along with a team of five and what looked to Tess like a van load of filing boxes. Just behind him was the Internal Affairs team and Field introduced former DI Trinder who had 'agreed to come out of retirement to advise'.

No further explanation was given and Field did not elaborate about the kind of advice he might be offering either.

Field set out his belongings on a desk that had been cleared for him and anyone capable of carrying a box set to work carrying files into a small office that had been requisitioned for the purpose.

'In there.' Field pointed to the office. 'A team will undertake a case review. That team will comprise Inspector Fuller, Sergeant Dattani, Sergeant Briggs, who was responsible for alerting us to the earlier offence, and DS Natalie Cooper from DI Trinder's team.'

Tess bristled, but said nothing. She knew this was an important job, but still resented being side-lined from the current investigation.

'DI Fuller will also be responsible for liaising with those officers who have now left the force, but who were involved in the Rebecca Arnold killing. DS Cooper and Sergeant Briggs will have particular responsibility for assessing the late DI Jackson's role in the investigation.'

There were two women in Trinder's team of six, Tess noted and wondered which was Cooper. She noticed Alfie Briggs standing guiltily by the door like a child caught listening in to an adult conversation. She dragged her attention back to what Field was saying. He was clearly taking charge, and so far the mysterious Trinder had spoken to no one outside of his own team. Tess was uncertain if that was a good sign or not. Field, she noted, was doing what he had done the last time she had worked with him and seeking to integrate the disparate teams, listing those of her colleagues and those from his team and from Trinder's who would be working together. No one looked particularly happy at the prospect, but Tess respected Field's wisdom. This way integration and communication might not be easy or welcome, but it would at least happen and being imposed from above and from outside meant that everyone could grouse about it with impunity.

'Any questions,' Field asked.

There were a few, mainly dealing with practicalities of computers and desks and the availability of bacon sandwiches and then Field suggested they all get acquainted with their new colleagues, and Tess caught Vin's eye and then headed towards the cramped space of their allocated office. She looked despairingly at the amount of material they would have to work through, stacked on desks, on shelves, on the floor in no discernible order.

'Wow,' Vin said. 'Where to start.'

'By sorting them into date order, I guess.'

Tess turned towards the unfamiliar voice. 'DI Cooper?'

'Natalie. Nat.' She held out her hand. 'Pleased to meet you.'

Automatically, Tess shook her hand and introduced Vin and Alfie who had now slipped sheepishly through the door and stood uncertainly beside one of the desks. Tess had never seen him look so uneasy or out of place.

Cooper was about mid-thirties, Tess guessed. Tall and, when she slipped off her jacket and revealed bare arms, athletic-looking with short dark hair and grey eyes.

Someone stuck their head round the door asking for coffee orders and discussing sugar and preference for hot chocolate seemed to break the tension. Surprisingly, it was Alfie who moved into action. He'd been scanning the labels on the boxes, looking at the dates and case numbers and scribbling them down into a notebook.

'We look like we've got five different case numbers,' he said.

'Five?' Cooper was clearly startled. 'My god.'

Tess decided she might actually like this stranger. 'So, six in all,' she reminded them.

'If we take the earliest date and put them on that shelf beside the door, then work our way round?' Alfie offered.

'Sounds like a plan,' Tess agreed. 'So presumably the Leanne Bolter casefiles will be kept in the main office . . . OK, let's do this.'

For the next half-hour they worked in near silence, sorting files and allocating spaces. Coffee arrived and was drunk and finally laptops and a scatter of pens and notebooks placed on the desks made the space look occupied. It was tidy just now, Tess thought. Sparse and neat and she looked forward to the time when that would change. Personal possessions would creep in. Mugs and photographs and tiny clues to personality and interests. She found herself wondering about Cooper and asked what seemed like the obvious question.

'Have you worked in IA for long? Have you worked with DI Trinder?'

To her surprise, Nat Cooper shook her head. 'Never met him before today,' she said. 'And I'm not IA, just on secondment. As of yesterday.'

She flushed slightly as three pairs of eyes turned to look at her. 'Secondment?' Tess asked. 'From where?'

'Peterborough, actually.' Nat grinned. 'I got the call late yesterday afternoon, packed a bag, drove up here.'

'And the rest of the team?' Vin asked.

'Kat Bains has worked in Internal Affairs for three years, apparently, but her specialty is fraud and computer crime. DI Trinder, well no one seems to know who he is or was, but like I said I only met him this morning. Peter Morgan, the tall black guy, he's a DS from Brighton, got the call same as I did. DI Dan Clifton and DS Vehn are from the Met and Manchester forces. Both Internal Affairs, but different regional forces and DS Clem Boroughs, he's the redhead, he's from Berwick-upon-Tweed.'

Tess frowned and exchanged a glance with Vin. But it was Alfie who nailed it. 'Looks like they've gone out of their way to assemble a clean team,' he said. 'No links with Joe Jackson, I'm guessing, and I'll make a bet that none of you come from anywhere these boxes refer to. Like I say, a clean team.'

'Sounds about right,' Nat agreed. 'With you, Sergeant Briggs, being the one anomaly. The one direct link back to both DI Jackson and one of the crimes.'

'DS Briggs was the one who alerted us to the link.' Tess felt the need to defend her colleague.

'And the link would have been made, sooner or later. But yes, he did and I'm not suggesting anything, so keep your hair on. I'm just observing. Tess, you and Vin are in charge of liaising with ex-officers. Any reason for that?'

Tess nodded. 'Ex-colleagues, people I'm still in contact with, so it'll be easy to resume. Field knows that. He's been SIO here once before.'

Nat looked curious, but Tess wasn't in the mood to elaborate. Nat's perfectly valid observations about Alfie Briggs had rattled her and Tess felt suddenly defensive.

'So,' she said. 'How do we organize ourselves.'

'I think,' Alfie said, 'that we should all be at least passably familiar with the whole narrative.' He gestured to take in the stacks of boxes surrounding them. 'There are five in here. Six counting the latest one, but we'll be briefed on that as we go. So, we assess what we've got, make an inventory, then look at the detail. We need to create a new book for each case. Like the man said. Fresh eyes. We feed back as we go and then—'

'Deliver a seminar to the rest of the group,' Nat said. She grinned at Alfie, softening what might have sounded like a patronizing response. 'Sounds like a way forward.'

'It's a hell of a lot of work, however you break it down,' Vin said.

'True, and we could do with some extra bodies,' Tess agreed, 'but the more people in the team the greater the opportunity for slippage. At least this way we can keep it tight, make sure we all talk to one another. Everyone stays in the loop.' Vin was right though, she thought, it was a crazy amount of work, especially as she and the others were going to be responsible for preparing their findings for the other teams.

'OK,' Nat said. 'So how do we break this up? Alfie—'

Suddenly Sergeant Briggs was Alfie, Tess noted. She wasn't sure she liked this other woman being so familiar. She told herself not to be so petty.

'Alfie, if you and I take the first two, see what came before the first case you know about.'

'It makes sense for Tess and me to take the next two,' Vin

said. 'See what the similarities are between those and our present case.'

'Then whoever deals with theirs first, moves on to the final one,' Nat picked up. 'We have two pairs of eyes on each so hopefully less will be missed and we review what we've got say, twice a day? Lunchtime and just before the evening briefing?'

It all sounded sensible, Tess conceded. 'I'm going out for a couple of hours,' she said. 'I want to speak to Naomi and Alec Friedman before we go any further.'

'And who are they?'

'Naomi was one of Joe Jackson's protégées,' Alfie told her. 'If anyone knows how that man thought it'll be Naomi. And Alec worked the Rebecca Arnold case with Joe Jackson. And from what I remember, he and Joe, they couldn't stand one another.'

'Must make for some interesting marital conversations,' Nat said.

SEVENTEEN

Patrick had to force himself to concentrate as he drove out to Bob Taylor's place. The route along the country roads was winding and the turn towards the house sudden and sharp. He realized how poor his concentration really had been when he nearly missed it. All the way Patrick had been thinking about Ginny and Sam and how they would cope when events quietened down and they were left to deal with the emotional aftermath alone. He knew his father had been affected by his, Harry's, sister's disappearance all the years that followed. That finally being able to bury Helen, having some idea of what happened to her had eased a little of the pain but it had also replaced it with new certainty. They knew for certain now that Helen would not be coming back. Harry and Patrick's grand-mother had a vision in their minds, now based on facts and not speculation of Helen's last hours and of how her body had been dumped after her murder. One pain replaced by another.

Sam and Ginny would never forget what they had seen. They would also never be able to cease from speculation of what their friend had suffered. Not be able to help themselves imagine her fear and pain, and the fact that they had been so close by would inflict guilt upon them not only that they had not helped but that they hadn't even known that Leanne needed their help.

There might be no logic to their pain but then, Patrick thought, since when do pain and logic share the same space?

Annie Raven opened the door to him and told Patrick that Bob had just taken the dogs out for a walk.

'He's left your stuff set out in the studio,' she said. 'But he said I should make sure you'd had something to eat before you started.'

'Thanks,' Patrick said, suddenly realizing he was actually really hungry. Annie's kitchen clock told him it was almost two thirty, more than an hour later than he'd normally arrive at Bob Taylor's place and he felt out of kilter and off balance now his routine had been interrupted. Patrick liked routine; needed order in his life, a trait he seemed to have inherited from his father.

The phone rang. Annie left him tucking into sandwiches and coffee. Annie and Bob's kitchen was always a warm and welcoming place, Patrick thought, with its range cooker and old dresser decorated with blue and white pottery and a selection of glass and ceramics Bob had picked up at craft fairs and flea markets. None of it matched and all of it was used, something that appealed to Patrick. He wasn't really one for 'ornaments', not unless they were paintings. Paintings were different, somehow.

Annie returned to the kitchen and poured herself a cup of coffee. 'That was Bob, he's on his way back.' She took a seat at the table and studied Patrick carefully. 'Are you all right?'

Then she laughed. 'Sorry, I always promised myself I wouldn't ask stupid questions, but what else do you say, huh?'

Patrick smiled. 'I don't know,' he admitted. 'Dad says it's like making tea. When a crisis happens someone reaches for the teapot and someone else sorts out the "box of appropriate platitudes".'

'Box of . . . oh I love that. It's so Harry, but I might have to steal it from him. He's right, though. That's exactly what we do.'

'And I am all right,' Patrick told her. 'I didn't really know Leanne, you know. She was just part of the group, so I feel terrible about what happened to her but also terrible that I can't feel as much as the others, you know?'

Annie nodded.

'I feel like I should be more . . . I don't know. I'm horrified, I'm a little bit scared. I'm grateful that I didn't know Leanne better because I can see what her friends are going through and then I feel like a real shit for being grateful for that—' He paused, poking at the crust of his sandwich left on his plate – 'and I'm really, really thankful that I've got people I can say this to and they won't think badly of me.'

'Thank you,' Annie said simply. 'For including me in that group.' She paused as though considering what she should say next. 'Gregory called,' she said. 'Nathan managed to get access to some of the crime scene photos and he's waiting on information from some contacts he has. But the consensus is—'

'That this isn't a one off,' Patrick finished. 'That he's killed before.' He noted Annie's surprise and shook his head. 'Look, two of our closest friends are ex-police officers, another two are . . . well, whatever you'd call Gregory and Nathan.'

'I suppose that represents a kind of balance.'

'I suppose it does. I suppose that's the best way of looking at it. Anyway, you don't have those sorts of people around you and not pick things up. Whoever killed Leanne wasn't scared. He was confident enough to do it with her friends sleeping next door. He took his time with it and he was in control. He must have been. So it couldn't have been his first time, could it? He'd had time to practise, time to get it right.'

Annie nodded. 'That's the assumption,' she said. 'Patrick, if you or Harry are worried about you being round campus, Bob and I, we'd be more than happy for you to—'

He was shaking his head. 'The place is crawling with police. Half my friends are going home, but I don't think any of that is going to help, you know?'

'How do you mean?'

'I mean, if a man like that is out to get you then he'll find a way, whoever you are, wherever you are. I mean . . . look, it's not quite the same thing, but a few police or you trying to run away wouldn't stop Gregory would it. I mean, not that he'd do something like this just for fun but, you know what I mean?'

'I know what you mean and no, you're right, that wouldn't stop Gregory or Nathan for that matter. But you're also right, neither of them would do something like that for fun. There would have to be a reason.'

'I guess whoever did it believes he had a reason,' Patrick said. 'Even if the reason was just that he wanted to.'

'People who just "want to" are the most dangerous of all,' Annie said softly and Patrick, looking at the woman with the long black hair and violet eyes seated across the table from him, wondered what she was remembering; who, in particular she had called to mind.

The sound of the front door opening and Bob coming up the hall broke the sombre mood. The two dogs skittered into the kitchen, greeted Patrick and Annie and then headed, tails wagging for their food bowls.

'Bob, they're muddied up to hell, where did you get to?'

'Walked along the ridge and then across the fields. I was thinking. I lost track of time.'

Patrick's interest was piqued. He had learnt enough 'Bob code' as Annie called it to recognize this meant a new painting was brewing. Bob reached beneath the sink and found one of the old towels they kept for drying the dogs. He rubbed them both down before washing his hands and starting a new pot of coffee. Only then did he remember to remove his damp and muddy coat.

'I found a tree,' he said.

'You walked through a wood,' Annie pointed out.

'Yes, but I mean I found a *tree*. He dug a small digital camera out of his pocket and switched it on. Annie and Patrick crowded close so they could see the screen.

'Ah, I see what you mean. It looks like an old ash.'

'It's the World Tree,' Bob said. 'See the way the roots reach down the bank like a network of snakes. It's exactly what I needed. And that sky . . .' He looked round distractedly and then seized his coffee mug and wandered out of the kitchen.

Annie laughed. 'Did he tell you what he wanted doing today? Because you'll not get any sense out of him now.'

Patrick nodded. 'We're not so different, are we?'

'From?'

'From whoever killed Leanne.'

'I might not be, Gregory might not be, but you? Patrick you are worlds away.'

He shook his head. 'No, I'm not. I know if anyone hurt someone I loved like that I'd not just want them dead I'd want them to be hurting when they died.'

Annie regarded him thoughtfully. 'Patrick, could you take the knife and drive it home?'

'I think I could, yes.'

'Then you have an insight that few people dare to have. It doesn't make you a bad person and it certainly doesn't make you like this killer, or even like Gregory for that matter. Gregory accepted what he was a long time ago. He knows one day it will probably catch up with him and he knows that in the eyes of many he'll deserve what comes. This man, he's just indulging in a game of 'I'm cleverer than the police, the victims, their families . . .' Gregory doesn't think he's better. You don't think you're better. That's what's different. You create, you don't destroy, not unless someone pushes you into a corner and you have to fight your way out and then, well, I'd be happy to have you at my back. But that would be you in extremis. Not you in the everyday. This man, he's *that* every moment of his life, even when he's doing something as innocuous as the super-market shop. Death shapes and defines him and causing suffering is the outward display of his power. So no, we're not like him.'

Gently, she squeezed Patrick's hand and then took their mugs over to the sink. 'Now, go and listen to Bob mutter for the afternoon, that's where you belong.'

Patrick nodded, but he was only half convinced. He could imagine himself as Annie put it, driving the knife home, not with any self-satisfied sense of vengeance but because it might have to be done and it scared him. Excited him too in a way and that recognition just scared him all the more.

EIGHTEEN

'Talk to me,' Tess said. 'Tell me about Joe Jackson. I never knew the man, he'd retired before I moved up here and all I know is the vitriol that followed his fall from grace.'

Naomi laughed uneasily. 'He didn't so much fall as crash and burn,' she said.

'And as far as I was concerned, there never was any grace,' Alec added. 'I hated the man, as Naomi will tell you.'

'I'd rather *you* told me. Look, you could say that Vin and I have been slightly side-lined, here. We're in charge of case reviews; anything Joe Jackson might have touched that impacts on the present case and on the one from eighteen years ago. Rebecca Arnold.'

'And the killings in between?' It was a calculated guess, but Naomi felt at once that it had hit the target.

'And the two before,' Tess said quietly. She took a deep breath. We think there are at least five over a period of twenty-two years. That's what we think so far. Six including Leanne Bolter.'

'Six? Fucking hell.' Alec rarely swore, something that had always amused his colleagues.

'Quite,' Tess said.

'Who's the SIO?' Naomi asked.

'Chief Inspector Field. It could be worse.'

'And who's dealing with the Internal Affairs investigation?'

'A former DCI. Name of Trinder. I don't know him at all. He's been brought out of retirement to head it up. I don't know why that is either.'

'I do,' Naomi said. 'Alec and Joe Jackson worked an under-cover case when Alec was still a probationer. Alec should never have been put in the position he was. The surveillance teams and Alec should have been pulled out before the raid took place. Joe knew there'd be weapons fired and he knew where Alec was and that he was in danger of being caught in the crossfire. But he gave him no warning, made no concessions for the fact they'd still got a man inside and he nearly got Alec killed. Internal Affairs was brought in, not just because Alec complained but because the whole operation was called into question. Trinder was in charge of the enquiry that followed. Joe was suspended and lucky to get away with just that. If I remember right at least two senior officers took early retirement.'

'Over that one incident?' Tess asked. 'Alec, I don't mean to diminish anything you went through but—'

'No, not just that operation. Joe Jackson, a DI called Ben Rackam and a DCI Pool, now deceased, I think, they saw themselves as some local version of *The Sweeney*, Joe felt he'd been side-lined, that his career was going nowhere. He had a wife who'd run off with a man who could give her more of what she wanted and he had lost custody of his daughter. Penny. Anyway, Joe Jackson's life was a mess. No one realized it at the time but—'

'So, did you meet Trinder?'

'Once,' Naomi said. 'At a conference just before he retired.'

'Must have done, I suppose.' Alec said. 'I was interviewed by IA. I nearly walked, if I'm honest. Suddenly being a PC didn't seem a healthy lifestyle choice.'

'But you stayed.'

'Couldn't think what else I wanted to do.'

'He's going to want to talk to you both,' Tess said. 'If you were still in the force, chances are you'd be off on gardening leave.'

'That might be difficult,' Alec said. 'No garden. Though we have applied for an allotment. You wouldn't believe the waiting lists.' He trailed off. 'Sorry, Tess. I thought I'd done with all this. So what do you want to know? How can we help you?'

Naomi felt Tess relax and was suddenly conscious that the other woman had been ready for them to tell her this was no longer their concern and she should leave them alone. They'd have been within their rights, Naomi thought, and her first instinct might have been exactly that.

'I need a start point,' Tess said. 'I feel like I'm all but excluded from the present investigation. I get to see the book and attend the briefings, but my hands are tied as far as actual investigation. So I thought I'd start with Rebecca Arnold. She was local, I have you two so I've got something of an inside track. I'm not going in totally blind.'

Naomi nodded. 'You need to talk to Alec about that,' she said. 'I wasn't even here when the investigation was happening. But I can tell you about Joe Jackson.' She drew a deep, somewhat unsteady breath. 'I can at least do that.'

'I'm grateful,' Tess told her.

'So, what are the parallels,' Alec asked. 'What makes everyone so certain these murders are connected? Why have the connections not been made earlier . . . or have they?'

'And the other cases?' Naomi added. 'All the same MO? The same victim profile?'

She was aware of the pause as Tess gathered her thoughts.

'I think we need more coffee,' Alec suggested.

'That would be good,' Tess agreed. 'And if you don't mind, can we run through what you know in isolation? I want to see what you and Jackson saw in the Arnold case. Know what the thought process was in that one instance before we muddy the waters with the rest. And then I'd like an insight into Joe Jackson, his thought processes, his investigative technique. Believe me, Alec, Naomi, I've been staring at case files since first thing this morning and my brain is about to explode. They're all running into one another. I need to focus on the one girl, the one instance, the one death and investigation and you two are the closest things I've got to an eyewitness account.'

'OK,' Alec agreed. He went through to the kitchen to make more coffee and Naomi turned her face towards where Tess was sitting. Something the woman had said had struck her hard. That the cases were all running together and she could no longer tell them apart.

'Are they all so similar, then?' she asked softly. 'Same MO, same victim profile?'

'That would be simple, wouldn't it? In a way? No. The victims are male, female, the youngest was fifteen and the oldest we know about eighty-six. But there's something . . . intangible, but there if you know what I mean. It's like he leaves a . . . an impression behind, a . . .' she laughed uncertainly. 'Sorry, I'm letting my imagination run away with me. I suppose it happens after a morning of crime scene photos.'

Naomi nodded. It did. She could remember the effect. 'So,' she said as Alec returned. 'Who do you want to start with? Me or Alec? Either way I think we should send out for pizza or something. I bet you've not eaten and I don't think we've got anything in the fridge worth making sandwiches from.'

'Thanks,' Tess said and Naomi understood she was grateful not just for the offer of food, but also for the tacit understanding that this would be a long discussion and that they were willing to give her the time to have it.

NINETEEN

It was DCI Field who attended the post-mortem in Tess's place. He had studied the crime scene photos but facing the actual corpse, Field thought, was always different. Always both more intense but also oddly easier. Field had analysed that many times but never come up with a satisfactory reason as to why that should be.

'No DI Fuller?'

'No, I'm afraid you're stuck with me.'

'She's prettier.'

Field laughed. 'Can't argue with that. How are you, Deacon?'

'Getting older. You?'

'The same. How are the family?'

'Grown and flown. It must be what. Ten years?'

'Easily that. The records say you did the PM on Rebecca Arnold.'

'I did,' Deacon agreed. 'I've reviewed the records and on the face of it, I'd say there are a lot of similarities.'

Field approached the table and studied the girl's face. There was bruising on the cheekbone and a small cut on the cheek but otherwise the face was untouched. Her hair spread out against the stainless steel and hung down over the end of the bench. It would have reached the girl's waist, Field guessed. 'He combed her hair.'

'It looks that way, and he cut a strand, probably a souvenir.' Deacon turned the head slightly and showed Field a small patch where the hair had been cut close to the scalp.

'Did he do that to Rebecca Arnold?'

'Not that I recorded. But a ring was missing. It was tight on her finger, so he took that too. At least that's the assumption. It was missing anyway.'

'And the wounds. Pre- or post-mortem?'

Deacon paused. 'She died when he cut her throat. Arterial blood was still pumping. The spray hit the ceiling and probably covered the killer, though it had lost some of its force by then. If you look at the crime scene photos, the bed was up against the wall, the cut was made from the victim's right, across to her left and was made with considerable force. He was almost certainly leaning over her and drew the knife towards himself.'

'And the order of the injuries?'

'Blood patterns from the crime scene indicate that there was bleeding from the incision, here to here.' Deacon indicated the opening in the abdomen from ribcage to pubic bone. 'I have to assume she was still alive at that point. Tox isn't back yet, but from the lack of defensive wounds I think we can assume she was unconscious or at least sedated and subdued.'

'I suppose we should be thankful for small mercies. How long would this have taken?'

'Hard to say. It depends how much of a hurry he was in. But, just speculating, he didn't rush and he knew exactly what he wanted to do. The incisions are straight and clean and there are no hesitation cuts. No sense that he had to think about it. He had a steady hand and a keen eye.'

'A doctor, maybe?'

'Or just someone with a lack of fear and a full measure of confidence,' Deacon said. 'Am I right in assuming there have been others between Rebecca Arnold and this poor girl?'

Field nodded.

'I'd have been surprised if not. According to my recollection, old Fincher was involved in the Arnold case, wasn't he?'

'The psychiatrist, yes. Joe Jackson consulted with him. Unofficially.'

'Which means he too is tainted, I suppose. For that matter, I should be as well. I was a friend of Joe's back then and my findings are in the case file.'

'DI Jackson knew everyone, seemed to have a finger in every pie going,' Field said. 'The question we have to ask is, does the fact that he seems to have been a murderer also make him a bad detective? How much should we call into question?'

'Well, good luck with that one,' Deacon told him. He signalled to his assistant that he was ready to begin. Field stepped back and watched.

TWENTY

'Jackson had a theory,' Alec said. 'He was convinced that whoever the killer was, he was either an investigator or in the medical profession.'

'And why was that?'

'Truthfully? I was too far down the food chain to be told. But I do know he had a particular suspect in mind. Hemsby or—'

'Hemingsby?' Tess said, recalling the name from her quick perusal of the case files. 'I don't remember who he was.'

'A shrink,' Alec said. 'I think, anyway. I don't recall if he was the psychiatrist kind or the psychologist variety or maybe a marriage guidance counsellor for all I know. Jackson was so convinced he was our man that he all but ignored two other suspects.'

'If Joe thought that was the best lead then there's every chance it was,' Naomi said thoughtfully. 'Whatever else he was he was a brilliant investigator. His clear up rate was—'

'Formidable because he coerced or otherwise persuaded just about every suspect that crossed our threshold to have other offences taken into consideration that just happened to be hanging around looking for a viable offender to own up to them. I saw him in action, Naomi.'

'So did I.'

'No. Sorry, he was very careful to keep you at arm's length. You saw the Joe Jackson that he wanted his protégé to see. He protected you, Naomi. Wanted to be Mr Clean in your eyes.'

'Alec, that's not fair.'

'I'm sorry, love. That's just how it was.'

'How you chose to see it!' Naomi frowned, wondering why she was still defending a man who had caused her so much pain. Probably because the child Naomi still remembered the man who had listened to her, seemingly cared about her, encouraged her when all she could feel was guilt and shame that her best friend had disappeared in part because she and Naomi had argued. Naomi should have been with Helen that morning. She had let her down.

Tess shifted awkwardly. 'The two other suspects,' she said. 'Why were they down-graded?'

'They weren't,' Alec said. 'Just shifted to other members of the investigative team. Joe headed up the focus on Hemingsby. He called in a man called Fincher, I think he was head of some university department or other to advise. I can't remember where—'

'It'll be in the records,' Tess assured him. 'And what did you think. Did you favour anyone?'

Alec laughed. 'Tess, I was barely out of my probationary year. I fetched and carried and made tea and did house to house. After what had happened with Jackson's little undercover stunt, no one seemed prepared to risk me crossing the road by myself never mind get properly involved in an investigation like this.'

'But you were one of the first to attend the crime scene. You were on the investigation. You attended the briefings.'

Alec nodded acknowledgement of that. 'We got called to the Arnold house,' he said. 'Briggs was out on his usual beat and I was with him. Alfie Briggs was and is a fantastic community officer. That's where his skills and his heart are and why he's never looked for promotion beyond sergeant and stayed in uniform. The parents had discovered her body, the father called the police and the ambulance and Alfie and I were only a street away. A general call went out and we quite literally ran down to the Arnold house. By the time we got there the mother was out in the street, screaming that someone had butchered her daughter.'

'Butchered? That was the word she used?'

Alec nodded. 'Which made it even stranger that she agreed to it being called a stabbing. Publicly, that's what it became and that's what the media reported.'

'But a lot of people would have been aware that it was more than that,' Naomi observed. 'Friends, family, whoever heard her shouting in the street and made their own connection.'

'Yes, but the details were still kept under wraps. Yes, I'm sure a few people would have been privy to the whole facts, but death was formally declared to be asphyxia, the so-called stabbing element was officially reported as happening after death and was in fact recorded on the PM as *post*-mortem.'

'Did he strangle her?' Naomi asked.

'No, he pushed her face down into the pillow and then put his full weight on her back, kept the pressure on while she suffocated.'

'God. That can take—'

'Too long.'

Silence fell for a moment, broken only by the tap-tap-sweep of Napoleon's wagging tail.

'And when you arrived at the house?' Tess picked up Alec's story.

'We got the mother inside. The father was sitting on the stairs. He was still holding on to the phone and the call taker was trying to tell him help was on the way, but he wasn't listening. Alfie Briggs told me to take the phone and report our presence to control and he led them both through to the front living room. A neighbour had followed us in. From next door. I tried to make her leave, but Mrs Arnold grabbed on to her and just carried on screaming and crying, so we let the neighbour through, put them all in the front room and just closed the door on them. I'd managed to shut the street door by then, but a crowd had gathered. It's one of those little terraced streets and back then it was a mix of retired people and young families, mothers and kids heading off for the school run, so there were plenty of people about to hear and see the commotion.'

'And you went to look at the scene?'

'Technically, Alfie and I were the first officers attending. It was our job to secure the scene, so we went up the stairs to the girl's bedroom.'

'What time was it? You mentioned the school run.'

'About eight thirty. Rebecca was usually up before eight, snatched a bit of breakfast and then went off to work. It was only a few minutes' walk from home. The parents had been out the night before. Mr Arnold was a member of some charity thing . . . Rotary Club or Buffaloes or . . . I don't remember, sorry. Anyway, they'd been out and slept later than they usually did. They woke at around eight and realized immediately that something was wrong.'

'Wrong?'

Alec hesitated, then said, 'For one thing Rebecca wasn't up. For another, you could smell the blood and shit from the landing. It was a small house, typical terrace layout, the stairs went up from the middle room and a door closed the stairs off. You know the kind of thing I mean?'

Beside her, Naomi felt Tess nod.

'We went up the stairs and along the corridor. The parent's room was at the front so you'd got the top of the stairwell separating the two rooms. The third, little bedroom had been converted into a bathroom. Rebecca was an only child.'

'And—'

'And the door was still open. The mother had gone to call her but they'd both realized that something was terribly wrong, so Mr Arnold followed. They'd opened the door and seen her. Mr Arnold had the presence of mind to stop his wife from going into the room. She said afterwards she just wanted to hold her little girl because that's what mother's do when their child is hurt.'

'So you just observed from the doorway?'

'I don't think she ever forgave him, you know. For not letting her go to their daughter. For holding her back—'

'He was right. There was nothing she could do and it would have perhaps contaminated the crime scene.'

'I'm not sure that's the point,' Naomi said softly. 'It's instinct, isn't it. To hold those you love as tight as you can, keep them safe. It must have cut her as deep as the killer cut her child.'

'And then?' Tess's voice had a shake in it and Naomi knew she must be visualizing the bedroom. Her memory of all the other violent scenes she had observed combining to make this all the more real.

'And then we went back down the stairs and waited for back up to arrive. Alfie posted me by the door and he went through to the front room to talk to the parents. Three patrol cars and an ambulance arrived only a few minutes later. SOCO, as it was then, turned up just a short time after.'

'And you kept the scene intact until then?'

Alec hesitated, thinking it all through. 'Procedure wasn't as tight as it is now. The strict handoff from FOA to CSI wasn't as controlled and if I remember right, Joe Jackson and another officer went upstairs before we handed over to the forensics crew. But I think they just did what we had done and looked from the door. I'd identified a path, I do remember that. Alfie and I had kept to the right-hand side of the stairs and the right-hand side of the bit of corridor. Jackson and the other officer did the same. I watched them go up the stairs and I'm pretty certain it was just before SOCO turned up.'

'And the other officer?'

'I think it was a sergeant Bryce. He retired not long after and I didn't really know him. It'll be in the records, though.'

'Bryce died just after he retired,' Naomi said. 'Lasted a year and then had a major heart attack. I remember the funeral. I was on duty directing cars at the cemetery. There was a good turnout.'

'There's always a good turnout,' Alec observed. 'It's just the way things are.'

Naomi recalled Joe Jackson's funeral. The world and his wife had turned up to pay their respects but that had been before . . . before anyone had known that her beloved mentor had been a murderer.

'And after that?' Tess prompted.

'I was on crowd control, the street was cordoned and only residents let through, then we escorted them to their houses. The press arrived and the rubberneckers and then, like I said, I was engaged to make the tea and do the filing and ask the neighbours if they'd seen anyone suspicious in the area. And that was that, really. I remember later that morning Jackson came out to talk to the press.'

'Joe was good with the media,' Naomi said.

'I'm sure he was,' Alec said. 'Jackson could have put a positive spin on the devil himself if he'd had a mind to.'

TWENTY-ONE

He had watched the two young men leave the university earlier and had followed them to the hotel, bought a coffee in the bar and settled down to read his paper. The boy called Patrick turned to look at him, idly curious as he entered the bar. He had glanced across again as the coffee had been delivered to the table and then removed his attention to his friends.

He had watched the little group. The girl and the boy who had found their dead friend and the two he had followed, joined shortly thereafter by a third. He watched them with regret. The boy would be so perfect, and there was still a little sadness that he had been forced to make the substitution. But you were dealt your hand and you played it and that was that.

He felt no urgency about the situation anyway, no pressure to act in the foreseeable future. He had, long ago, learnt to exercise self-control. To wait out the time between and to cover his tracks. He knew, of course, that connections had been made and that the police had looked for a pattern and no doubt found several; some real and some imagined by those who fancied themselves to have a little psychological insight – an idea that amused him greatly. A little knowledge was not just a dangerous thing, it also served, more often than not as a misdirect. A template against which expectation could be measured.

The girl left the group and soon after that it broke up. He followed the object of his interest for a while, but then turned and headed off to have lunch before his afternoon appointment.

All was well, he thought. All, in fact, was very well.

*   *   *

'Tell me about the three suspects,' Tess said. 'Anything you remember.'

Alec moved restlessly and Naomi guessed he was getting impatient with all the rush of past memories. 'Your records will tell you more than I can.'

'But I'd welcome your impressions.'

'My impressions. Right.' Alec reached for a slice of pizza and munched pensively for a moment, gathering his thoughts.

'What was it about Hemingsby that appealed to DI Jackson? What made him stand out?' Tess prompted.

Alec shook his head. 'I don't know that,' he said. 'The other two were local men, known to have been in the area and one had previous. Greening, I think the name was. I don't recall the first name. He was a local butcher, known to get aggressive after a drink and he'd narrowly escaped jail, if I remember right. GBH. The victim claimed to have been threatened with a knife, but Greening had used his fists and both were drunk. There was something else as well, but . . .' He shook his head. 'Sorry.'

'And he was in the frame because?'

'Because he'd been seen hanging around outside the Arnold house and making a nuisance of himself. He fancied his chances with Rebecca, apparently. I think they'd been at the same school though he was a few years older. She had a steady boyfriend and made it plain she wasn't interested.'

'And the boyfriend was alibied?'

'Must have been. I don't remember anything about him.'

Alec frowned, trying to drag the memories to the surface. 'Greening had a sister. Younger. Rebecca and the sister were friends, I think.'

'And because he was a butcher he'd be comfortable with knives and have a knowledge of anatomy,' Tess said thoughtfully.

'Didn't they reckon the same thing about the Ripper cases? No evidence that old Jack was a butcher either in the end. But yes, I suppose that would have made him an acceptable suspect. That and his background and the fact that the parents had already told him to bugger off and leave their little girl alone.'

'Still, it's one hell of a leap,' Naomi commented.

'And suspect lists have been drawn up on a lot less.'

'True. Everything has to start somewhere. Who was the second suspect?'

'Dilly Hughes,' Alec said.

'Dilly?'

Alec laughed at Tess's tone. 'Named for Frank Dillinger,' he said. 'I kid you not.'

'And, apart from having an unfortunate name, he was liked because?'

'Because he had a history of sexual . . . escapades is probably the best way of describing them. Nothing violent that we knew about, but he liked to expose himself to young girls in the park and had an unfortunate habit of standing, buck naked, pressed up against his bedroom window in full view of the street. He lived on Landsmoore Road, that little enclave of 1970s houses with the big windows, so you can imagine the full impact.'

'And exposure is often a precursor to sexual violence,' Tess said with a nod.

'Statistically, yes. The family moved away pretty smartly after the Arnold murder and there were a half dozen girls who came forward to say that Dilly had grabbed at their breasts or made lewd suggestions. Psychiatric reports, if I remember right, suggested that our Dilly wasn't all there but he'd been seen in the vicinity of the Arnold house on several occasions and Rebecca was certainly one of the young women he targeted. She'd lodged two or three complaints with the police. Alfie will probably remember it better. He was probably one of the officers tasked with going round to have a word with the family.'

'And no charges were brought? Just the complaints?'

'Far as I remember, yes. But I may be wrong. As I say the family moved away and I don't know what happened after.'

'And of those two, Dilly Hughes and Greening, the general opinion was?'

Alec shrugged. 'They rose to the top of the list because they'd been in the right place at the right time and they had contact with Rebecca Arnold, but we also brought in the usual suspects. Anyone with a conviction for knife crime or sexual violence. There was no suggestion that Rebecca Arnold had been raped or sexually assaulted but consensus was that there was a sexual component to the crime. It was so bloody . . .' he searched for the right word.

'Intimate,' Naomi said.

Alec nodded thoughtfully. 'I suppose that would be a good way of describing it,' he said. 'Perversely intimate. Horrifyingly so.'

'And this Hemingsby? Was he in contact with Rebecca Arnold? How did he make the list?'

'Now that,' Alec said, 'was always something of a puzzlement to those of us not in Jackson's inner circle. I was just suddenly aware that he was on the board as a person of interest and then as a suspect. Beyond that—'

'But you must have been present at the briefings,' Tess objected.

'And very little was said beyond the fact that Hemingsby was a suspect. Look, you have to understand the way Jackson worked.'

Naomi shifted uncomfortably. She wanted to object but in truth found she could not. In some ways Joe Jackson was unpredictable and difficult, even she had to admit that. He led an investigation from the front, confiding in a select few who could be relied upon to agree with his reasoning and not question his methods. He was very much in favour of defining a 'need to know' and his opinion was generally that very few people needed to know very much. She bit her lip, vaguely annoyed with both herself and with Alec that she should be forced to come over, even slightly, to his way of thinking.

'Jackson had certain colleagues that he trusted with his ideas. The rest of us were just worker ants. He gave out his instructions and we followed them. But over Hemingsby he was even more close-lipped than usual and I suppose that was understandable in a way. Hemingsby was respectable, had friends who might intervene on his behalf and create a lot of noise, according to Jackson. We should tread carefully. Understand, this was the impression I got, I knew very little about the man or his background though I vaguely recall that he thought Dilly Hughes might have been a patient of his and I think that might have been how the initial connection was made. Something like that, anyway, but what I remember is mostly gossip I picked up so don't hold me to it.'

'And how did he go from being a witness to being a suspect?' Tess wanted to know.

'Sorry. I just can't tell you that. Only that he did. Meanwhile we plebs continued with our house to house and our interviews and with chasing the likes of Dilly Hughes and interviewing members of the public who came in or phoned in and were certain they'd seen something that might crack the case . . . and you can understand, the local community took this very personally, very much to heart and everyone and his dog wanted to help out any way they could.'

'Information overload.' Naomi smiled. 'Who kept the book?'

The book; a collation of all leads, all information received, all interviews and suspicions and tasks completed or left undone. It was the bible; the core text for any major case.

She felt rather than heard Alec hesitate. 'Well,' he said at last, 'Alfie Briggs acted as collator for the general enquiry.'

'But?'

'But not for Hemingsby.'

'No,' Alec agreed. 'Not for Hemingsby.'

They fell silent for a few moments and then Tess said, 'Look, I'll get this from the records when I go through, but tell me. Surely DI Jackson wasn't SIO on this? Who headed up the MIT?'

'If I remember right, the new structure for Major Incident Teams had just been established up here. We were a twelvemonth or so behind the Met in getting the full structure in place,' Alec said. 'It was a DCI called Frearson, I think. But Jackson had day to day control of the enquiry. Rumour was, he and Frearson went way back.'

'Which doesn't mean—' Naomi started to object.

'Which means only what I've just said,' Alec said firmly. 'Naomi, Tess, I was a very junior officer in a very big team. I saw what I saw and Joe Jackson appeared to be the one calling the shots. What DCI Frearson got up to behind the closed door of his office was an unknown then and it certainly is now. I think he wasn't far off retirement at the time and I think he went back to wherever soon after the investigation began to wind down.'

'And it remained an unsolved,' Tess said.

'Just like all the rest,' Naomi added.

'Just like all the rest.'

TWENTY-TWO

Tess returned to the office in sombre mood to find that DCI Field had returned from the post-mortem and was waiting to brief her.

'The tox screen has yet to come back, of course, but the post turned up a couple of needle marks, one just below the chin and one beneath the armpit, so we can assume she was drugged and unable to fight back.'

'Conscious?' Tess asked. Her mouth felt too full of saliva and she tried hard to swallow it.

'Until we know how high her cortisol levels were we won't know for sure but—'

'And do we know' – perversely, her mouth had dried now, lips sticking to teeth. She tried again. 'Do we know the order that the injuries occurred?'

'From the preliminary analysis of the blood spatter it seems he cut her open first. Cut her throat after . . . the blood pressure had already diminished. She'd have gone into shock, her body would have been shutting down. Cutting the throat made the end quicker but it was already inevitable.'

'She could still be alive through all that. Jesus! It doesn't bear thinking about.'

'Then don't. Focus on what you can change, not what's already gone.'

She nodded automatically. It was good advice but she didn't have a hope in hell of following it. She wondered if Field did either.

'How did you get on with the Friedmans?'

'Naomi is a bit touchy. Understandably, I suppose.'

'Touchy? How.'

Tess shrugged. 'She and Joe Jackson had history before she

joined up. When Naomi was twelve or thirteen her best friend was kidnapped and murdered. Naomi and Helen had been arguing and separated in a huff. Helen waited for her on the way to school the following day, but Naomi went another route. Helen disappeared, Naomi had a hard time forgiving herself. Joe Jackson helped her pick up the pieces, apparently.'

'Ah,' Field said. 'And that's the case that—'

'That Joe Jackson is now a suspect in – for murder. He left a note of confession. It came to light after his death. His daughter brought it in and—'

'And the famous Joe Jackson fell from grace – albeit post-humously. There were two killings linked to Jackson, weren't there? The girl Helen Jones and a man. Wasn't he supposed to have been the daughter's boyfriend?'

Tess nodded. 'They were found at the site of two adjoining houses, they would have been new builds at the time. Helen in one, Robert Williams under the patio of the one next door. Williams was the older lover of Jackson's daughter, Penny. It seems that Jackson tried to scare him off and when that didn't work took more direct action.'

'Right.' Field was thoughtful. 'Well, I'll familiarize myself with the background but might it be a good idea to talk to the daughter as well. Penny Jackson might remember something, might have spoken to her father or overheard him talking to someone else.'

'It's a long shot,' Tess commented, 'I'll track down a current address.'

'You were telling me about the Friedmans.'

'Um, yes. Alec, on the other hand . . . anyway, they both cooperated as best they could and I'm sure will continue to do so. But I'm not sure they can tell us very much. Naomi was not involved in the case at all and Alec was a very green, very new officer kept on the periphery.'

'And I understand was not a Joe Jackson acolyte.' He smiled. 'I've been chatting to Sergeant Briggs.'

'No, he was not.' She hesitated. 'Alfie . . . Sergeant Briggs . . . he's—'

'Internal Affairs will interview him on the record, but word is he's not under any suspicion. Alfie Briggs was incidental to

Jackson. Lacked the ambition and the drive to be of any interest. I don't think he's got anything to worry about and IA are in agreement that he's more use to us than he is any kind of threat to integrity.'

Tess bristled. 'Alfie Briggs is the definition of integrity,' she told him. 'Right, well I'll get all this written up and then get back to the case reviews.'

She collected a coffee on the way and returned to the cramped little office in which the rest of the team were poring over the records.

Tess flopped down in front of her computer and opened a new document, began to type up her conversation with Naomi and Alec.

More paperwork, she thought, glancing round at the stacks and boxes already divvied up among her colleagues. More information, when they were already drowning in the stuff.

TWENTY-THREE

Nathan still had a few contacts left in the police force up and down the country, people he had worked with or who had worked for Clay or who owed Nathan or his one-time mentor a favour. It was not as easy as it had been when he had the full weight of Clay's organization behind him but Nathan still had some leverage and by lunchtime he had a dossier compiled to show Gregory.

Nathan watched as Gregory dug into his lunch and flipped through the photographs and preliminary reports.

'Does nothing put you off your food?'

Gregory had the grace to look slightly apologetic while he thought about that. Then he shook his head. 'Sorry. Not really.'

Nathan shrugged. 'So, what do you think? What the killer did indicates experience. He was relaxed. There was no rush.'

'No. This is not a first-time kill, that's for sure. Not even a second or third, I'd say. So the question is, how many times before? We need to find that out and track the cold cases.'

'What makes you sure they'd be cold cases?'

'So cold they're dead and buried,' Gregory said. 'Failure to find a murderer capable of this kind of callous, careful behaviour would be a career killer. Finding the killer, on the other hand, would make you untouchable even if you never got anything right again. So, he's not been found yet, this is most likely not a copycat either.'

'I agree,' Nathan said. 'Copycats generally rely on the media to give them the details of what they are emulating. I think we'd both have remembered if something like this had hit the media. I did a quick search, didn't find anything that looked similar so far.'

'My guess is that he operates at long intervals, and over a wide geographical area. And that the police keep the worst of the details out of the public domain.'

Nathan nodded and took another bite of toast. 'Chances are he'll be satisfied for a while and there's no danger to Patrick or his friends. At least we'll be able to reassure Harry of that.'

'On balance, that's likely to be true. Chances are he'll also hang around to watch the police operation. He'll like to see what effect he's had. That'll be part of his game plan.' Gregory flipped through the notes Nathan had managed to acquire. A summary of the crime scene reports and initial findings from the hastily arranged post-mortem. No tox screen yet, no blood work or chemical analysis. He turned one of the photographs around and peered closely at it.

'Cause of death is currently presumed to be exsanguination,' Nathan remarked. 'What are you looking at?'

'Her face,' Gregory said. He put the image down beside Nathan's plate and tapped at it with his index finger. 'Look at the mouth.'

'I don't see anything?'

'Exactly. If there'd been a tape or a gag, there'd be trace, there'd be abrasions, maybe traces of adhesive or even splits at the corners of her mouth if she'd struggled against a gag. Which she would have done. Her friends heard nothing. He kept her quiet somehow. Not,' Gregory added, 'that any kind of gag would have shut her up. Not while he . . . well.'

'She wasn't dead when he cut her,' Nathan observed. 'The arterial spray hit the fucking ceiling.'

'So, we hope she was at least unconscious, don't we? She wasn't able to struggle or fight back, that's for sure.'

Nathan looked again at the pictures and pushed his plate away. He nodded, not really trusting himself to speak. He was aware of Gregory watching him, observing the pallor and the reaction to the pictures. Not judging; Gregory was merely curious and, Nathan knew, also very conscious of the emotional responses that he found lacking in himself and that, on a purely intellectual level, he sought to understand. It wasn't that Gregory was incapable of feeling. Gregory's loyalty to friends was unparalleled. But, Nathan thought wryly, Gregory was still a bloody sociopath.

'How many more,' Nathan said. 'And over what time frame?'

'We can be certain there are a few and my guess is that this killer has as long a career behind him as I do. Think you'll be able to get the tox reports when they come in? And a full post-mortem report?'

As long a career, maybe, Nathan thought. He doubted he'd have left Gregory's body count in his wake. 'Probably,' he said, in answer to the post-mortem question. 'Gregory, Harry doesn't need to know all the details of this. You do know that?'

'*I* won't tell him if you think I shouldn't. But you're forgetting Patrick. *His* friends found the body. They won't be able to keep something like this to themselves.'

'They'll have been warned by the police not to talk about it.'

'To keep clear of the press, certainly, but if you were a normal teenage kid and you'd seen something like this for the first time, who would you turn to? Would you be able to keep your mouth shut? Not relieve the pressure by talking to your friends?'

'Fair point,' Nathan conceded.

'So his friends will talk to Patrick and Patrick will talk to Harry because that's what he does. He and his dad are close. And he'll know it's alright to confide in Bob and Annie too, because they know about this kind of business. And they know how to keep their mouths shut.'

Nathan disagreed. 'They know about violence, yes. Annie

spent a good chunk of her childhood living in war zones and most of her adult life photographing them but this is something else. But you're right. Patrick will see them as safe to talk to. But I think he might censor the details for Harry and frankly, I doubt his friends will want to describe a scene like this in detail. It happened to someone they cared about, Gregory. They'll want to block as much as they can.'

He could see Gregory considering all that. Finally the older man nodded. 'I'll give Harry a call later,' he said. 'He works away from home on a Thursday. I doubt he'll want to be phoned while he's bean counting.'

'You memorized Harry's schedule?'

'And Patrick's timetable,' Gregory said.

Nathan shook his head. 'You just can't help it, can you?'

'It's intel,' Gregory said. 'You can never have too much intelligence.'

TWENTY-FOUR

After Tess had gone, Naomi felt restless and irritable. Alec suggested a walk, but that wasn't what she wanted either.

'If we walk, we'll just end up talking about this.'

'If we stay here, we'll just end up talking about it.'

'I know, so what's the point.'

Alec took her hand and squeezed it gently. 'I'm sorry,' he said. 'I know this must be—'

'No. No you don't. You have no idea how this makes me feel. You have no idea how bloody angry I am, how . . .' She wasn't sure what the 'how' was, just that she felt it. She pulled her hand away from Alec's and got up, went to stand by the window as though staring out at the view.

Naomi had moved here after she had lost her sight. The flat had been ideal, with its simple layout, small kitchen where she could have everything within reach and smooth wooden floors. The view from the window had been described to her by her sister, Sam. A narrow street of terraced houses, some larger, like this one on the corner that had been converted into flats and even holiday lets. A little playground where she could often hear the kids playing when the school day ended and, down the gap between her street and the one running crosswise to it, a glimpse of the promenade and the beach only five minutes' walk away.

The flat had felt safe. A security pad on the front entrance and then a key to her own, very solid, front door. It had felt easy and comfortable. It wasn't the first time that the realities of the world had come crashing through into her sanctuary but this time it felt so much more personal. This was her past as well and not since that day, nearly four years ago when she had heard that Helen's body had been found had she felt so exposed to it. So intruded upon. And somehow it didn't help that Alec was now caught up in that intrusion.

'Is there anything I can do?'

Naomi frowned, suddenly irritated by the tone, by the fact that he really cared, that he was worried about her and equally irritated by how irrational that was. She should be glad that he understood or at least tried to understand the way she felt.

She shook her head, wishing she could tell him to just go away and leave her alone for a while. Knowing that she couldn't.

'Look,' he said. 'I'm going to walk down to the shops, we're short of milk and bread and . . . and other bits. OK?'

She nodded, not quite trusting her voice, both annoyed and relieved that he should have read her so well.

'Joe Jackson,' Naomi intoned as she heard the street door slam shut. 'Joe bloody Jackson.' Dead and buried and yet still causing pain.

She threw herself into her favourite chair beside the window and felt Napoleon nuzzling at her hand, upset that his people were unhappy. She stroked the silky head and closed her eyes leaving her mind free to wander. She had joined up after the Rebecca Arnold case had gone cold, but was surprised at how much she remembered of the atmosphere that still permeated. A skeleton team reviewed any new evidence that came in, but the Major Incident Team had been dissolved. It was still talked about, though. Officers that had been involved unable to let go, and Joe one of them, gnawing at the bones of the case, checking in almost daily with those still involved to see if there was progress.

'We'll get the bastard,' he had told Naomi. 'We'll get him. He'll make a mistake and I'll be there.'

'He'll do it again, won't he?'

'They always do. His type, they can't help themselves. It's a compulsion, an addiction. It's not like your common or garden murderer. He or she is focussed on the single reason – might be money, might be lust, might be that they feel someone's done wrong to them, but it's a single reason and a single victim. Bang, it's done and the chances are they'll never step out of line again.'

'Murder isn't exactly just stepping out of line.' Naomi remembered being amused and a little bit shocked.

'Compared to the likes of this bastard it is. This wasn't passion or anger or desperation or misjudgement, even. This was planned. This was done just because the fucker wanted to do it. This is a whole different animal.'

'Stepping out of line,' Naomi said softly. 'You certainly did that, didn't you, Joe. How did what you did to Helen fit in with passion or anger or desperation. Was it one of your 'misjudgements'? Fuck it, Joe, how could you do something like that? How does it make you any different from—'

She shook her head, feeling the tears prick at the corners of her eyes. Even now she couldn't believe that he had done it. Even now, with all the evidence, with the confession, with the finding of the body, she still couldn't equate the Joe Jackson she had known with the murderer of her best friend. And the guilt of that was sometimes overwhelming.

Naomi gave in. As she had done so often in the past, she slid down from her chair and buried her face in Napoleon's soft coat and she wept, bitterly.

TWENTY-FIVE

'There are six victims that we know about.' Tess glanced up from her notes and surveyed the room. 'As DCI Field has already told you, we'll be bringing in a Behavioural Investigative Adviser and they'll be able to talk through the possibility of other victims, but our initial assessment is that the killer's behaviour at the first crime scene we are aware of is too practised and confident for this to have been a first run. For now, though, we're taking it as our start point.

'Victimology is inconsistent. There have been two males and three females, now four females including Leanne Bolter. I have to stress that even the collation of these cases is speculative. There are no, I repeat, no clear forensic links between the scenes, in fact our forensic information is very limited. The similarities between scenes, between the methods used to kill and a few more abstract features that may only link one or two of the murders are what bring these together. That being said, we have to start somewhere.'

'Can I just ask?'

Tess looked towards the speaker. It was Clem Boroughs, the red-headed DS who had come with the Internal Affairs squad. She nodded. 'Go ahead.'

'Who initially collated the files? Who made the initial selection; linked the investigations.'

Tess took a deep breath. 'That would, in part, have been DI Jackson,' she said. 'During the Rebecca Arnold investigation he submitted data to HOLMES and came back with a single link. To Martia Richter, the first known of our cases. When the new Home Office system came online in 2000, he resubmitted and two other cases were linked. Since then, with the final review in 2004, when all forces were linked up to the system, two other unsolveds have been added to the list. I'd recommend we stake another run at it now, the system has improved considerably since the last request was made, that was only three years ago, but you never know . . .'

Boroughs nodded. 'Can you write up the process for me? Who requested what, inputted what data, what force and so on? I'll take another swipe at it.'

'Thanks,' Tess said, ticking one job off her list at least, though, at the same time, not sure she wanted to be hands off. The Home Office Large Major Enquiry and its newer counterpart, ViCLAS, the Violent Crime Linkage Analysis System could be awkward to navigate. Like all databases, the results you got could depend so much on the way you searched and she'd have liked to know what parameters were being used.

'So the first victim was?' Field prompted her.

'First known victim was an eighty-six-year-old woman called Martia Richter. Unmarried, lived alone. PM has cause of death as blood loss. She was eviscerated and the presumption is that she died of shock and blood loss. He didn't cut her throat or smother her – as he did with Rebecca Arnold. PM records that there were no hesitation injuries and the body was posed, sitting upright against her bed. He'd combed out her hair. Friends and neighbours testified that she'd always worn it up, though she'd kept it long and that she braided it before bed at night. The braid had been carefully undone and the hair combed and fanned out across the bed behind her.'

Tess took the photo of the crime scene that showed the final position of the body and affixed it to the board. She heard the shocked murmur of response. Get used to it, she thought bitterly. It won't be getting any better.

'Who found the body,' someone asked.

'Her niece. She had a key and when she couldn't get a reply to her knocking, she let herself in. They'd been planning a shopping trip and lunch. A regular fortnightly thing, though apparently someone from the extended family made contact every day, even if it was only a phone call. No one reported strangers hanging around, no forensics that can be directly attributed to the killer. She was drugged with ketamine, but unlikely to have been unconscious. There's one thing worth noting, maybe, that's the niece saying that her aunt had been worried about someone she had seen the last time they had been out together. She'd not mentioned it at the time, but a few days later confessed that 'a man' she had spotted when they'd been out for tea with friends had been preying on her mind and that she was sure she had seen him since. The niece wasn't sure what to make of it and suggested that if she was worried she should report him, but the thing was, there was nothing concrete to report. Her aunt just had a feeling, a sense that there was something strange or odd or dangerous about this man. That was all.'

'Do we have contact details for the niece?' Field asked. 'It might be worth talking to her again.'

Tess nodded. 'She's made sure she's kept in the loop, apparently. Even when she moved house she made certain the local police knew where she was going and she called the SIO on a regular basis until he retired.'

Another murmur, a brief burst of laughter, out of place but relieving the tension.

'The next we know about was Rebecca Arnold, almost ten years later. So I'll hand over to Alfie for that as he was first on scene.'

First, with Joe Jackson, she thought. She listened as Alfie outlined for the team what he has already outlined for her. How they had been only a street away and run to the Arnold house. The mother screaming and the father on the phone desperately calling for assistance.

'Tox from the Leanne Bolter murder suggests that ketamine was used to render her partially unconscious whereas he pressed Rebecca Arnold face down into the pillow and smothered her.

'Blood spatter indicates Leanne Bolter was still alive when he cut her, but only just. There was less arterial spray than might have been expected. The pressure was already lowered.'

'So he can improvise,' Field said. 'Differences in MO.'

'And which might indicate that he can occasionally be impulsive. Choose a victim without time to go equipped,' Alfie agreed.

'And the third was male. After a three-year gap. Thirty-two-year-old William Trevenick. IT support for a local computer retailer. He came home from a night out to find his killer waiting for him. Friends shared a taxi with him, watched him to his door and then went off home. Apparently he was very drunk, barely managed to make it up the garden path and get his key in the door. He wouldn't have put up much of a fight. No ketamine, but the throat was cut and the body posed. On the bed. His hair was short but it seems to have been combed. William's friends said he used a lot of product in his hair. Wet look gel. The killer had found a bowl in the kitchen, brought it to the bedroom and washed the hair before combing it through.'

'That's just fucking creepy,' someone commented and Tess nodded. Strange, she thought, how it was sometimes the smaller details that got to you. 'Afterwards he emptied the water out in the bathroom and left the bowl there, together with a wet towel that he'd used to partially dry the hair.'

'And no evidence that William Trevenick was worried or scared?'

'None,' Tess confirmed. 'He'd had a night out with friends, had too much to drink, gone home.'

'Fourth was two years after and another male. Keith Allen, thirty-seven, a mechanic at a family-run garage. Keith was a cousin of the owner. The set up was the cousin had a house next to his business premises and the cousin Keith Allen had a flat, like a granny annex, next to the house. If you look at the photo of the premises it looks like it was originally an old coaching inn with the gateway with a padlocked gate through to what would have been the stables and was converted into a workshop.' She pointed. 'Keith Allen's flat is that bit of the building, there. You had to come into the yard to get to it. The door faces on to the yard and there's only a small window on the outside wall and that runs alongside a road. Not a busy road, but . . . best guess was that the killer had come in through the front door.

'Keith Allen was expecting his girlfriend so he'd left the door on the latch and the padlock off the gate.'

'So, the killer was familiar with him. With his habits?' Boroughs speculated.

'It seems a fair assumption.'

'And the girlfriend?'

'Found the body. Just missed the killer. He'd been dead less than an hour. His cousin had spoken to him only two hours before. There was a narrow window of opportunity and the killer took it.'

'Maybe he didn't know about the girlfriend?'

'He seems to have known about everything else.'

'Unless it was a chance thing? He spotted the gate, let himself in, found the door on the latch.'

'Ketamine?' Field asked.

'Was used this time.'

'Which suggests preparation. Mitigates against it being opportunistic.'

'Allen put up a fight, the place was a mess. He also had a head wound so it's likely he was subdued first and then injected. None of the victims seems to have been tied up or gagged but all show signs of petechia which is associated with asphyxia. So, the possibility that breathing was restricted in some way. One of the side effects of ketamine is that it actually opens up the airways and improves rather than depresses circulation, apparently. A couple of the PM exams point this out and that it may have an evidential effect that they can't predict. So there's a good chance he did something else. Something that restricted their breathing but left little obvious trace.

'The last death we know about is the present case. Leanne Bolter.' She paused, waiting for questions. 'Crib sheets will be available after the briefing.' She pointed to the side table where the notes had been laid out. 'There are a couple of names that are worth following up,' she added. 'The consultant forensic psych on two of the cases and who did a review after Keith Allen was a guy called Reg Fincher. He's since retired but . . .'

'Follow it up,' Field said.

'And there's a witness statement from a woman called Deborah Tait who said she saw Keith Allen having an argument with a tall, bearded man outside the garage a couple of days before the murder. I also think it's worth reinterviewing the relatives. You never know.'

Field nodded. 'Your team can handle all that? Good. So, where are we with the current investigation? Don't go away, Tess, I want you to brief us on what the Friedmans had to say.'

Tess nodded and stepped aside, waiting for her next turn.

Patrick and Harry had wandered over to see Naomi and Alec that evening and they had all walked down on to the beach.

Naomi let Napoleon off his harness and took Patrick's arm. Behind them, she could hear Alec and Harry chatting as they threw a ball for Napoleon, their pace slowed by the game, their voices grew more distant as Patrick and Naomi strolled on.

'So,' she asked him. 'How are you? What have you been up to?'

Patrick laughed. 'Well that's another way of asking,' he said. 'I'm fine. Everyone is upset and a lot of people are scared and some have gone back home.'

'Understandable, I suppose.' She felt Patrick nod.

'Oh, sure, but we both know it wouldn't make any difference. If someone had targeted you it would take more than a change of address to stop them and if you're not a target, then you have nothing to worry about. And as none of us, at any time, have any idea that a crazy might have us in their sights, well it's kind of academic, isn't it?'

'You've spent far too much time around the likes of me and Gregory,' she said. She tried to keep the comment light, but the truth was, Patrick's statement had concerned her. 'You're far too young to be thinking like that,' she said at last.

'Age has nothing to do with it,' he said.

'Then you are far too experienced.'

'Maybe. But there's nothing anyone can do about that is there.'

'Unfortunately not. How are things with your artist?'

She felt him relax a little. 'Bob has started a new body of work,' he said. 'The central theme is The World Tree and it's going to be amazing. He's starting to teach me some restoration techniques. He reckons it's a good fall back for times when no one wants to buy pictures.'

'And did Bob ever need a fall-back position? I thought he'd been successful forever.'

Patrick laughed. 'No one is successful all the time, especially not at the start. But working with Bob will give me a real leg up. I know that. I just love it, Naomi. I'm just learning so much.'

'I'm glad. You have a talent and you work hard. You deserve the attention.'

He shrugged. The arm holding hers jerking a little as the shoulder raised. 'Bob has to verify works of art sometimes,' he said. 'There's a picture that arrived that is probably a fake and he's got to do a report on it for the owner, but the thing is, it's so beautiful. The man who did it . . . who Bob is pretty certain did it . . . he was a real master. He understood so many techniques and Bob says he could copy about a dozen other artists so perfectly that he's certain some of the fakes have made their way into national collections. And I don't get it. He was so bloody brilliant, Naomi, so why didn't he make a success of his own work? How come Bob Taylor made it big – I mean, Bob is amazing and deserves it, but this other artist, Bob says he was a genius but . . .'

'I suppose a lot of it is down to luck,' Naomi mused. 'And consistency and reliability and maybe just down to being identifiable. I mean, you look at a Bob Taylor work and it's instantly recognizable. You look at one of your pictures and it has Patrick Jones written all over it. Maybe if you dissipate your efforts . . . maybe if no one knows what you are, it's harder for them to get into what you do?'

'Maybe. The picture Bob's looking at is a Madonna and child with St Anne. It's small, the sort of picture you'd keep for personal devotion, Bob says. So you'd like, keep it in your bedroom or whatever.' He laughed. 'That's where I'd keep it, anyway. You can't look at it and not feel happy. It's got a kind of glow to it. There's an egg tempera underpainting and then oil glazes and it's on a gesso panel so the light just bounces back through all the layers and Bob says that if it turns out to not be genuine then the owner has the legal right to just destroy it. I hate that idea, Naomi. And you know what scares me? About me, I mean?'

'Is that the thought of that picture being destroyed hurts you almost more than the idea of that girl being killed,' she said softly.

She felt him nod.

'That's fucking awful, isn't it? I mean, what kind of person thinks like that?'

'Patrick, listen to me. You grew up in the shadow of loss and grief. It overwhelmed your life and the lives of everyone around you. Since then you've seen more, done more than anyone of twice your age should have ever done. And now you've started to carve out a niche for yourself, to discover who you really are and where you belong and that's all separate from the stuff you've grown up with, from what you've had to take on. It's yours, it's precious, it's intense. Of course you feel some things more acutely than others. Your life is overwhelmed by things that matter, by life and death and loss. You can only take so much of that before you need to escape from it.'

'Yes, but—'

'Patrick, you are one of the most loving, caring and compassionate people I have ever known. You have nothing to feel guilty about.'

They walked on in silence for a while. The wind had changed direction and was now blowing off the sea, cold and chilling and heavy with salt. Naomi turned to face the ocean, relishing the sharpness of it.

'I take it you've talked to Gregory about the murder,' she said.

'Dad has. Gregory wanted to come down but Dad said no need. I think he just wants the reassurance that Gregory is there, you know. They like each other, which is weird, considering.'

'The hired killer and the accountant.' Naomi laughed.

'Except Gregory isn't for hire these days and Dad is a very reluctant accountant. Gregory's promised to teach him to sail, did you know that?'

'What, boats!'

'I think that's usually what people sail. Yes. Dad's dead keen.'

'Well, you do surprise me. I suppose we'd better turn back. I think it's going to rain, you can feel it in the wind.'

They turned, Patrick on the shore side this time, Naomi closest to the sea. Ahead of them they could hear Alec and Harry laughing about something and Napoleon barking as he chased in and out of the waves.

'Wet dog,' Patrick said. 'And he's found something to roll in.'

'Oh, joy. Never mind. I've got an old towel in my bag. We're used to cleaning him up before we head home. He loves it down here.'

Patrick nodded. He was watching the dark as it crept in from the horizon, clouds promising rain as Naomi had predicted.

The cloud shadow moving across the water, blurring the vanishing point. Up ahead the beach narrowed and the promenade wrapped around, ending at the fairground, the rides still cloaked and covered before the tourist season began in a few weeks' time. A few people wandered along the promenade, some hurried, fleeing the coming rain or simply wanting to get home from work, Patrick supposed. One figure stood beside the railings, looking back out to sea and Patrick was drawn to the stillness of it. As Patrick watched, the man straightened and moved away and something in the way he walked reminded Patrick of the man who had come into the hotel when he had gone to see Ginny and Sam. He tried to think what it was that was familiar, but could not quite define it. Something in the way he consciously straightened his body, in the way he moved so purposefully?

'Penny for them.'

'Not worth it,' Patrick told her, but the feeling nagged that something was wrong. That there was something he should be able to remember.

Napoleon ran up to them, greeting Naomi with a happy and sodden tail and Patrick let the thought go as he bent to pet the wet dog and help Naomi dry him off before putting his harness back on.

When he looked again the man was long gone.

They were getting closer now and the boy glanced his way again. Tom turned and walked back through town towards where he had left his car. The boy, Patrick, would recognize him and he wasn't ready to be recognized. Not yet.

He had watched the four of them and the big black dog descend the steps from the promenade and walk along the beach. The dog's harness had been removed and the dark-haired boy, Patrick, had taken the blind woman's arm. He did so naturally and easily as though this was a familiar thing and the two of them walked ahead of the men, their path along the firm sand newly wetted by the slow, incoming tide. The two men chatted and threw a ball for the dog, lagging behind as they occupied their canine companion. The dog looked happy, he thought. Running in and out of the shallows, rolling on the

sand, chasing his toy, like a child just let out of school and
chasing across the playground.

He knew now who the woman was, and that their paths had
crossed a long time ago and that intrigued him. He liked to
look for patterns and coincidences, finding them oddly pleasing.

'So you were the child that Joe Jackson made such a fuss
about,' Tom murmured. 'Little Naomi Blake.'

He had gone back over her records and discovered that he'd
done two assessments with her before handing her on to a
female colleague for counselling and that DI Jackson had been
very concerned about her progress, checking in frequently to
see how she was coping. She had been thirteen, Tom recalled
and her best friend had disappeared. Everyone knew that she
must be dead. Naomi had felt so guilty, had withdrawn into
herself, taken the pain of it inside of herself and been a long
time learning to open up to life again.

And Tom had played a part in that recovery. Was that a good
thing? He thought it probably was. Did that mean she owed him?
He thought it probably did.

He watched from the promenade railing, the strong wind
blowing in off the sea chilling his face and hands and uncovered
head until the party turned back and began to walk towards the
steps. At one point the boy had looked in Tom's direction and
he could read in the young man's body language that something
caused him concern. A sudden stiffness and caution though Tom
fancied not one in a thousand people would have registered it.

Interesting, he thought. And he was the nephew of Naomi's
dead friend. How would his aunt have felt about him had she
survived. It fascinated him to speculate about what might have
been had circumstances changed. That was, in part, why it was
so satisfying to change those circumstances. To have the power
to make them impossible, non-existent. To make an end as he
saw fit and not one left to dumb chance. It pleased him to think
'*I have made this so*' whether that concerned the recovery of
a child or the ending of a life and therefore of potential for
change. Either way it was emblematic of a job well done. Either
way he took pride in his work.

TWENTY-SIX

Doctor Fincher lived in a retirement village some fifty miles from Pinsent and Vin and Tess left early to go and visit him, intending to see the witness, Deborah Tait, in the early afternoon. She had been the woman who had witnessed the argument between Keith Allen and the unknown man. Deborah Tait was another sixty miles further on than Fincher and that reminded Tess about the breadth of geographical spread of the crimes.

The appointments had been made by DCI Field the evening before and local constabularies had also been informed. Tess had names and numbers she could use to liaise should the need arise.

The morning was wet but bright. Heavy rain overnight had cleared and now the road glistened ahead of them. Even with sunglasses, it was dazzling. They seemed to be driving straight into the sun.

'So, what do we know about this Fincher?'

Vin consulted his notes. 'Sixty-eight years old, consulted on two of our cases. The Allen murder and William Trevenick. Seems he was also briefly involved when Martia Richter was murdered, but the consultant forensic psych on that was someone called Doctor Elia Vincenza, now deceased. Natural causes,' he added. 'She came out of retirement to look at the Richter murder. I wonder why.'

'Maybe Fincher will know.'

'He's an emeritus professor, apparently. Does that mean he wanders about between universities?'

'Maybe. I think it might just mean he's retired and just does a bit now an again, but I may be wrong.'

Vin laughed. 'Whatever. It's good to get out of the office for a while. You can hardly move in that little room, not when we're all in there.'

He was right, Tess thought, though there wasn't a lot anyone could do about it. Space was at a premium and her usual desk had been taken over by Field who had added a table alongside that he had allocated to DI Trinder, the Internal Affairs team leader. Another one who had been brought out of retirement. She knew that a lack of really senior and experienced staff at the top level meant that a number of officers had been coaxed away from their fishing and football and gardening and assigned to look over cold cases, carry out periodic reviews and assist open cases in an advisory capacity but it seemed odd, nevertheless.

'What do you think of Trinder?' she asked.

'Barely spoken to him.'

'I think that goes for most of us. I thought it would be all formal interviews and him breathing down our necks, but he doesn't seem to be playing it that way.'

'I almost wish he would,' Vin said. 'The man prowls. I mean, you look up and there he is. It's like being sixteen again and taking my GCSEs and having the exam invigilators walking up and down the rows. You've done nothing wrong and you still feel bloody guilty.'

'Yeah, I know what you mean. None of his team seems to have met him before, even those from IA. Field knows him, I think.'

'And Joe Jackson did. Don't you find that a bit weird? That they bring in someone who knew him when everyone else has been selected because they didn't.'

'I suppose it depends on whether he was a fan or not,' Tess speculated. 'Far as we know the pair of them hated each other's guts.' Like Alec did. She wondered about the conversation that would have played out after she had left Naomi and Alec the day before. It could not have been comfortable.

The retirement village was well signposted. Apparently it was for the active over fifties and the little bungalows set in parkland looked expensive and carefully manicured. The park was entered via a large gate and a manned gatehouse. They were greeted with smiles and asked if they would like directions – a loaded question, Tess thought, that was a scarcely concealed 'who have you come to see'. The road through the parkland passed a manor house that she guessed would once have owned all the land.

'Looks like they have a golf course,' Vin commented. 'Bet it costs a pretty penny to retire here.'

'Not on a police pension, that's for sure.'

'Not sure it's my cup of tea anyway. It looks too . . . organized. I'll bet no one grows Dahlias.'

'Dahlias? What, the flower?'

'My old man has an allotment. He grows these bloody great multi-coloured things and shows them every autumn. Very serious it is. But this doesn't look like a Dahlia growing area.'

Tess giggled as she imagined Mr Dattani senior and his giant flowers. 'No,' she agreed. 'This looks more like orchids in the conservatory. I think this must be the one.'

She pulled into one of the parking spaces beside Fincher's bungalow and cut the engine.

'He grows those too,' Vin told her. 'You'll have to come round, and admire.'

Doctor Reg Fincher was waiting by the door as they walked up. He was a tall, thin man who stooped slightly as though used to hitting his head or having to bend down to listen. He leaned on a heavy and rather gnarly walking stick. The handle was carved into the shape of a dogs head and worn smooth by long use. Fincher limped as he led them into his home and Tess noticed that his left shoe was built up at the heel.

'I was born with a club foot,' Fincher said and Tess got the impression that he'd got used to explaining himself and preferred to just deal with curiosity straight off. 'Had several operations to straighten my ankle and improve mobility, but . . .' He shrugged. 'Fortunately, I've never had a yen to climb mountains or run marathons. Come along through.'

They followed him into a large and light front room. Beside his chair a trolley had been set out with a kettle and cups and the makings of tea and coffee. A bottle of milk stood in a polystyrene tube. 'Keeps the milk cold,' he said. 'The trolley keeps everything handy. I picked it up for two quid at a car boot. I've become an avid car-booter.'

Tess laughed.

'Oh you'd get on well with my parents,' Vin said. 'Every Sunday they're off somewhere.'

Dahlias and car boot fairs, Tess thought. She wasn't really familiar with either.

Fincher made coffee and then asked what he could do to help. 'Your DCI Field scanned and emailed the crime scene pictures,' he said. And he's given me an overview of your notes. I remember the Trevenick and Allen cases, of course. Terrible. Terrible.'

'And you were briefly involved in—'

'The old lady. Martia Richter. Yes. But only briefly. My colleague, Elia Vincenza, she did the reports on that one. I was fully committed elsewhere so I only did the preliminary write up. Elia took over within a few days and she, of course, went back over everything I'd concluded and made some revisions. I think that must have been the last thing she worked on.'

'She was already retired, wasn't she?'

'Yes, but only recently. She still had her accreditation so there was nothing untoward. It was at a difficult time for the profession, many people left or took different directions. For a while we thought it would collapse in on itself . . .' He paused, a look of concern and sadness drifting across his face.

'Was that after the Colin Stagg affair?' Vin asked.

Fincher nodded. 'There were several years when the profession was in chaos. We undertook root and branch revision and, frankly, it was about time it happened. Even before that there were too many egos riding for a fall. And the media didn't help, of course. The idea that criminal profilers had some sort of magic wand . . . of course, that was because the early practice was so influenced by the American model and the work the FBI had been doing, interviewing serial killers, building their model on what was really quite a narrow sample. And there was the perceived glamour of it all.

'The new professional model is much more Euro centric. It takes more account of regional variations in crime and criminal behaviours and what a Behavioural Investigative Adviser can and can't say and do is now much more clearly defined and very closely peer-reviewed. I'm glad to say that the likes of myself and Elia had a part to play in that. We must be realistic. No one is infallible and no one should place themselves on a psychological pedestal.'

He sat back and Tess felt that he was satisfied now he'd got that off his chest. She was vaguely familiar with the events surrounding the Colin Stagg affair, but made a mental note that she would ask Vin about it when they left.

'So, what do you remember about the cases you were involved in?' Tess asked. 'It would really help to have someone who actually saw the scene. Crime scene photos can only tell us so much and—'

'Absolutely.' Fincher nodded. 'Now, where to begin.'

He closed his eyes as though the better to remember and Tess exchanged a glance with Vin. Fincher was in his element, she thought. It must be hard to retire from what must have been an all-consuming profession and then not have anyone to talk to about it. To have to keep silence because of the nature and confidentiality of his work.

'Well, I think I should start with the Martia Richter case, if that's all right with you. I was involved only in the initial stages but went to the scene on that occasion before the body had been removed. You know how unusual that is? Especially now. Usually our opportunity to walk the scene comes a few days later and we brief ourselves from the crime scene photos and the PM report.'

'Why was that?' Vin asked. 'Why were you there so early?'

'In part it was a sign of the times,' Reg Fincher said. 'This was in 1990, so two years before the Colin Stagg debacle led to the majority of us being persona non grata with many forces. The SIO was a DI Trinder—'

Tess was momentarily taken aback. She exchanged a quick glance with Vin, relieved that Fincher's eyes were still closed.

'It was his first major case as SIO and he was newly promoted to DI. I suppose he wanted to make a good impression. Since the late 90s, of course, all Behavioural Intelligence Advisers have to be ACPO approved, but back then it was all media excitement and anyone with a degree in applied psychology looking to jump on the bandwagon.'

'That's a rather scathing view,' Vin commented.

'Perhaps,' Fincher agreed, opening his eyes and grinning at DS Dattani. 'But I'm an old man and I've seen a lot of changes. Plus, no one listens to me any more so that grants me a certain freedom of expression.'

He looks like a mischievous kid, Tess thought.

'Anyway, we 'profilers' as we were termed in those days, before we became BIA we were looked upon by some as near magicians and by others as interfering idiots who wouldn't know a criminal if they fell on us.'

'And DI Trinder—'

'Was shocked enough to bring in all the big guns he could find. You've seen the crime scene photos?'

Tess nodded, remembering the image of the old woman propped against her bed, her hair spread out around her, hands resting on what was left of her abdomen. 'Had you seen anything like that before?'

'Not like that, no. It was shocking. A visceral scene that evoked a visceral reaction. What struck me about the scene was how neat and tidy it was as though the killer had defined an area of operation and kept all the mess and brutality and . . . and focus very, very tight. It was an impression Elia shared, something she commented on independently when she took over a few days later.'

'And why the handoff?' Vin asked.

'Oh, pure practicality. I was due to spend the term lecturing in the US, it just wasn't possible for me to continue.'

'And that compared to the other crime scenes, in what way?' Tess would never have described the Leanne Bolter scene as neat or tight.

'Utterly different,' Fincher said. 'I've had a good look at the new scene photos that you sent me and also reviewed the old ones you so kindly emailed and they just reinforce my memories. There was a progression between the Richter scene and the William Trevenick scene and then again with Keith Allen. But you've got to remember, with the Allen murder, the victim was a big man who fought back. He didn't give his killer an easy time. Allen was a real break in the pattern. If you look at the other victims that we know about, they are small, slight, easily overpowered. Keith Allen stood six three, was heavily built, muscular, he would not have been easy to subdue and the scene reflected that.'

'You said, that we know about,' Tess commented.

Fincher nodded. 'There's what looks like a ten-year gap between the Richter killing and Rebecca Arnold. Another four between that and William Trevenick and then two between Trevenick and Allen. Then a longer period of what, nine years before he killed your young student? It doesn't follow what we'd see as a usual pattern. It's the opposite of escalation and yet the level of . . . skill, for want of a better word, seems to have developed as does what I suppose you might term the theatricality.

'The Richter killing, though I'm pretty sure it wasn't the first, was almost modest. It was controlled and, as I said, focussed. Consciously restrained and confined in comparison. By the time he killed Leanne Bolter, he seems not to care about that any more. He wants to make a big impression. It's a major display of power and the sole object seems to be to set out to create maximum impact. Maximum shock.'

It certainly did that, Tess thought. She imagined she could still smell the scene on her clothes and skin. 'You are certain it's the same perpetrator?'

Fincher shrugged. 'No one can be certain of anything. The balance of probability is, yes, the same hand, yes it's a male. In all probability he would have started in his mid to late twenties and he chose an initial victim or victims that could be easily subdued and dealt with.'

'So, that would make him in his fifties?' Vin asked.

'In all likelihood. Mobile and at ease in a variety of settings, I would say. He doesn't stand out in either a terraced street, a university or the sheltered housing development that Martia Richter lived in, which, when you consider he would have been a considerably younger man, is interesting.'

'Do you think there will be a link between victims?' Vin asked. 'They seem like such a disparate group, both in ages and occupations and where they are geographically.'

'Maybe,' Fincher said. 'But my feeling – and that's all it is – is that our man selects on some criteria of his own. That he has his own agenda and process that makes sense to him but might not show up as a pattern that any of the rest of us could recognize.'

'A doctor, a butcher, a—'

Fincher was shaking his head. 'It takes only minimal skill to do what he did. These days you could find instructions on the internet for gutting an animal. Prior to that you could have found it in your local library. There's no particular level of skill here. Just a hell of a lot of confidence and that confidence has only grown over the years and, if he's not dealt with, it will just continue to grow.'

'Maybe he'll become overconfident? Slip up?'

'Which implies there would be further murders,' Fincher pointed out. 'I wouldn't count on that, to be honest. Even if we are wrong in the assumption that we're missing some bodies, he's still been active for a long time and he's paced himself carefully. He's controlled and organized and doesn't seem inclined to rush. The one break in the pattern is Keith Allen and I've always suspected that to be anomalous in some way. It felt more spontaneous—'

'He went prepared. He injected Allen with ketamine,' Tess objected.

'And he rushed the job. He barely left in time before the girlfriend got there. It stands out.'

'If I pressed you on that?' Tess said, sensing there was more.

Fincher shrugged. 'As I say, I'm an old man and no one takes any notice of what I say any more. But I'd always felt . . . sensed . . . maybe imagined that it was personal. If I was asked to pick out a weakness in his oeuvre, then that would be it. Keith Allen.'

Tess absorbed that before asking, 'Was there a BIA on the Rebecca Arnold case? I don't recall one from the records. Sorry, you probably wouldn't know anyway. It's just suddenly struck me that I didn't see a note of that.'

'I'm sure there would have been,' Vin said, suddenly puzzled.

Fincher shrugged. 'Sorry, can't help there. I was called to the William Trevenick scene because by then our computer link-up had improved and I was identified as someone who'd worked on the Richter scene. Elia was too ill to come herself. She died not long after, but I attended the scene and did the write up and the advisory report.'

'And did it seem familiar when you first saw it? Would you have identified it as related to the Richter murder?'

'An interesting question,' Fincher approved, looking at Tess. 'I think I would, yes. The Richter murder stayed in my mind, as you might expect. I hoped not to see anything like that again, but I thought I might. Someone who enjoys his work as much as our perpetrator does won't be able to resist.'

'Work?' Vin asked. 'You think he has a purpose in doing this?'

'Who can say? It was just a figure of speech. But I'm sure that the killer will have a certain internal logic to his actions. It will mean something to him even if that meaning never becomes clear to any of us.'

'And would it help? If we understood what drove him?'

'Possibly. Possibly not. If he had a particular victim type then you might be able to make predictions. I'm not an expert in geographical profiling, but from what I've seen there seem no obvious geographical links – though that is a line of enquiry you should have analysed, you know. It might be possible to identify a centre from which he's branching out. But as the victim profile is so varied and there are no obvious links between them I'm guessing – and I hesitate to use that word – that he's picking his victims according to some game plan of his own. He must be recognizing something about each one that fits with an internal checklist. What that might be . . .'

Tess nodded. 'And the Trevenick case. What do you remember about that?'

'That he was younger. Mid-twenties. Gay, but only a few close friends knew that because his family wouldn't approve. He worked at something in computers, I think.'

'The investigating officer thought he might have picked someone up on a night out and brought them back to his flat.' Vin noted, 'but friends said that would be out of character and there was no evidence to suggest that. He'd been out that evening with friends who'd dropped him off home and watched him go inside. He'd have had to go out again to pick someone up and there was no evidence of that.'

'I think a little personal prejudice crept in,' Reg Fincher said carefully. 'Whoever it was that killed him, Trevenick let them in. There was no sign of forced entry and no sign of a struggle. Injection sites beneath the arm and in the chest, which I think is what you've seen with Leanne Bolter?'

'Beneath the armpit and under the jaw.'

'Which means in each case the killer got up really close before the victim knew what was happening.'

'Which either implies a degree of trust or it implies a threat which made them compliant. A gun, a knife—'

'And no one heard anything. The occupants of the flat below said they could sometimes hear him moving around.'

'And they were alerted to the death when blood dripped through their ceiling,' Fincher remembered.

'Yes, that's right. In fact that's another thing that struck me. With everyone else there was a fair certainty that the body would be found quickly. Someone from Martia Richter's family visited every day. Rebecca Arnold still lived at home. Keith Allen's girlfriend was due to come and see him that night. Leanne Bolter's flatmates would realize something was wrong.'

'And if it hadn't been for the blood, William Trevenick might have gone undiscovered for days. The smell would have drawn someone eventually, one assumes, but that isn't always the case.'

'You think that's why his other kills haven't been logged,' Vin said. 'You think his other victims might have been people who weren't missed.'

'I think it's a possibility,' Fincher said. 'I think ten years is a long time to wait. A long time for the need to build.'

'Then why have some victims that are sure to be found. Why risk killing in such close proximity to other people? Why not always keep it hidden? Pick those victims that no one will miss.'

Would anyone miss her? Tess wondered. Someone would notice she'd not turned up for work, but apart from that . . . she had no regular routine. No friends she made a point of contacting regularly. No family that would miss her occasional phone call.

'Perhaps, in his mind, they are not as satisfactory,' Vin speculated. 'Maybe they're like . . . God, I can't think of an appropriate analogy. It'll sound crass, but maybe it's like a snack when what he really needs to be satisfied is more like a full meal. Sorry,' he apologized, seeing the look of disgust on Tess's face.

'I think you have a point,' Fincher nodded. 'Distasteful as it sounds I think you may well be accurate in the analogy. He makes do with the simpler, less risky activity, but every so often. Every so often he has to indulge himself. Your young student seems to have been his latest indulgence.'

'The Colin Stagg case,' Tess mused. 'That was 1993?'

'Nineteen ninety-two. Rachel Nickell, killed in front of her little boy on Wimbledon Common. A profile was mapped out but the psychologist's role kind of spread into other areas. It all got out of hand.'

'Entrapment,' Tess said. 'Wasn't that it?'

'From what I remember. Colin Stagg was identified as the most likely suspect and no one looked any further than that. The investigation took on its own momentum, I suppose. The investigating team got a young officer to work undercover, get to know him, see if they could elicit a confession but it all went tits up. He had nothing *to* confess. It didn't do the discipline or either profession any good and it put an innocent man through hell.'

'I wonder what Joe Jackson's opinions were on profilers by the time of the Rebecca Arnold murder. If he trusted them. If his interest in the Hemingsby link, about which we know practically nothing anyway, was influenced by whatever that opinion turned out to be.'

'The practice had changed by then,' Vin pointed out. 'The shrinks were getting their act together again. What's happening about Hemingsby and the other Rebecca Arnold suspects, anyway?'

'Alfie Briggs and Nat Cooper are chasing them up which might be difficult in Hemingsby's case. Jackson left surprisingly little detail about him in the records. His last known address was a B & B that's been closed for at least the past three years.'

'Have you asked Sergeant Briggs about him?'

Tess shook her head. 'Not had a chance yet. It might be interesting to find out what Joe Jackson's opinion on forensic psychologists was back then too.'

'I think we should mine our resources for all they're worth.

The Friedmans and Alfie Briggs are our links to the past, if you like, they are our eyewitnesses.'

And we all know how unreliable eyewitnesses can be, Tess thought.

'What do you make of Fincher's idea that the Allen killing was personal?'

'It might fit with our witness who saw him arguing with someone.'

'Well, we'll see what our witness has to say soon. How long do you reckon from here. Fancy stopping for something to eat?'

Tess, not driving on this stretch, peered at the sat nav. 'It reckons about an hour and fifteen, so yes, I think lunch is definitely in order. What did you make of Fincher?'

'He enjoyed his job,' Vin said. 'I don't know, he seemed almost gleeful at times but maybe that's just a coping mechanism. I suppose it's like any profession that brings you in contact with the worst that people can do day after day, you find ways of lessening the impact.'

'And what's your method?'

Vin shrugged. 'I spend time with my family, I eat good food. I don't talk about work in the house.'

'Not at all?'

'No, I sit in my dad's shed on his allotment and I watch him fuss with his Dahlias or whatever and I spill my guts to him when I need to. Then I imagine he's digging all of that crap in, like fertiliser, turning it into something good.'

He must have seen the incredulous look on Tess's face because he laughed self-consciously. 'Sounds ridiculous when I say it out loud.'

'Maybe I should get a frigging allotment.'

'There's a hell of a waiting list,' Vin told Tess, reminding her of Alec telling her the same. 'What do we know about this woman we're off to see?'

'Deborah Tait. Lived a few doors up from the garage where Keith Allen was killed. She knew him to say hello to, she said. Knew his cousin better. She was twenty-five at the time of the murder, married the following year and moved away. Her parents still live in the same house they did back then, which is how we got in touch. Field spoke to her on the phone, but he reckons the personal touch is needed which is why we are on the way to hear her tell us what we've already got in our records.'

Vin glanced at her. 'That's a bit jaundiced,' he said. 'It's always better to talk to people. You know that. Odd memories can surface. Different questioning styles can elicit different answers.'

'You sound like a training manual,' she said sourly. Then apologized. 'Sorry, there's just something about Fincher that's left me feeling out of sorts.'

'Anything in particular?'

'Hard to say. Just the feeling that I didn't ask the right questions. That I didn't elicit the new response, you know?'

'I thought he was doing his best to be helpful. And if you missed an opportunity then so did I, so—'

'Maybe it wasn't even that.' Just before they had left, Fincher had promised to make arrangements for them to access his records, currently in storage. 'Maybe it's the thought of more filing boxes to go through,' she said. 'That's enough to make anyone feel sour.'

Vin laughed. 'There was a sign for a pub that does meals just back a ways,' he said. 'Look, there's another one. Shall we?'

Tess looked at the brown sign emblazoned with a silhouette of a knife and fork. 'It's called the Black Dog,' she noted. Somehow that really suited her mood.

TWENTY-SEVEN

Reg Fincher turned on his computer and opened the files Tess had sent to him. He had managed to keep his emotions under control while the police officers had been in his home, but receiving the images and reports the night before had been like a punch in the guts and he knew he could not go on in denial.

He knew who had done this. He had known for a long time in his heart of hearts however impossible and ridiculous it might seem to suspect such a man of anything violent or cruel. Reg Fincher *knew.*

He closed his eyes, blocking out the pictures on the screen and then he made up his mind.

The mobile number he rang was answered on the second ring. 'Reg, this is a surprise. How are you?'

'A surprise? I don't think so. I had a visit this morning from two police officers, came down from your neck of the woods, wanted to talk about Martia Richter and Rebecca Arnold. Oh and William Trevenick and Keith Allen. You see the connection, I'm sure.'

'I know the cases, yes. Reg, I'm not sure—'

'You assured me you had nothing to do with Martia's death and I believed you. You had alibis; more alibis than any one man could possibly require for the others and I believed that too. I chose to believe that anyway.'

'Reg. What's all this about. You sound hysterical.'

'Is that your professional opinion? I didn't think we liked to use that terminology these days.'

'Reg, what's brought this on? It isn't like you to jump to ridiculous conclusions and they are ridiculous, you know.'

'Are they? Are they really. Time was when I'd have done anything to believe that. When I *did* do anything to believe that. I never told you that I consulted on the Rebecca Arnold murder, did I? Off the record as it happened. A detective called DI Jackson came to me asking questions. About you. He knew it was you even if you did have enough witnesses willing to swear you'd been somewhere else at the time.'

'I'm ending the call now, Reg. You're getting yourself upset over nothing. Take yourself for a walk, calm down. You're meant to be retired, remember. You always told me you wanted a long, peaceful retirement, so why are you spoiling it for yourself?'

The phone went dead.

Reg Fincher put his head in his hands. His whole body shook with the emotion of it.

He won't let this go, Reg told himself. He's right. I'm a bloody fool.

He picked up his phone again and this time he called his

solicitor. His papers were lodged in secure storage, Reg no longer remembered exactly what he had packed away in store but he knew that this might be his last chance to hand them over to someone who might make use of them.

The courier would deliver them to DI Fuller by Monday, he was told. Was everything all right?

'Yes,' Reg assured his solicitor, an old friend who'd taken care of his occasional legal requirements for years now. He wondered if he should confide, wondered if he should pack a bag and run away. Wondered if he should call Tess Fuller and tell her what he suspected and could not prove.

He ended the call and sat down, staring again at the computer screen.

He didn't deserve help, he told himself. And anyway, where would he run to that he could not be found?

TWENTY-EIGHT

Deborah Tait – or Needwood, as she was now – seemed relieved that they had not arrived in a marked car and didn't look like police officers. Her home was on a new estate, the roads still not fully tarmacked and teams of landscapers still busy in the communal areas.

'This is nice,' Tess said.

'It is isn't it? It's a bit small, but at least it's got us on the property ladder. It's a shared ownership scheme with the housing association. Only way we could ever hope to do it. I mean I work too, but only part-time at the moment with the kids being little and still at school.' She glanced at her watch.

'What time do you have to collect them?'

'Oh, not till three. I'm all right for a bit. Sit down, can I get you anything?'

She was hovering nervously and Tess shook her head. There seemed no point in prolonging the agony. Deborah obviously didn't want them there, intruding into her new life with memories of the old one. Tess could imagine the indignation when

her parents told her they had given her address to the police
and that it was about Keith Allen.

'We won't keep you,' Vin said, sitting down. 'And we'll keep
it all as brief as we can.'

Deborah Needwood nodded and took a seat. 'It's just that I
don't know what more I can tell you. I told the police at the
time and I talked to that Inspector Field on the phone so I don't
see why—'

'We have to be seen to be doing everything by the book,'
Vin said. It was a phrase he used a lot, Tess knew, but one
which did seem to placate nervous or indignant witnesses.

'I suppose you do,' Deborah agreed, but she still looked
unhappy. 'So what can I tell you?'

'If you could just run through what you told our colleagues
that would be really helpful.'

'Well. I don't see how it would, but . . .' With a deep sigh,
Deborah Needwood began.

The afternoon he was killed, she saw Allen and a man she
didn't recognize arguing about something. They were standing
on the pavement just outside of the garage.

'I had to pass by them to get home,' she said. 'I felt uncomfortable. But Keith had spotted me and I didn't want to cross
the road in case that looked . . . well . . . Look it sounds silly,
but I didn't want to draw attention. I didn't want the man he
was arguing with to . . . make him think . . . to look like I was
judging him in some way.' She laughed nervously. 'That sounds
so silly, I know. But it was the way I felt. I wanted to get by
them as fast as I could.'

'It can be embarrassing, seeing people you know arguing in
the street,' Tess soothed.

Deborah seized on that. 'Yes,' she agreed eagerly. 'It can,
can't it? But I didn't know the other man. I'd only thought I'd
seen him around once before and I wasn't sure about that either.'

'You'd seen him before? Did you tell the other officers that?'

Deborah shook her head. 'I don't remember. I suppose I must
have done. I saw him in the corner shop a few days before. I
didn't think anything about it at the time only when I saw him
arguing with Keith I remembered him. I remembered his coat.
I remember thinking it was a nice coat. Expensive-looking.

Double-breasted wool. Dark grey. It stuck in my head because Dad had been looking for a new winter coat and I knew he'd like one like that but I knew we'd never be able to afford it. Not really like the one the man was wearing. You could see it was expensive. You know how you can tell sometimes?

'I didn't tell the other officers that. I felt really stupid saying something like that. They'd have thought I was a right idiot, wouldn't they?'

'So, what made you tell us?' Vin asked gently.

'Because my husband said I should tell you everything, even if it sounded stupid. He said, you never knew. A little thing might be important.'

'He's right,' Vin nodded encouragingly and Tess sat back willing to let him take the lead. Vin could be really persuasive.

'Do you remember anything more about him? His age, what he looked like. What he sounded like? You said he and Mr Allen were arguing. What was his voice like?'

'Arguing but not shouting. It was like they were tense, like they were trying to keep it quiet, but Keith looked furious and he was waving his arms about, you know? The other man, he was really still. He just stood there, not moving, like he was trying to be really calm but that was just winding Keith up more. You know what it's like when you lose your rag with someone and they try to take the high ground and tell you to calm down and be reasonable?'

Vin nodded. 'My mum,' he said. 'Still drives me mad.'

Deborah laughed. 'Mine too. So I went past them and I could feel him looking at me.' She looked away, suddenly nervous again.

'How did he make you feel, Deborah?' Vin asked.

Tess frowned at the odd question but Deborah nodded.

'Scared,' she said. 'Exposed. I suddenly didn't want to go straight home. I didn't want him to see where I went. So I went to the corner shop and bought milk I didn't need and chatted to Wendy, the owner, for a little while and when I looked out before I left, he'd gone and Keith was still standing in the street looking furious. I made sure I couldn't see him anywhere and then I went home.'

She had lost all the colour in her face, Tess noticed. She looked scared, just remembering.

'Can you remember anything about the way he looked?'

She shook her head.

'How about when you saw him in the shop. Did he scare you then? Did you notice anything about him then?'

Deborah shifted in her seat. 'His hair had some grey in it, but he wasn't old. Forties, maybe? Pale skin, not like he worked outside or anything. Taller than me. About the same height as Keith. Keith was over six feet tall. I think. Not as broad as Keith, even in the coat he didn't look as wide. Keith was wearing his work fleece. It had the garage logo on it. He had it on over his overalls.'

'And his voice?'

'Quiet. No accent. He told Keith that he should think about . . . something. Just that he should think about it. Keith blew up after that, said he'd thought all he was going to and that was that. He told the man to fuck off. I heard that when I hurried by but that was all. Even then Keith was trying not to shout, not to be loud. Like neither of them wanted to be heard.'

'Then why not go into the garage?'

'Probably because Bri would have been there. Keith's cousin.'

She pulled herself together then, physically withdrawing into herself, like she was gathering her composure about her and redressing in it. Deborah glanced at her watch again. 'If that's everything. I have to pick up the kids in a bit.'

Tess rose and Vin followed her example. The clock on the mantelpiece said it was only a few minutes after two and Deborah had previously told them that she didn't need to leave until three, but it was clear that Deborah had said all she was going to. The door had closed.

'What do you think?' Vin said as they drove off.

'Interesting, though it doesn't get us a lot further.'

'Her reaction to the man she saw?'

'Might well be heightened in retrospect. She's talked about it with her husband. Recently. It must have occurred to her that instead of seeing just some random stranger she might have spotted Keith Allen's killer. That thought would leave anyone feeling very vulnerable and it would be easy to project that feeling backwards to the time you actually saw the two men arguing.'

'Still, it's possibly something as opposed to possibly nothing.'

'True, and I suppose that's a small step in the right direction.' Tess agreed.

TWENTY-NINE

Three seminar groups for the same module had been brought together and crowded into one of the lecture theatres. Patrick took his seat beside Daniel. 'Know what's going on?' he asked.

'No. Did you get a text from Hank last night?' Hank had gone home at the weekend and not yet returned.

'Yes, said he wants to come back but his parents are trying to persuade him to wait a few days.'

'Here's Sam.' Daniel waved him over and their friend flopped down into the vacant seat beside him.

Their tutor, Paul Metcalf, came in. He had a man with him that Patrick vaguely recognized. Tall, neatly bearded, very correctly and smartly dressed. Patrick closed his eyes for a moment and the image of the same man coming into the hotel the day he had gone to see Sam and Ginny came into focus.

The man stood, surveying the lecture room and the students in their tiered seats, waiting to be introduced.

'Good morning everyone. I know this is a little unexpected but times have not exactly been normal. Now, you know that counselling services are available within the university, but I also know that it can feel difficult and awkward being the one that goes to seek them out. So I've brought in a friend of mine. You might well have seen him around campus. This is Doctor Tom Reece who lectures in applied psychology and also knows more about trauma and the effects of shock than just about anyone I know. He's also going to talk through what's available on campus and why you should be accessing it. So, if you'll welcome Tom Reece?'

Sporadic clapping as an uncertain and slightly awkward group stared down at this stranger. Patrick didn't clap. He was trying to fit the shape of the man in front of him into the shape of the man he had spotted on the promenade the night he and his father had walked on the beach with Naomi. The figure fitted very well.

Tom Reece took his place at the lectern, not bothering with the computer desk. He took in the room with a sweeping glance and silence fell, everyone curious now.

'Violent death is, thankfully, not part of most people's everyday experience here. It's something we believe happens to other people. It's something that happens in some mythical 'out there' place that we read about or see on the television and which is separate from us so when it comes and lands quite literally on our doorstep, the vast majority of us have no coping strategies in place. No framework within which we can act. It's unknown territory and because of that it's very frightening. Very frightening indeed.'

Patrick switched off the words at that point, guessing what was coming. Talk about coping strategies and seeking help if they felt overwhelmed and being there for one another. Instead, he watched the man standing there in front of them all. And when he had watched enough to fix Reece's features, his body language, his attitude in his head, Patrick began to draw.

At the end of forty minutes the students began to file out. Some stayed back to talk to their tutor and to this visitor, taking the leaflets he offered and accepting the concern. Patrick's friends moved past without comment but Patrick held back, curious now.

'You OK, Patrick?' Paul Metcalf asked.

'Fine thanks, I just wanted to ask something.'

'I'll leave you to it then.'

Patrick waited until the tutor left. He saw him pause outside to exchange a few words with Sam and Daniel and a handful of others who had stayed to chat in the assembly area outside of the lecture theatre.

'You were in the hotel bar,' Patrick said. 'I saw you there.'

'The White Hart? Yes, I remember you.'

'And on the promenade. I saw you on Friday night.'

'You're very direct, aren't you?' Tom Reece sounded amused.

'Sorry. Yes, I forget I'm supposed to lead into things.'

'I don't mind. And yes, that was possibly me on the promenade. I stood and watched the sea for a while. It relaxes the
mind. You have a good visual memory.'

Patrick nodded. 'It's what I do,' he said. 'See things, draw
them. I'd better go now.'

'All right. Have a leaflet?'

'No thanks.'

Patrick left and went through the automatic doors to join his
friends and Tom Reece watched the group walk away. He wasn't
surprised that Patrick had recognized him or even approached
him to tell him so, but he was intrigued.

The boy interested him more and more.

THIRTY

I t had been one of Naomi's mornings for working as a volunteer at the local advice centre. Her taxi dropped her home
just after two and Alec announced he'd made sandwiches
and the kettle was on.

'Busy session?'

'It always is.'

'I've been thinking, you know. I've got the same experience
legal wise and so on that you have and they're always looking
for volunteers—'

'You'd have to do the training course. Be a bit like going
back to school.'

'I know, and that's fine. I just think I could be useful. Not
that I want to tread on your toes or anything.'

'I wouldn't mind. Like you say, you have all the right quali-
fications. You could be very useful. What brought that on
anyway?'

'I don't know. Restlessness, I suppose. A need to be doing.
A need to feel useful. It still gets to me when ex-colleagues
start dashing round working on important stuff and I'm left
standing on the side-lines.'

'You miss the force?'

'No, I miss the sense of purpose. I suppose I miss the challenge. I feel like I'm stagnating a bit, that's all.'

'So, do something about it. Retrain. Or rejoin.'

'Not in a million years. I don't miss the hassle or the paperwork or my boss.'

'No one would miss him. You could do consultancy work. You've had enough offers. If you don't take them up soon they might stop coming in.'

'Security and risk assessments. Right. I really see myself growing old doing that.'

'I'm not suggesting you do it forever. Just to give you something while you figure out where you actually want to go. It's a networking opportunity if nothing else.'

The kettle had boiled and Alec made tea and they took their late lunch through to the living room. Naomi sat in her favourite seat beside the window, Napoleon leaning against her leg for a moment before harrumphing and slipping down on to the floor. 'We'll take him out after lunch,' she said. 'Then you can give McCormacks a call, tell Dale you'll come over and go over the plans for the new system. He'll be glad to see you.'

'OK,' Alec agreed. 'Harry called, said Patrick was fine and at uni and Gregory and Nathan were looking into things. Whatever that means.'

'Better not to ask.'

'And DI Trinder called.'

'The Internal Affairs guy Tess was telling us about?'

'The same. Would like an informal meeting.'

'And you said?'

'That I supposed so, but I didn't see how we could help any more than we had.'

'We don't have to talk to him.'

'No, but he's asking that the two of us and Alfie get together with him to "kick some ideas around".'

'Sounds like he's treading carefully.'

'Sounds like he's a wanker. I must have met him before, I suppose, after the debacle that nearly got me killed, but I've no memory of the man. You said you'd encountered him?'

'Um, yes.' Naomi took a bite of her sandwich and tried to remember exactly. 'The last time was just before the accident.

He was a keynote speaker at a conference I went to. A training thing on technology, I think.' She shook her head. 'Can't remember. I had a conversation with him at dinner. You know, they did that 'you will mix whether you want to or not' thing, seating senior officers and the rest of us round the same tables? Well, I ended up next to him. Can't remember what we talked about. I was probably just trying not to slur my words.'

Alec laughed. 'So, what do we tell him? Do we go and have a chat?'

'I suppose we do. It's Alfie I feel for. We both dug the tunnel and escaped, he's still in the thick of it.' Not, she reflected, that she'd had any choice in the matter. The accident that took her sight had made sure of that.

'Alfie will be fine,' Alec said. 'Tess said he's part of the review team, so the mud can't have stuck – not that he deserves any mud. I told Trinder that we were free tomorrow. Hope that was OK?'

'So that's what made you so fidgety. I suppose that's all right. Frankly, Alec, I'm reluctant to be drawn in. I know nothing about the Rebecca Arnold case, you and Alfie Briggs were pretty incidental after the initial discovery of the body and I'm beginning to think that I can't even tell anyone anything valid about Joe Jackson. I thought I knew him, but it turns out I didn't and every new question that comes along convinces me even more that I knew nothing about him really. He put on a good show but it seems like that's all it was.'

They finished their lunch in silence until Alec eventually said, 'I can ring him back?'

'And what would be the point. Let's get it over with, have the conversation and then be done with it. I suppose he's just being thorough. Now, let's go for that walk and then you can call Dale McCormack and arrange a time to go and see him. It's time we moved on, Alec. I'm sick of being dragged back into what's past and gone.'

Tess and Vin arrived back at headquarters to find that the BIA who had been allocated to the case had already arrived and was asking to view the scene. Field had decided that as Tess and

Vin had been, technically, the first officers attending, that Tess should be the one to take her there.

'Can I grab a coffee first?' she asked Field.

'You can, and you and Vin can brief me on what Fincher and the witness—'

'Deborah Tait—'

'Right. Yes. What they had to say.'

Tess glanced at her watch. Three forty-five. They had made quite good time from their last appointment but she was tired now and really not enthused about going out again – especially not back to the scene.

Half an hour later and she was off again with Caroline Towser in tow. The BIA was a woman about the same age as Tess, she guessed. Short red hair – dyed a very vibrant shade – and an abundant scattering of freckles across her nose. She clutched a folder containing the crime scene photos in her hand.

'It was a messy scene,' Tess said, indicating the photos.

'Looks it. I'm glad not to have been there, believe me. Bad enough seeing the pictures.'

'All part of the job,' Tess said and noticed Caroline smiling at her. 'What?'

'Just thinking how many times I've heard that phrase today,' she said. 'I think it's a kind of mantra. I'm not sure anyone notices they've said it anymore.'

'You could be right. I've never thought about it like that.'

'You visited one of my old professors this morning.'

'What, Fincher?'

'Uh uh. He was an emeritus professor by the time I heard him lecture. Just came in from time to time, but he was a major figure before he retired. What did you think of him?'

'Um . . . what did you think of him?'

Caroline Towser laughed. 'Intense,' she said. 'Determined to drag us all kicking and screaming into the scientific age. Utterly committed.'

'Enthusiastic,' Tess returned. 'I got the feeling he was good at separating himself from the reality of what he was seeing?'

'Probably. I suppose that goes with the territory, maybe. You have to be mindful but detached, at least that's what we're taught to be. Actually doing it takes a bit longer.'

'Definitely,' Tess said. They had arrived at the scene and Tess waited for the officer manning the barricades to let them through, aware of the media interest at a new arrival.

'We're up on the second floor,' Tess said. 'I don't suppose you know someone in your field by the name of Hemingsby, do you?'

'Doesn't ring a bell. Why?'

'Just a name that came up.' She led the way up the stairs to the shared flat. The CSIs had gone now and the place was deserted. Caroline stood in the doorway as Tess had done two days earlier, studying the kitchen and communal area. The smell of blood and death still permeated, still hung in the air and Tess noticed that Caroline wrinkled her nose, a slight frown between her eyes.

'Stinks,' Tess said. 'You go away smelling of it and it stays in your nose for days.'

'I know. But it surprises me every time. So, shared kitchen and seating area. Who slept where?'

Slowly, methodically they walked the scene, Caroline comparing what she saw to the photos of the crime scene and taking more of her own. She asked about Ginny and Sam and about the girl who had been at her boyfriend's that night. About the statements from those who had found the body. She was calm and thorough and Tess found herself liking the other woman. They stood together at the bedroom door, studying the image of the girl who had lain on the bed, her life ripped away from her with such violence and Tess could almost see the slight figure of Leanne propped up against the pillows.

Tess watched as Caroline stepped into the room and crossed to the bed, comparing the photos to the remaining reality. Her hand moved as she visualized how the wounds had been inflicted from Leanne's right side to the left, the assailant drawing the knife towards himself as he finally ended her life. She looked upward at the arterial spray on the walls and ceiling and finally she turned away.

'Finished?' Tess asked.

'For now.' Caroline's voice was steady but her face was very pale, the freckles standing out against white skin.

They returned to the car and Tess drove her to the hotel where Caroline had booked in for the night.

'Are you all right?'

'Yeah. I'll be fine, thanks. Are you?'

Tess smiled wryly. 'I'm doing OK. When will you have something for us?'

'Preliminary summary tomorrow, but I need to consult on this one. Talk to my supervisor and get another perspective. It's a mistake to rush.'

Tess nodded and watched as Caroline walked into the hotel, scuffing her feet on the steps outside as though wishing to wipe what was left of the scene off her shoes before stepping across another threshold.

Tess drove away wishing it was as easy as that and suspecting that Caroline didn't think so either.

THIRTY-ONE

Tom Reece slipped his key into the lock. He could hear music coming from somewhere in the house and his daughter, Hester, singing along to a song he didn't recognize. He should keep up with his daughter's taste in music, but since Hester moved on from the succession of boy bands and Rhea got a boyfriend who was into vintage rock, he'd pretty much given up. They were very much young women now, whether he liked that or not, and his role seemed to be shifting on a weekly basis from participant observer to observer that was occasionally invited to participate.

Hester was in the kitchen, prodding at something in the oven. The scent of baking cake filled the room.

'Hi Hes, how are you. Is that chocolate cake?'

'It is.' She straightened up and came over to give him a quick kiss on the cheek. 'Mum's out in the garden hacking the roses down.'

'I think it's called pruning,' he said.

'Whatever. There's less of them than there was an hour ago.

She said we'd be getting pizza and chips out of the freezer for dinner so I thought I'd make a cake.'

'Is Rhea coming back for dinner?'

'Don't think so. Steve has a gig somewhere.' She turned up the radio and proceeded to sing along to yet another unfamiliar track. Tom went out into the garden to rescue the roses from his wife. Hes was right, hacking down might have been a better description. 'You know you have to leave something above ground, don't you?'

'Says the gardening expert. Had a good day?'

'Not so bad. You?'

'I could rant. I won't. I've come out to do some gardening instead.'

'So, this is a displacement activity. And who are you really mutilating when you chop these poor defenceless plants to pieces?'

'Oh, you're exaggerating. *They'll* grow back.'

'And your preferred victims might not?' He slipped an arm around her shoulders and kissed her forehead. 'I'm told it's just the three of us tonight and it's going to be pizza and chips in front of the telly.'

'Hes is making cake and we can open a bottle.'

Tom nodded. 'Sounds fine to me.' They wandered back inside and Tom smiled fondly at the women in his life – the absent one included. He'd done a good job as a husband and father, he decided and it was the source of some professional pride that he could say so. Pride was at least an emotion he could fully comprehend even if there were oh so many that he could not. Pride in his work kept him on track, kept him doing the right thing, created a level of admiration and loyalty in others, made him acceptable.

And pride in his work made him careful, thorough. Out of reach and hidden from those that might want to do him harm.

THIRTY-TWO

G regory sifted slowly through the mass of printouts on the dining table. Nathan had stacked the paperwork on a case by case basis, but Gregory had his own notion of what was useful, placing images side by side that came from different crime scenes.

Nathan watched him, silently. Nathan had long ago learned not to interrupt a thinking man. He wondered what Gregory was seeing that he had not but was willing to wait for the explanation. His contact had sent him seven different sets of information garnered both from HOLMES, the Home Office Large Major Enquiry System and ViCLAS, the Violent Crime Linkage Analysis System and from her contacts in other forces. She was an ex-colleague of his one-time guardian and mentor, Gustav Clay, and high enough up in the system that she could collate intelligence from a variety of sources without anyone questioning her reasons. She was one of the few contacts left operating at such a high level and Nathan was grateful that his relationship with her had continued uninterrupted after Clay's death. Slowly, Nathan was compiling a network of his own, but such enterprises took time and Nathan made use of anything he still had in that direction.

Nathan watched as Gregory compared the images of Leanne Bolter and the old lady, Martia Richter with that of Rebecca Arnold and Sadie Rahman, a young woman whose death had happened three years before Rebecca Arnold had been killed. He had found those images that depicted the most similar poses and laid them out side by side. Below those he placed the images of William Trevenick, Keith Allen and the youngest of the group, fifteen-year-old Trey Baxter. The only black victim. Sadie Rahman's parents had come from somewhere in the Middle East though the police report conflicted as to whether that was Israel or the Lebanon. Nathan wondered how anyone could have got those two such disparate cultures confused and wondered if it had relevance.

Gregory stepped back and Nathan judged it safe to talk. 'You think they're all the same man?'

Gregory nodded. 'I think we're missing three,' he said.

'Three? How do you work that out?'

He stepped over to the table and stared at the images, hoping to see what it was his friend had spotted.

'I'll make it easy for you,' Gregory said. He rearranged the photographs in date order speaking as he did so. 'I think there must be at least one before the old lady.'

'Martia Richter.' Nathan nodded in agreement.

'Then we've got the youngest victim. Fifteen years old, went missing at a street carnival. His friends assumed he was with his family, family assumed he was with friends. Found dead eight hours after he went missing. Found in the flat of the older sister of one of his friends – which implies intelligence gathering before the act and a deliberate attempt to unsettle.'

Nathan thought the word 'unsettle' might be a bit mild, given the circumstances, but he let it pass.

'This wasn't connected,' Nathan said. 'Why?'

'Not all old cases or cold cases have been uploaded on to the system yet. There have been several revisions of the HOLMES and ViCLAS systems,' he said, 'and the rate at which that happened varies from force to force. Anyway, next we know about is Sadie Rahman. The boy was killed just on two years after Martia Richter, the girl, Sadie Rahman, nineteen years old, was killed three years and four months before Rebecca Arnold.' He placed the picture, leaving a deliberate space between the images of Sadie and Trey. 'Our second missing person,' he said.

'Why.'

Gregory ignored him, laid down the picture of Rebecca Arnold. Then William Trevenick and Keith Allen. 'I think there's a missing piece between Allen and the student that's just died,' Gregory said. 'Now look.'

Puzzled, Nathan looked at the sequence, trying to see what Gregory had spotted. Trying to visualize those missing in between. 'Try thinking like Patrick would,' Gregory said.

'Like Patrick?'

'Like an artist. Like someone who sees patterns, sequences, relationships.'

'I don't—'

Suddenly he did. 'Oh.'

'Yes. Oh.'

Nathan studied the pictures closely, the poses were at first glance very similar, victims resting either on or against a bed, laid open from sternum to pubic bone. The women's hair had been combed out. But now Nathan could see that there was movement between the pictures, a flow from one to the other. The old lady had her hands resting on her thighs, palms up, face turned slightly to her left. Trey Baxter had one hand, his right, palm down, his face turned out towards the viewer, but still a slight tilt to his left. Sadie Rahman faced the viewer straight on and her right hand rested on her thigh, palm up, the right rested on the floor had been turned palm down.

'There's a gap between Trey and Sadie. The hands . . . the sequence is incomplete.'

Gregory nodded. 'I might be wrong. It might be chance, but the posing seems precise and deliberate. From image to image we get the little changes, like he consulted the last images and then made a tiny change. One leads on to the next.'

'Two of them are posed on the bed, the rest beside it.' Nathan felt he ought to play devil's advocate.

'And look at the layout of the room in both cases, what you can see from the door.' Gregory tapped the appropriate photos. 'What matters is what those who found the bodies saw first. The position is designed to cause the biggest impact.'

He had a point, Nathan thought. 'So, if you're right, there are ten victims,' Nathan said.

'Plus whatever practice runs there were before he got it right.' Gregory speculated. 'Minor assaults to start with, probably, moving up to murder as the confidence grew.'

'I don't like your thinking,' Nathan said. 'The locations of the Rebecca Arnold and Leanne Bolter murders are only a couple of miles apart.'

'And Martia Richter and Keith Allen were in the same town. The rest seem scattered. Furthest south is Sadie Rahman in Haringey. Furthest north are Rebecca Arnold and Leanne Bolter.'

'How many murders do you think Alec's colleagues know

about? My contact is going to send an additional briefing, but it's possible they have the missing ones?'

Gregory shook his head. 'I think your contact is in a better position to gather the intel,' he said. 'But we'll have a chat to Alec and Naomi later, see what they know.'

'Probably a lot less than we do,' Nathan observed.

'Then we'll have to bring them up to speed, won't we,' Gregory said.

Patrick was in his bedroom, painting. Harry brought him a hot chocolate and the suggestion that it was time to turn in for the night. Patrick's desk was scattered with photographs Bob had taken for him together with colour notes and articles on techniques. A board, ready prepped with chalk gesso sat on Patrick's easel and he had begun to transfer a drawing, the paper pricked along the lines of the drawing and placed in position ready for the charcoal and chalk mix to be pounced through.

'You're not going to do that tonight,' Harry said. He knew the process took time, the dots that were transferred to the board then had to be joined up with dilute ink or paint and it was a process better done in one operation before anything had the chance to smudge.

'No, I'm too tired. I'll get on to it in the morning. Then I suppose I'd better get the essay finished ready for Monday.'

'How's it going?' Harry asked.

Patrick shrugged. 'It's OK, I'd just rather be painting.'

Harry set the mug down on a bare corner of the table and leaned in to scrutinize the photographs. 'It's really something, isn't it? Are you planning on making a copy or—'

'A copy first,' Patrick said. 'I want to get to grips with the technical stuff before I try experimenting. One day I might be capable of making a proper copy, just now I'll be glad just to figure out how the hell he did it.'

Harry laughed. 'How are you?' he asked.

'I'm OK, everyone's anxious and on edge, but I suppose that's inevitable. Sam's moving into his new digs this weekend. Ginny's gone home. I doubt she'll be back.'

'You'll keep in touch?'

'We'll try. It won't last. She wants to get away from everything.

She doesn't understand that it's inside of her now. She can't run away from what she saw and she's better off keeping close to the people who understand it. But she doesn't know that yet.'

'I wish you didn't know that,' Harry said.

'Dad—' Patrick picked up the mug of chocolate and sat down on the edge of his bed – 'Dad, I am what I am because of everything. It's all right. I'm OK with it all.'

Harry nodded. 'I'm proud of you,' he said. 'Well, goodnight. Don't stay up too long.'

Harry made his way back downstairs, checking the locks and making sure the world was closed out for the night.

Patrick's phone chimed. It was a text from Daniel. *'Want to help Sam move on Sunday? My uncle's letting us use his van but only if he drives.'*

'What time?'

'Be about three. Meet up at union building?'

'OK. Does Sam have to get his stuff?'

'Police are getting it for him. See you then?'

'OK.'

He'd have to make sure the essay was finished, Patrick thought. He wondered how Ginny was doing and if any of them would hear from her again.

THIRTY-THREE

Reg Fincher was not used to late-night guests and he had heard no car pull up outside the bungalow. He twitched the curtain aside and peered out, trying to see who was standing at his front door. Perhaps attracted by the sudden light through the curtained window, his visitor stepped away from the door and turned to look at him.

Fincher let the curtain drop.

It's late, he thought. Do I really want the bother of him this time of night?

Do I really want to let him in at all? Do I really have the options?

Reg Fincher closed his eyes and when he opened them again a familiar figure was standing in the hall.

'I still have the key you gave me,' he said. 'I thought I'd better ring the bell first, though. I didn't want to give you a fright.'

It's a bit late for that, Fincher thought. You've been scaring the living daylights out of me for years.

'I don't remember giving you a key.'

'No? Well, I can leave it with you when I go. It's not a problem. I brought a bottle with me. Thought we could have a glass or two and talk about old times. I miss working with you, Reg.'

Fincher wasn't sure he could say the same. He fetched tumblers, knowing the bottle would be Scotch and that it would be a good one. Macallan or Dalwhinnie, perhaps. He knew Reg didn't like the really peaty varieties. His guest had taken off his coat and sat down in the chair that had been occupied by the policewoman who had come to see him the day before. Tess, Fincher thought. Her name had been Tess.

He'd been right in his guess about the whisky. He set the glasses down not offering ice or water. One thing they both felt was that if a Scotch was good enough to drink then it was an insult to dilute it, though Reg had no such qualms about drinking ginger with a blend.

He raised his glass. 'Good health,' he said.

'Good health indeed. This is not the kind of place I expected you to move to. Not your sort of thing at all.'

'I like the quiet. I like to walk. I like the security of it.' He thought how stupid that sounded considering who his visitor was. 'I didn't hear your car.'

'I didn't want to disturb the neighbours. It's late. I walked through the wood.'

So, he'd come over the wall, Fincher thought. He felt a tightness cramping in his belly. No one had seen him at the gate.

'You know about the student. The girl who got herself killed the other day?'

Reg Fincher nodded. 'Know about her, seen the pictures. Poor little sod. What did she do to deserve that?'

'Wrong place, wrong time. What it comes down to for all of

us in the end, I suppose. That or old age, or sickness . . . and I've always wondered about that, you know. If sickness is down to being in the wrong place at the wrong time and something gets triggered to go awry that wouldn't do if you hadn't been there.'

'That's nonsense and you know it.' Fincher poured himself another drink. If this was his wrong place, wrong time, then he was going out with a bellyful of the good stuff inside of him. His guest watched as Reg knocked it back.

'It's meant to be sipped,' he said. 'Enjoyed.'

'Is it. Is it really?'

Silence fell between them for a while and it was an oddly companionable one . . . considering. Reg Fincher could feel himself getting sleepy, his vision blurred. 'It's bad form to spike a man's drink,' he said, but his voice slurred and he wasn't sure the words made any sense.

'So, drink a little more.'

Fincher lifted the glass. His hand was unsteady and the glass chinked against his lips and then his teeth. He managed to swallow but he could feel the tumbler sliding from his fingers, then feel a hand gently taking it away.

Blinking, trying to focus, Reg Fincher noted that his companion's glass had not been touched.

'You should have stopped,' he said. Or tried to say. His lips felt loose and dry and then wet as he realized that he could no longer close his mouth and saliva dribbled down on to his chin.

'Sit back in your chair.' The man rose, eased Reg back into his seat, leaning his head gently against the wing of the armchair. Wiped his face and closed his eyes.

By the time he left a half-hour or so later, walking back the way he had come, Reg Fincher was dead in his chair. He had cleaned the glasses and the bottle but left them on the little table they had used and, as promised, he had placed the front door key beside the glass. It pleased him to provide another puzzle, a further irritation. Reg would have appreciated it, he thought as he drove away. It was just the sort of detail that gave him a thrill.

*   *   *

There was a back entrance to the house. Strictly speaking it led up a fire escape, one of two attached to the back of the building. The lower flats shared one but when the conversion had been made a separate fire escape had been built, leading only from that top flat beneath the eaves and it was this rear door that he had always used. The official front door, the one that led through the main body of the house and gave access via communal stairs was rarely opened. Deadbolts secured it from the inside and any post the flat might receive – junk mail excepted, of course, and that, like all the house mail, was simply dropped on the hall table by whoever noticed it first – was diverted to a PO box.

He rarely even saw the other occupants of the house. He visited once or twice a week, usually in the evening and on no regular basis. Paid his rent regularly and was known to the landlord as some kind of rep or commercial traveller with a lifestyle that took him away a lot.

Tom let himself in and stood in the kitchen listening to the familiar silence. The kitchen was equipped with basics and he even made use of lights and cooker and electric fire enough that the flat attracted a low but viable bill. It was simply furnished with a mix of items owned by the landlord and a few bits he had picked up at charity shops and flat-pack outlets. He slept occasionally in the small bedroom and watched television sitting in one of the old armchairs in the small living room.

It looked acceptably inhabited should anyone visit, but so far, no one ever had.

Tom propped the walking stick he had brought with him against the unused front door. Maybe he should buy a stick stand, build a collection around this one lonely souvenir? He quite liked the idea. Reg Fincher's stick, robust though it was, did look a little odd on its own. A clearly personal item in a very impersonal environment.

It was a more substantial souvenir than Tom usually went for but then, Reg Fincher had been a more substantial part of his life than any of the others which was why it had been appropriate to give his old friend a peaceful and non-traumatic end.

As he usually did when he came to this small, secret place,

he checked on his other remembrances. Nestled in a sideboard
drawer were small boxes and packets, none of which he had to
open to know their contents. Strands of hair tied with ribbon,
a ring, a key on a chain that used to be worn around a neck.
A poetry book that had sat on a bedside table and was inscribed
to a lost love. A postcard of Llandudno. His choice of objects
eclectic and usually small, chosen because they must have meant
something to those whose lives he had taken.

He did not stay long this evening. Friends were coming over
for supper and he didn't want to be late home.

Checking that all was well, Tom Reece switched out the
lights and locked the door, pausing at the top of the fire escape
and listening to the faint sounds of televisions and voices and
people in the street before descending once more into their
world.

THIRTY-FOUR

Tess headed back to Fincher's home mid-morning. News
of his death had been relayed via the local police –
professional courtesy having led Field to let them know
previously that Tess and Vin would be making enquiries on
their patch.

'Found dead by the window cleaner, this morning,' Field had
told her. 'The curtains were partly open and he could see Fincher
sitting in his chair. He thought it was unusual. Fincher usually
came out for a quick conversation while he worked and was
always ready with the money when he'd done. He knocked,
thinking the guy might be asleep but getting no answer came
to the conclusion that the professor might be ill, so he called
the gatehouse. The doctor came, thought he might have had a
heart attack.'

'So?'

'So, there was a bottle with two glasses on the coffee table
in front of him and a front door key and a note.'

'A note? Suicide?'

'Security guard on the gate thought it looked wrong. He knew you'd been to see him, so he called it in. Fortunately, someone took notice. The glasses had been wiped clean but there was still a residue in the bottle. It's been fast-tracked.'

'And the note?'

'Well that was another thing that raised eyebrows. It said "You should have stopped me." And it wasn't in Fincher's handwriting.'

'Should have stopped who?'

'Well, that's the question, isn't it. Tess, some bastard's playing games. That's the way I read it. Caroline Towser is waiting to be picked up at her hotel and she'll be going with you to take a look.'

'This is being treated as a crime scene.'

'As a possible crime scene. But my bet is—'

So, Tess had collected the BIA and driven back the way she and Vin had travelled the day before.

The security guard recognized Tess from the day before and told her that DS Denny was waiting for them at the professor's bungalow.

'Think you could live in a place like this?' Tess asked.

Caroline shrugged. 'I suppose I could retire to it,' she said. 'Though probably not on the pension I'll be getting by then. It's a bit off the beaten track though, isn't it? It's what, five miles to the nearest village and ten or so to the closest town. What do they do for shopping?'

'Get it delivered, I suppose. Though there's a little shop on site, up by the clubhouse on the golf course.'

'No, I mean *shopping*. Like at the end of a bad day and you need like shopping *therapy*.'

Tess laughed. 'I suppose they go and beat seven shades out of a golf ball.'

'Nope. That wouldn't do it for me.'

They pulled up outside of Fincher's bungalow. A young man with very black skin stood talking to the other security guard Tess remembered from her previous visit. They turned to greet the two women.

'DS Denny. Ryan. I spoke to your boss on the phone.'

Tess introduced herself and Caroline. 'Do we know any more?'

'Bottle tested positive for barbiturates. He could have overdosed but—'

'You don't think so?'

'He had a visitor. Come along inside. Ben, here, it seems he was right to be suspicious. The body's been taken but the rest of the scene is intact. CSI will be coming over later in the day.'

'The scene's not been handed off yet?'

'No, our chain got broken, unfortunately. Ben called the paramedics. They declared death, it looked like a heart attack. Private ambulance was called and the Prof was taken to the morgue. Ben had noticed the scene looked odd and called it in, but as it didn't look like a suspicious death from the outset, we were a little slow on the uptake. Ben told my boss that you'd been round making enquiries, he checked the system and he talked to . . . Field, is it? Right. So he sent me over. Ben had locked the door after the paramedics and ambulance had gone, so there'd been no further interruptions after that and the items on the coffee table are untouched, as far as we can ascertain, apart from the bottle. I photographed that in situ, bagged it and couriered it over to the lab. I've been on the advanced crime scene, preservation of evidence courses, so I should have done it right,' he added. 'Since then I've not been further than the living room door so—'

'So we'll stay in the hallway,' Tess confirmed. 'There was a note?'

'Yes, left in place, weighted down by what looks like a front door key. It matches the emergency key they keep at the gatehouse but it's not Professor Fincher's. His is still hanging on the hook by the back door. The note says, "You should have stopped."'

'Not "stopped me"?' That's what Field had told her.

'No. Just *stopped*. Nothing's covered by the key, you can see the whole message.'

Tess stood in the doorway and looked. The coffee table was set between the two chairs as it had been when they visited. It was small and square and looked like a flat pack. Two glass tumblers had been carefully set one on either side of the table. A single sheet of what looked like A4 printer paper lay in between the key placed carefully dead centre. She couldn't read the words on the paper but she could see that they had been written about a quarter of the way down the page in a single line.

'Where was the bottle?'

'Beside the left-hand glass.' He showed her the pictures he'd taken on his smart phone. Caroline looked over her shoulder and Tess moved out of the way so that she could see the room more easily.

'A handwritten note?'

'Looks that way.'

'So, handwriting analysis.'

'Will suggest similarities, if we get an exemplar,' Caroline said. 'It's still considered far from an exact science. But it can be helpful.'

The sound of a van pulling up drew DS Denny back outside.

'CSI have arrived,' he told them. 'I'll hand off, soon as you're done.'

'What do you think?' Tess said.

'It's not as dramatic as the other scene.'

'You think it's the same killer?'

Caroline shrugged. 'I'm not in the business of speculation,' she said. 'But it's one hell of a coincidence, isn't it? And there's something . . . I think it's the precision of it, you know. It feels the same.'

'I'd not have said that Leanne Bolter's killing was precise,' Tess argued. 'It was just a bloody mess.'

Caroline shook her head. 'It was precise,' she said. 'The placing of the body, the deliberate, unhesitating action of the cuts. The sense of drama. It was precise.'

The CSI were waiting and they returned to the front of the bungalow, releasing the scene.

'So, what now?'

'We drive back but I want to make a detour on the way and pick up Fincher's notes. We'd have done it yesterday but we had a witness interview in the opposite direction and no time to loop back. His papers are lodged with a solicitor. Field's cleared it with them for us to collect everything. Fortunately Fincher wrote us a letter of authority yesterday.'

'He definitely didn't come in by the front gate,' Tess said. 'The security guy reckons it's possible to come over the wall and through the woods.' She pointed in the opposite direction to the golf course.

'I'll need to take a look,' Caroline told her. 'I need to see the complete scene.'

'Sure, but I'm not sure how we'll figure out exactly where the killer came over. It's a long perimeter wall and quite a big lump of woodland.'

'A lump? Is that a technical term? Come on, we'll need to take a look anyway. The probability is that the killer will do what most people do and have taken the path of least resistance. Chances are people walk in the woods regularly, there'll be tracks that are easier to follow than others. He'll have followed where other people have already led.'

'All right. So where do we start? Oh, is that a map?'

'Not really.' Caroline opened the glossy brochure she was holding. 'It's a sales brochure. Ben gave it to me. But it's got a sketch map of the site in the back, look. And it shows how the road curves round the wall, away from the main gate.'

'So, if you didn't want to be seen, you'd go over the wall about here,' Tess pointed.

'That's what I thought.'

'Security cameras?'

'Apparently not, only on the main gate and on the clubhouse and shop on the golf course. Apparently some of the house owners install their own and they can have them linked up to the gate for a fee. Fincher didn't, unfortunately.'

'So—' Tess glanced about, trying to get her bearings – 'we're here, if we head off in that direction . . .'

'Should have brought wellies,' Caroline observed ruefully.

It took them ten minutes to get to the wall. The wood was still bare and open, leaves just starting to green the branches but not yet open and the ground was sodden for most of the way raising Tess's hopes that there might be footprints close to the wall. Looking back, it was possible to get a view of Fincher's bungalow and the two closest to it and the golf course clubhouse up on the rise beyond.

'He'd be able to see the lights in the bungalow. And this time of year, there's very little undergrowth, you could walk pretty much direct,' Caroline said. 'We just need to find where he came over the wall.'

'And we need to go slowly,' Tess said. 'I don't want to risk us disturbing a secondary scene.'

Caroline nodded. 'It would still have been pitch black out here,' she said. 'The moon was still new and it was pretty cloudy last night. Out here too, apparently.'

'You think he'd have risked using a torch?'

'I don't see why not. People would have had their curtains closed and if he kept the torch pointed down and shielded it with his hand he could have kept a good view of where he was treading, kept the bungalow in view and headed for the lights in the window. It would probably have taken longer than the ten minutes it took us, but it would have been easy enough.'

Tess nodded. The two women moved carefully now, looking down, trying to avoid the deepest mud and wettest grass. It was Tess that spotted the prints. 'Look. There.'

'Oh, my god. Yes.'

On the ground close to the wall were two clear impressions. Deep and side by side as though someone had landed hard on both feet. Then tracks leading away and leading back just a few yards from the first.'

'So he came over there and went back just a little ways up,' Caroline said. 'You got an evidence bag or something to cover them down with? You can bet your life it's going to rain before the CSI get out here.'

'Nothing big enough with me, but DS Denny is still on scene. I can see his car. He can get the call put through and he might have something in his kit. I think we should head back, go the way we came.'

Caroline nodded. She took off the bright red scarf she was wearing and tied it to a tree. 'Make it easier to spot,' she said.

Tess finished her call and then used her phone to take pictures of the footprints and surrounding aspects. 'He's sending two of the CSI over, I told him we'd be heading back. They'll meet us at the edge of the wood and follow our path back through.' She took a last look at the tracks. 'Looks like you were right,' she said. 'He took a direct path. The footprints are headed straight towards the bungalow.'

They turned and followed their own footprints back to the perimeter of the wood. Two CSIs arrived just as they did and Tess showed them the pictures she had taken and pointed to the red scarf on the birch tree. Then they headed back to Tess's car.

'Any insights?' she asked after they had taken their leave and driven away.'

Caroline laughed. 'We don't do insights. BIAs do comparisons and statistical probabilities. Everything we suggest or advise is based on empirical evidence from studies that are as scientific as we can make them. This isn't *Cracker* anymore.'

'You can't tell me that you don't wish it was sometimes,' Tess teased her.

'Oh, the maverick profiler who's always right. It would be lovely. Make the job so much easier. As it is, it's like being back at university. Everything we say has to be backed up by referencing some study or other or an earlier successful report or what our supervisor thinks and then we get the joy of yearly assessments.'

She grinned at Tess. 'So yes, it would be more fun, but it is better the way it is now. Hope I can prove that to you?'

'I hope you can too,' Tess said fervently.

THIRTY-FIVE

'Doctor Hemingsby?'

The man in green scrubs looked up from the charts he was scrutinizing. 'Yes?'

'Sergeant Briggs. I wonder if I could have a word.'

Hemingsby ticked off something on the chart and replaced it in the rack. 'Come on in here,' he said leading Alfie into a tiny closet of a room fitted out for tea making and dish washing.

'Parents use this space if they're staying overnight,' Hemingsby explained. 'And family waiting for their kids to come out of surgery.' He grinned. 'It's hard to find a quiet spot.'

'Dr Hemingsby, I believe you knew an Inspector Joe Jackson. In fact I believe you might have been involved in an enquiry he was leading—'

'Rebecca Arnold.' The smile had vanished now. Hemingsby nodded. 'I knew Joe,' he said. 'I knew Rebecca's family. My sister was a friend of hers.'

'And you were a suspect in her murder,' Alfie said flatly.

For a moment, Hemingsby seemed to be considering that. 'You're here because of that student that's been murdered,' he said.

'I am. You took a bit of tracking down.'

'I don't see why. I've been working here, in the same hospital for the past ten years.'

'Because Inspector Jackson left very few clues as to who you were or where you might be found. The address you gave him was false. The interviews you did with him are missing. And because everyone that remembers that investigation says that he kept his suspicions about you very close to his chest.'

Hemingsby nodded as though none of that was a surprise. 'It wasn't a false address,' he said. 'It was where I stayed while I was up here looking for a job.' He paused as though considering his options. 'I thought this was all over,' he said. 'I thought after Joe died all of this would be dead and buried.'

'Like Rebecca Arnold was, you mean.'

'An unfortunate turn of phrase. Sorry. But you know, that's not the way I meant it. This isn't what it looks like. It isn't what it looked like then.'

'So, maybe you'd like to come in and tell us how it was?' Alfie said.

When Tess got back she was told there'd been developments. 'Nat Cooper and Alfie Briggs tracked down the suspects in the Rebecca Arnold murder. The butcher, Greening, he has a shop down the coast and a solid alibi for the night of the Leanne Bolter murder. Dilly Hughes is locked up at Her Majesty's

Pleasure. Robbery with violence, he'll be out in another five years.

'And Doctor Keith Hemingsby has come in to talk to us. Alfie found him at St Almas. He's a paediatric surgeon, been there for the past decade. At St Luke's as a houseman when Joe Jackson added him to the suspect list.'

'And?'

'And he has an alibi for the night of the Bolter murder. Was in surgery. An emergency call, so . . . he's off the hook for that. And what he has to say about the original investigation is, shall we say, revealing.'

Field led them down to the operations room from where they could see the interview on CCTV.

Hemingsby had changed out of his scrubs. He was in company with Alfie Briggs and Nat Cooper and he looked a little anxious as most people, in Tess's experience, did in a police interview room. It was clear, though, from both Alfie and Nat's demeanour that this was more than a suspect being interviewed by two officers.

'So, what's going on,' she asked.

'Listen in, it's getting interesting.'

Puzzled, Tess took up position in the room adjoining the interview suite and watched as Hemingsby continued with his explanation.

'So, there was me and Joe and a psychiatrist he'd dragged in to consult on the quiet and we were sitting in this pub in the middle of nowhere. The Red Lion as it was then out on the coast road.

'Sounds like a bad joke put like that, I suppose, but Joe wanted to keep our meetings quiet and out of the way.'

'How long had you known Joe Jackson?'

Hemingsby paused. 'Must have been about five years by that time. My mother was a civilian worker, transcribed interviews and that sort of thing and I'd got to know him through her. She'd got to know him because she was one mean pool player and—'

'Joe Jackson organized the inter-station tournaments,' Alfie said.

'So, it was one of those coincidental things. Joe got on well with my mother, and with my dad, and Joe came over from time to time. He was just part of the landscape, growing up, but the thing was, not many people knew that. Local officers knew my mum and anyone that played pool, but you know as well as I do, civilian staff and non-civilian staff don't mix much at work and my mum had left by the time I got involved in Joe's scheme.' He paused, frowning. 'Well I didn't so much get involved as Joe involved me.'

'He could be a persuasive bastard,' Alfie observed.

'He could be a bastard, full stop.'

'You didn't like him then. I'm surprised you—'

'I didn't volunteer for the role, Sergeant Briggs. I was conscripted. I wake up one morning and there's a couple of policemen at my door *inviting* me to come to the station and tell them where I'd been on the night of the Rebecca Arnold murder. Didn't even give me time to get properly dressed. I was scared to hell and my mother was frantic.'

'I thought you were living in the B & B?'

'No, not at that point. I moved out of home soon after. I'd been coerced into going along with Joe's scheme but I didn't want my parents taking any of the flack. They put it about that I wanted to be closer to the hospital and had moved away because of that and fortunately, not many of the neighbours had witnessed my supposed arrest that morning. Those that had were used to seeing coppers coming and going to my mum's place and thought nothing of it.

'So why go to the trouble. Why not just ask you on the QT?'

'Because he wanted it to seem authentic. He wanted there to be a paper trail should anyone go looking. Look, I've lived with this thing for years now, been scared to death in case it all came up again. Joe promised he'd put it right, make sure there was nothing substantial in the paperwork.'

'Which he did,' Alfie told him. 'There seems to be no record of him bringing you in that first morning and the records after that are patchy. But *I* remembered and so did others. Joe couldn't erase us from the record.'

Hemingsby grimaced as though he wished that was otherwise.

'So, you were sitting in this pub . . .'

'Yeah. But before that. The morning I was brought to the station the sergeant that had brought me in, he left me in an interview room and a few minutes later there was Joe, bringing a cup of tea and grinning all over his bloody face. He said he'd phoned my parents and cleared things up with them and I said what things and he said he'd told them that I wasn't really a suspect for murder. That he needed a favour.'

'A favour.'

'He had a suspect in mind for Rebecca Arnold, but he couldn't pin anything on him even though Joe "knew" he'd done it and knew he'd killed at least once before. He wanted to put it around that he had a suspect, hope that this other person of interest as he called him, would relax, give something away or something.'

'And you went along with it?'

'Not at first. I didn't want to. The thing was, I worked with the guy Joe was talking about. I mean, not closely, but I was starting my specialty in paediatric medicine and the bloke Joe was after worked on the mental health side. Kids who are long term in hospital and their families and siblings, well they often need a lot of support on the emotional side of things. It can be really tough on brothers and sisters as well as the child involved. So—'

'So Joe thought you could confide in this man. Act as though you were scared, see if a reaction could be provoked?'

Hemingsby nodded. 'That was Joe Jackson's grand plan.'

'Seems sketchy?' Nat observed.

'Oh, it was. I think he was clutching at straws, hoping if he grabbed enough straws he'd be able to build a bloody raft.'

'But you agreed to go along with it.'

'No,' Hemingsby said flatly. 'I didn't agree. I wasn't given a choice. Jackson said that if I didn't help him out he'd make sure my arrest was made public. Leaked to the local press. He would have destroyed my life, sergeant and the fact that I didn't have any real alibi for the night of the killing pleased him even more.'

'Where were you that night?'

'On my own, at my parents, catching up with my reading and listening to music. I saw no one, my parents were away, I called no one, I ate what I could find in the fridge so there wasn't even a takeaway order to verify I'd been home. I had nothing and Joe Jackson. He relished that.'

'You must have been angry.'

'Angry doesn't cover it. I was also scared. Scared of what this might do to my life, my career, everything. I was also scared that Joe might be right and this suspect of his might actually turn out to be a killer. Talk about hanging me out to dry.'

'And this meeting in the Red Lion,' Nat Cooper prompted him.

'Was between me and Joe and this Fincher. Joe had a problem that his suspect had an alibi. Fincher had a problem that he'd convinced himself that Tom Reece, Joe's suspect was incapable. But the trouble was, Joe, could tell that Fincher wasn't as sure as he said he was. That he had doubts. He was playing devil's advocate, I suppose, this Fincher, talking about conferences that Tom Reece had been to, all the people who'd be prepared to alibi him for some other dates and times they were poring over.'

'Do you remember details?'

'No. I was just thinking how I could get out of this one. I'd got Joe on the one side blackmailing me into finding out that this bloke I worked with was a serial killer and Fincher on the other trying to find ways of convincing himself and Joe Jackson that he was pure as the driven and I got the feeling neither of them really had a clue as to how they could prove their argument.'

'What hard evidence did DI Jackson have?'

'I don't know. I think something had made him suspicious and he'd followed up on it. He talked about Tom Reece appearing at one of the scenes and something about three of the killings being in university towns, but what does that mean? Since all the polytechnics got university status it's hard to find a sizeable town that doesn't have at least one university associated with it. Like I said, he was clutching at straws.'

He paused and rubbed his face with his palms as though trying to clear the memory.

'And now it's all come back,' he said. 'Joe Jackson's dead

and buried and discredited and he still manages to reach out and try and drag me down.'

'You said he and Reg Fincher talked about other deaths. Do you remember any details?'

Hemingsby thought about it. 'There was an old woman,' he said. 'With a foreign . . . maybe a German name? Jackson kept saying something like "you had your doubts. You keep having your doubts." But I was thinking more about how I could get out of the situation than I was paying attention, though I think the idea of taking me out there and having me involved in their debate was supposed to persuade me this was the right course of action. It didn't, I ended up thinking that Joe Jackson had finally lost it.'

'And did you tell Tom Reece what had happened to you?'

Hemingsby nodded. 'I saw him in work the day after that. We were both at the same meeting. He could see something was wrong. I'm better at hiding my emotions now, I suppose. You learn to when you're dealing with frightened parents, but back then . . . anyway, he asked if I was OK and I did exactly what Joe must have wanted me to do, must have known I would, I told him what had happened and then . . . and then I told him what Joe thought Tom might have done.'

'Why did you do that?' Nat asked him.

'Because I was angry, I suppose, because Tom Reece is bloody persuasive. Because I was more swayed by Fincher's arguments than I was by Joe's, I don't know. Maybe because I was scared and scared people do some strange things.'

'And what happened after that?'

Hemingsby had paled. He rubbed his face again, his stress evident.

'He laughed. He actually laughed. He told me that DI Jackson must be delusional and that if I needed an alibi for the night in question he would happily give me one.'

'And what did you make of that?' Nat Cooper asked him.

Hemingsby took a deep breath. 'I can't exactly tell you why but I began to wonder if Joe Jackson might be right,' he said.

THIRTY-SIX

The late afternoon brought Naomi and Alec back to what had been their place of work. Alfie Briggs met them in reception and escorted them both past the front desk.

'Sorry your appointment got changed,' he said. 'It got a bit exciting here earlier on.'

'Oh? Developments. But you can't say what? Right?'

Alec sounded tetchy. Naomi had grown used to being excluded from what had once been her world, but Alec had less practice at it and although he had left the job voluntarily it still stung.

'Come on through,' Alfie said. 'I've borrowed an office so we don't get stuck in an interview room. Trinder will be along shortly.'

He organized coffee and Naomi sat in one of the low visitors' chairs that Alfie had fetched into the room. She tried to figure out whose room it was but the building was no longer familiar territory. DI Trinder's voice was oddly familiar though, especially considering the fact that she'd met him only a couple of times. She decided it was because he reminded her of the morning DJ she heard on local radio most mornings. The Scottish accent modified by a long time living among Sassenachs. She shook his hand, feeling odd calluses on the palm. She wondered if he played golf. The door closed, she heard Trinder take a seat behind the desk and Alfie pull up a chair beside hers.

'So,' Alec said and the tetchiness was still apparent. 'Alfie said you wanted to talk to us. I think we've already covered everything we know—'

'And I'm sure you have,' Trinder said. 'But we didn't know what questions to ask you before. Now we do. As Alfie may have intimated already, there have been developments today and to be honest we don't know what to make of them yet. The three of you knew Joe Jackson. Two of you were around during the Rebecca Arnold investigation and now—'

'What developments,' Alec sounded impatient now.

Naomi reached out to take his hand, but he didn't take hers and she realized she wasn't certain how far away his chair was from hers. She let it fall. 'Alec, calm down. What developments. What's changed?'

'Sergeant Briggs brought Doctor Hemingsby in for interview.'

'Doctor? What kind of doctor?'

'A well-regarded paediatric surgeon. With an alibi. And a very interesting story to tell.'

Alec and Naomi listened while Trinder brought them up to speed though, Naomi noted, he was careful not to name the new suspect.

'The question I have,' Trinder said, 'is: is that the kind of behaviour DI Jackson might have indulged in? Would he have set up something like this, below the radar?'

I want to say no, Naomi thought. But he would, wouldn't he.

Alec had no such qualms. 'It sounds exactly like a Joe Jackson scheme. Jackson told no one anything he didn't consider they needed to know. Even if that lack of knowledge put them in the line of fire. He was an egomaniac. A—'

'Mr Friedman, I can understand why you might be inclined to feel that way,' Trinder said cutting him off. 'Sergeant Briggs thinks it's entirely likely that Jackson played his cards so close to his chest that even close colleagues might have been kept in the dark.'

'It sounds like Joe,' Naomi said quietly. 'He liked the game. He liked to feel he knew things that others didn't. He liked to be the one in control and he trusted very few people. Not really trusted them. I think a lot of people in Joe's life had let him down and he didn't like to be in that position. Of being the underdog, the one who hadn't seen it coming, you know. If Joe really believed that this man was a murderer then he'd move heaven and earth, he'd lie and cheat and hide evidence in order to make his plan work. To catch the killer. Joe didn't play by the usual rules; Joe made his own rules and most of us went along because they worked. He got results. And he made those of us who followed him feel like we were privileged. Like we were on the inside track.'

'Doctor Hemingsby spoke about him as persuasive,' Trinder said. 'He said that Jackson promised he wouldn't risk Hemingsby's reputation or career. So he kept it quiet, made it look as though he was a suspect but only a handful of people were privy to his identity. But he made sure the suspect knew. Had Hemingsby tell his colleague that the police had taken him in for questioning. That he thought we were trying to fit him up.'

'And what evidence did Jackson have against this other man,' Alec asked. 'Is he another doctor?'

'A medical doctor, no. He was, at that time, part of the child psychiatric team.'

'Part of CAMHS,' Naomi asked. 'Working with kids?' She was horrified.

'And there's no evidence to suggest any impropriety in the workplace.'

'No evidence! If Joe suspected—'

'Suspected. Could not prove. He hoped Hemingsby might be able to lure him out into the open. Might be able to give Jackson an edge, but nothing came of it. The case went cold, then Jackson retired, died and, well you know the rest.'

'He left a confession to murder,' Naomi said quietly. 'He became what he tried to prevent.'

'So what happens now?' Alec said. 'Is this suspect still working for CAMHS?'

'No,' Trinder told them. 'He moved into a teaching role. Now, he lectures, writes authoritative texts on child mental health and is a well-respected member of the community with a wife and the obligatory dog and two kids.'

'And he's local,' Naomi guessed.

'Moved back this way two years ago. Lectures at the university, consults at two of the local hospitals. Plays golf with the chief constable for all I know. And we have only Hemingsby's word and Joe Jackson's suspicions to say he's done anything.'

THIRTY-SEVEN

Daniel's Uncle Ephraim had picked them up and driven Sam to the new flat. Patrick had been to Daniel's place a few times. His parents were dead and he lived with his uncle and aunt and grandfather in a Gothic-looking building on the edge of town and Patrick had been fascinated and delighted by the fact that it had two waterspout gargoyles projecting from the roof.

Sam didn't have a lot of stuff to move but the police had packed his clothes, kettle and cooking stuff and other belongings into a clutch of black dustbin bags and the thought of moving a half dozen well-stuffed bin bags and a suitcase a half mile from the university, had seemed pretty daunting.

Sam's new flat was on the third floor of a converted hosiery factory overlooking the canal. It was one of the latest blocks taken over by the university and Sam would be among the first occupants. Unlike the old flat, this wasn't shared accommodation but a simple bedsit-style apartment with a tiny kitchen area and a separate bedroom with en-suite shower.

'It's nice,' Patrick said. 'Think you'll be lonely on your own?'

'I know people in the block. It'll be OK,' Sam told him. He dumped the final bags next to the window and looked around. Daniel came in with another bag, followed by his uncle carrying a box Sam didn't recognize.

'Aunt Vi figured you'd need basic supplies,' Daniel said. 'So she sent some groceries over.'

Sam, taken aback, tried to say thank you and that he'd pay for them.

'No, it's a housewarming gift,' Daniel said. 'Fresh start and all that.'

'It's a bit crowded in here,' his uncle said. 'I'll wait in the van.'

Sam thanked him again and the three of them stood in Sam's flat suddenly at a loss as to what to do next.

'Have you heard from Ginny?' Patrick, the most domesticated of the three switched on the fridge and began to unpack the grocery box.

'Yeah, sort of. I'd sent her about a dozen texts and she finally said she was all right. I don't think her mum and dad want her upset any more so they're getting at her about talking to me on the phone.'

'It's not your fault,' Daniel said.

Sam just shrugged and it was clear to Patrick that a part of him thought that it was.

Tom Reece watched Sam and his friends unloading the van. He recognized Ephraim Goldman, of course and his nephew, Daniel. Daniel was such . . . was so untouchable. He'd not paid much attention to the dark-haired one before, the one they called Patrick. Though he'd noticed the boy in the hotel that day and then at the university, and felt that there was something about him. Something . . . older, wiser. Interesting.

Ephraim Goldman came back out of the block and got into his van, glancing around as he did so. He saw him, of course. The dog, spotting a friend, had pulled at the lead and yipped happily.

'Doctor Reece. Tom.' Ephraim closed the van door and crossed the road, hand extended ready to shake. 'How are you?'

They shook hands and Ephraim bent down to pet the spaniel. 'It's a nice walk along the canal.'

'It is. I can cut back through towards home without having to deal with the main roads. She's still not brilliant with the traffic.'

'Well, she's still a pup. She'll learn. How are you all anyway? Sheila? The girls?'

'Oh good, all good. Growing like weeds. Hester is in sixth form now.'

Ephraim jerked his head towards the van. 'Just doing my good deed for the day,' he said. 'A friend of Daniel got caught up on that dreadful business. He was a flatmate to the girl that was killed.'

'I've heard about it. The campus has been buzzing.'

'They've moved him in here. Needed transport, so.'

'That's good of you.'

'Oh, it's nothing. He's a nice kid and his family are miles away. And I don't think they get on all that well. His mum and dad came up for a day, Daniel said, then they had to get back to work or whatever. Sam didn't want to go back with them so . . . had it been my son caught up in something like that I'd have been out on the streets looking for the bastard.'

Tom Reece nodded. 'I know you would,' he said. 'And I don't think they'd benefit from the experience.'

'Damn right they wouldn't! Anyway, shouldn't keep you, you'll be wanting to spend your Sunday with the family. Give them my best.'

Tom Reece said he would and walked slowly on. Ephraim wouldn't just be out on the streets, Tom thought, he had contacts, connections. Men not afraid to get their hands dirty. He thought about how that made him feel and decided that it excited him. Not enough to risk harming Daniel but . . .

He helped the puppy down the steps and on to the canal path. She was still all paws and ears and uncoordinated limbs and steps baffled her.

Not yet, he told himself. Now was not the time. He stayed ahead by being careful, being in control and he wasn't about to ruin all that now.

Not *yet*.

THIRTY-EIGHT

Field looked grim at the morning briefing. 'We have two more names to add to our list of victims,' he said.

'Two? Where from?'

Tess looked to see who had spoken, figured it was Trinder.

'Arrived on my desk this morning. The Met did another run through the computer analysis and these came up. It's possible they won't be the last. Trey Baxter, fifteen years old. April 1992 and Sadie Rahman, age nineteen. Jan 1996. I'll get the reports copied and circulated.'

Which means my team will, Tess thought, and she needed to start on the Fincher box files. Apparently they had arrived that morning as well. She'd spotted them taking up most of her desk. And now, two more murders to appraise, collate against previous known cases and a set of notes to prepare for the evening briefing. She shouldn't feel resentful of the dead, Tess thought, but sometimes it was hard not to feel at least overwhelmed by the sheer quantity of paperwork and information.

'And now, we have to deal with other developments,' Field said. 'As you should be aware, Dr Keith Hemingsby came in voluntarily to speak with us about the Rebecca Arnold investigation. What he had to say threw the focus of our investigation in a somewhat different direction. Whilst we will not be completely writing off Doctor Hemingsby as a person of interest, another name has come up, one that will require more careful consideration and Will. Not. Go. Out. Of. This. Room.'

Tess felt the frisson of interest flutter through the assembled group. She wondered how long it would be before the phrase 'pillar of the local community' came up.

'Doctor Tom Reece.' Field affixed his picture to the board. It appeared to have been lifted from a group shot and she guessed he'd found it on the internet.

'Unusual in that he's both a medical doctor and a PhD. Specializes in the mental health of kids and adolescents. Teaches at the local university and as a visiting professor at several more. Writes for prestigious journals and, well, you've guessed it, is considered to be—'

A pillar of the local community, Tess thought. Right, that's got that out of the way.

'Now, this may be nothing but mud-slinging for reasons we're not aware of yet. It could be that DI Jackson was chasing shadows or had some bee in his bonnet about Reece or that Hemingsby has over-egged Jackson's interest in Reece in order to deflect from himself. It could also be that Reece is guilty.'

Tess listened as Field handed out tasks for the day. She knew already what hers would be. She and her team would spend what looked through the mucky windows to be a bright spring morning ensconced in a stuffy little office raising dust from long-closed files.

She exchanged a glance with Alfie Briggs and knew he was missing his usual routine too. He should be out there in his community, not in here trawling through archaic notes.

But, she supposed, someone had to do it.

'Who's taking what,' Nat Cooper asked as they settled in for the duration.

'OK, you and Vin work the Trey Baxter enquiry. 'Alfie and I will do the overview of the Sadie Rahman case. We'll get them written up and then take half of the Fincher stuff each. I've not even looked at it yet.'

'OK,' Nat said. 'I had a quick peep into the boxes. Looks like lecture notes, notebooks, bills and lord knows what else.'

Tess groaned. 'First things first,' she said. 'Do we know who turned up these two murders?' she asked Nat, hoping that as a member of Trinder's team she might have been told.

Nat shook her head. 'All I know is they turned up this morning. I think, from his reaction, even DI Trinder didn't know about them.'

That was true, Tess thought. He'd seemed genuinely surprised.

'Onwards and upwards then,' she said. 'We'll break for lunch and compare notes at, say, twelve?'

THIRTY-NINE

Gregory had arrived at Naomi's flat just as she and Alec came back from walking Napoleon.

'Wondered when you'd show up,' Alec said. 'Where's the other half of the double act?'

'Nathan's gone to see Annie and then book us into a hotel,' Gregory said. 'How is everything?'

He waited until Napoleon had his harness removed before greeting the dog and Naomi could hear the happy tail wagging as her guide dog made the most of meeting an old friend.

'Everything's as fine as you'd expect it to be,' she said. 'We've been interviewed a couple of times and it won't be the last. DCI Field is the SIO, you may remember him from your last little adventure down this way and Tess is checking back through old files. I think they've uncovered five deaths so far.'

'Seven,' Gregory said. 'They should have two more by now. And there'll be others, maybe not as dramatic, but others none the less.'

Naomi nodded. 'And you know this because?'

'Because a contact of Nathan's ran another search for us. What she found has now been added to the local enquiry. There are five different forces in on this, including the Met. And a span of twenty-odd years.'

'Really? Jesus wept. I know they found Hemingsby, supposed to be Joe Jackson's number one suspect in the Rebecca Arnold murder, but it turns out to be a different kettle of fish altogether.'

'Make me a cup of tea and a sandwich and tell me all about it,' Gregory said, 'and I'll share what we've got so far.'

Patrick had driven over to Bob's and taken his preliminary work on the Madonna with him. He set it up on his studio table, and stepped back. Somehow, everything looked very different in Bob's studio. It was probably just the light, but simply being in that space seemed to lend clarity to Patrick's thoughts and enable him to get some perspective on his work. Sometimes that was a good thing; sometimes not, but today he decided was a positive one.

So far he had only begun to lay in the base colours. It was a time-consuming job as the underpainting was done in egg tempera and the process of working in many tiny, cross-hatched strokes was not one that could be rushed. For a long time, Bob had told him, it would look all wrong, would feel as though he was getting nowhere. It was only by building and shading successive micro thin layers that the right effect could be created. Then it would be a question of laying in sheer, pure glazes of oil colour over the top and dammar varnish to bring unity to the whole and prevent dead – dry and matt spots – from spoiling the clarity of light bouncing through the layers.

It was slow, precise and calming work, Patrick found, rather like drawing and shading with a pencil but far more demanding as you couldn't smudge to shade or change from hard to soft to get a different effect.

Leaving his own work he crossed to the table where Bob left instructions for what he needed Patrick to do. This could be anything from editing photographs of Bob's work, emailing information – Bob left a crib sheet as a Word file from which Patrick could cut and paste – to grinding pigment or preparing canvases. Patrick loved the work, the mix of modern technology and medieval tradition. He was alone in the house today having let himself in through the studio door. The day Bob and Annie had presented him with a key had been the proudest moment he could recall. This was one of Annie's regular teaching days and Bob had to deliver some prints to a gallery, a job he tried to do in person whenever possible. Increasingly often, he took Patrick with him.

Today, Bob had left a recipe for Patrick to mix. A bleach for removing the foxing and cleaning the end papers he and Patrick had harvested from the rattiest of the auction books and he'd left a few other instructions for emails that needed sending and photographs taking. He started with the chemicals mix, taking care to get the proportions right. When he heard the front door open he assumed it must be either Bob or Annie returning. Then a voice called out from the hall that belonged to someone else entirely.

'Anyone home?'

'In here.'

Nathan came into the studio. 'You on your own?'

'Yes. Bob's doing a delivery and Annie's teaching. She'll be back in about an hour.'

'Right. I'll make us both a coffee. What's that stuff you're mixing?'

Patrick told him.

'And what's that?' Nathan asked going over to take a look at the picture Patrick was working on. 'That's definitely a Bob project and not an art school exercise.'

Patrick laughed. 'The original's over there. It's fantastic. Bob says it's a fake but I really don't care.'

Nathan withdrew the cloth from the little painting and gazed at it. 'I don't imagine Bob cares either,' Nathan said. 'So, why's it here?'

Patrick told him about the authentication Bob was doing and found himself confiding his worries that the beautiful little object might be destroyed.

'No, that's not right,' Nathan said. 'Someone created this with skill and a lot of love. Don't worry, Patrick, Bob will find a way out of the dilemma. He's a good man.'

'You think so?'

'I think so.'

'And are you and Gregory here to catch the killer?' Patrick asked, an ironic smile twitching at the corner of his mouth.

'Let's say we're going to give it a try. Your dad's worried, I know that much.'

Patrick nodded. 'He gets scared about a lot of stuff these days,' he said quietly. 'It's like he's been overloaded by things to be afraid of.'

'I can sympathize with that,' Nathan said softly. 'Overloaded is a good word. I sometimes think that life will reach critical mass one day and just blow up in all our faces.' He smiled, tried to break the mood. 'Listen to me. Sometimes the whole mortality thing feels like a big joke. A really bad joke. I'll go and make that coffee.'

By the time Annie got home Nathan seemed to have broken out of his mood but Patrick could see the pain behind his eyes.

FORTY

Naomi had been surprised when DI Trinder turned up and even more surprised by what he asked.

'Does the name Tom Reece mean anything to you? Joe Jackson might have mentioned him.'

She laughed. 'Oh, you mean Doctor Tom. Yes, he was lovely. I think Joe knew him, yes. Why do you ask?'

Trinder paused. 'Doctor Tom . . . how did—'

'After Helen went missing. I was a mess for a while. My GP referred me for counselling and Tom Reece did my initial assessments. All the kids called him Doctor Tom. My main counsellor was Beatrice . . . Toon, I think her last name was. But Doctor Tom tended to follow up his kids personally so I still saw him on a semi-regular basis for quite a few months. Why?'

Trinder still hesitated. 'And what did you think of him? Have you seen him since? Met with him as an adult?'

'I thought he was nice. He was gentle and persuasive and patient, I suppose. You're still not telling me why—'

'And have you seen him since then?'

'Um . . . only once I think. It was at work, he and Joe were talking about something and I recognized him, of course. Went over to say hello and thanks.'

'And how did Joe take that?'

How had Joe taken that? Naomi frowned, worried now by the direction the conversation was leading. 'How should he have taken it?'

'You tell me.'

'Actually . . . actually he wasn't too happy about it. At the time I thought it was just because I'd interrupted them and maybe he thought I was being rude. I apologized and went on my way.'

'And do you still think that?'

'What is all this about. What's Tom Reece got to do with anything?'

'He was the man Joe Jackson suspected of killing Rebecca Arnold. The real suspect.'

'He what? No, that's just crazy. Joe would never think . . . Tom Reece would never . . . You're serious, aren't you?'

'And you have no contact with him now?'

'No. Why should I have?'

'Good. Don't let that change.'

'You really are serious. On what evidence?'

'Circumstantial as yet.'

'So, nothing then.'

'Nothing but Jackson's suspicions and a few things that don't add up. For instance, why would a man need two completely separate alibis for the same night?'

'What do you mean?'

'The night Rebecca Arnold was killed Tom Reece stated he

was home with his family. A colleague stated he was out having a drink with him until the pub closed at eleven and then that Reece went back to his place.'

'A mistake. People get their times and dates mixed up all the time.'

'And that's true, but the colleague came forward voluntarily when he heard on the grapevine that Tom Reece had been questioned by the police.'

'He was brought in for questioning?'

'Once, yes. Jackson interviewed several medical professionals who might have come into contact with Rebecca Arnold. He made it look as though it was an innocuous element in a complex investigation.'

'Which it might have been. What contact did Tom Reece have?'

'Which it might have been. Rebecca's mother worked as a cleaner in the Stainford wing, which was then used by the CAMHS unit. Rebecca went to help her out a few times when they were short-staffed. And in the school holidays when they needed extra cover for absences.'

'So?'

'So it gave Jackson an excuse to speak to several members of staff, including Tom Reece.'

'And a friend heard about this and thought he might need an alibi. Trinder, that's stretching things. People overreact to police involvement, however peripheral, you know that, especially when they've had minimal contact previously. It's a traumatic event when a policeman knocks on your door, even more so if you or someone you know is actually questioned. People close ranks, get protective.'

'Perhaps.'

'Is that all you have? That he has too many alibis. It's so thin you can see through it.'

'And Joe never mentioned anything to you?'

She began to shake her head and then paused, a half-formed memory worming its way forward.

'Remember, I wasn't around for the Rebecca Arnold murder. So I must have run into the pair of them talking a couple of years later. I knew nothing about the operational events of the

Arnold killing . . . Joe talked to me the day after I'd spoken to Tom Reece, asked me what I knew about him and I told him he should know the answer to that. He and Tom Reece had come into my life at pretty much the same time. He warned me off. Told me I should stay out of his way. That people around Reece had a nasty habit of getting hurt. I had no idea what he meant and he wouldn't say, but I remember how serious he was. I gave it very little thought though. Joe was protective. He was my mentor. I thought he was my friend.'

'He was maybe just recognizing a fellow predator,' Trinder said.

FORTY-ONE

'Trey Baxter, fifteen years old. Out with friends at a street carnival. When he disappeared it was assumed he'd just gone off with another group of friends or was with family so it was a couple of hours before anyone realized anything was wrong.

'He was discovered four hours later at the home of a girlfriend of a family friend who'd been with them that afternoon. The young couple had alibis for the whole day and were never suspects but it was always assumed that the killer must be someone who knew the flat would be empty and therefore knew something about Trey and his family and social group.'

'How was he killed?'

Tess glanced at her notes, but she knew the details by heart. 'Signs of partial asphyxia and on that occasion tiny bits of plastic were found wedged between his teeth as though he'd tried to bite down on something. Speculation was that a plastic bag was placed over his head. He was then injected with keta-mine and killed in pretty much the same manner as Leanne Bolter. As you can see, the crime scene photos are very similar.'

'We've prepared detailed notes,' Nat Cooper said. 'But there were no obvious suspects and no leads from the interviews with friends and family. Police put out a call and the family requested help from the community which was forthcoming but which generated only false leads so far as the original investigation was concerned. We're still sifting but so far, we'd have to agree with them.'

Tess took up the narrative. 'A standard review on day eleven suggested that there may have been a gang-related element. The young woman whose flat was used for the killing had, when she was much younger, had some gang associations. This was rapidly dismissed. There simply wasn't anything to support it and the SIO went on record as saying that he thought the review was trying to shift potential blame in a misleading direction. It caused a lot of ruffled feathers, but the SIO looks to be in the right here.'

'Sadie Rahman was nineteen when she died. She was studying to be a teacher and had been on her way home from university when she disappeared. As you can see from the map, her route took her through central Manchester and then she should have taken a bus home. She's seen several times on CCTV, as you'd expect. There was also a CCTV camera on the traffic lights exactly where she should have crossed to her bus stop, but she never appeared on it. So the theory is she disappeared between here and the bus stop.' Tess indicated a point on the map outside a McDonald's where Sadie had last been picked up on camera.

'She was a creature of habit, apparently. Always took the same route, went straight home after classes unless she was meeting friends, in which case she always texted her mother. And there's every suggestion that she was simply heading home on the day she died.

'Her body was found in a hotel room the following day. The hotel was just a few hundred yards off her route. And CCTV in the hotel lobby shows her talking to a tall, bearded man – sound familiar? Keith Allen was also reported talking to a tall, bearded man before he died. The pictures unfortunately aren't worth a damn. He's aware of the camera, never looks towards it and the image quality is pretty awful anyway and as it's pre-digital attempts at enhancement have been pretty bleak.'

'She must have known him,' Nat says. 'Everything family and friends say about her indicates that she'd never have gone to a hotel alone with a man, and looking at the CCTV footage, she seems quite at ease with him. She's certainly not afraid of him at that point.'

She and Nat fielded a few questions, knowing there would be more after the briefing notes had been read and her colleagues had time to absorb the information.

'Whoever the killer is, he is not someone they feared. He got in close, in some cases he seems to have been invited into their homes. He's organized and not afraid of risks, the BIA preliminary report emphasizes that he is capable of risk minimization, even in circumstances where that conclusion seems counter-intuitive. It's likely that he enjoys the sense of power that comes with knowing other people are in close proximity but he then does all he can; subduing the victim, working silently, to keep from being discovered.

'He is likely to be someone in his forties or fifties and educated, professional, having status in the community he lives in. This is not some misfit with a grudge, this is a man who probably has it all but still wants more. And, above all, he's capable of great self-control. There are wide gaps between murders. There's no indication that he needs to escalate or that the impulse to kill is getting out of control. This is not a man who makes obvious mistakes. He is intelligent and devious and—' Tess took a deep breath – 'he's good at what he does, hideous though that might be. We've just got to try and be better.'

FORTY-TWO

'You're lucky,' the blonde woman escorting Tess told her. 'She's having a relatively good day.'

'Thanks.' Tess looked at the name tag the woman was wearing. It was small and discreet and pinned to her cardigan and it said that her name was Doctor Kirkwood. 'What's wrong with her, I mean—?'

'Dissociative Personality Disorder. It's what people used to call multiple personality syndrome, but that's never been a very accurate description. Sufferers don't necessarily switch between different personalities. Sometimes, like Penny, they have simply lost hold of who they are, or were. If you can imagine, it's like losing your definition of self. In Penny's case, it drifts and shifts, and some days, like today, she seems to have a handle on who she is or at least part of who she might be.' Dr Kirkwood smiled gently. 'What I'm saying is, don't expect too much. There are some days when she'll happily talk about her father; others when she is quite convinced that Joe Jackson was father to another woman, someone Penny calls Naomi?'

'Naomi Friedman.' Tess nodded. 'She was Blake back then. Penny was terribly jealous. She tried to kill Naomi.'

'A fact she no longer associates with herself. And if it's not relevant, I'd appreciate it if you don't bring it up.'

'It's not. I'll leave it well alone. I want to ask if she ever heard her father mention a man called Tom Reece. He's—'

'A psychiatrist. Yes, we consult with him from time to time. Can I ask why?'

'What do you think of him?' It was a clumsy question, Tess chided herself. The doctor frowned.

'He's excellent with patients and very helpful if we need a consult. Goes out of his way to do a good job. Why? And why should you want to ask Penny about him?'

'I can't really say.' Tess wished she'd not mentioned him now. She thought fast and tried another tack. 'Does he have any enemies? Professional jealousy, maybe? Someone who'd want to blacken his reputation?'

Dr Kirkwood laughed but she still looked puzzled. 'There's always professional jealousy,' she said. 'We're all only human, but no, Tom Reece is well thought of. He's produced some of the primary research and set teaching material for students and medics looking to work with young people. I can't imagine anyone wanting to do him harm.'

Tess thanked her. They had walked the length of a long corridor, a nursing station at one end and another halfway down. The corridor ended in a bright room with big windows overlooking a very pretty garden. Outside, staff and patients wandered, still wrapped against the cold and damp that came with the fag end of winter. A half dozen people sat in the bright room. Two played cards, one stared out into the garden and another at a television, on but muted. He wore what Tess recognized as infrared headphones, a small sender unit had been fixed to the wall beside the TV.

A woman Tess recognized from an old photo as Penny Jackson sat opposite a member of staff, a young woman in jeans and sweatshirt, differentiated from the patients only by her name tag. She got up as Tess and Dr Kirkwood approached.

'I've told Penny that she has a visitor,' she said. 'Penny is happy to have a chat with someone new.'

She put gentle emphasis on the word 'chat' and Tess nodded. She had been asked to leave her bag, her phone, anything in her pockets back at the reception. 'Sally will take notes for you,' Dr Kirkwood had said. And this, it seemed, was Sally.

The young woman smiled again and indicated the seat she had just vacated. Tess sat down and Dr Kirkwood departed. Tess saw her stop at the first nurses' station and assumed that was as far as she planned to go. Sally took a chair close by, out of Penny's eye-line but close enough to intervene if she got upset, as Dr Kirkwood had said she would. She held a small notebook and a pencil in her hand.

Tess felt uneasy, both at the thought of questioning Penny Jackson, a woman who was obviously out of reach of any reality Tess could recognize, and at the thought that someone else was listening in, making decisions about what to record and how to set it down. It was so far from her usual working practice that it felt improper, somehow. Unprofessional.

Penny was watching her.

'Hello,' Tess said. 'My name is Tess. Thank you for agreeing to see me.'

Penny's expression did not change.

Tess wasn't sure how to proceed.

'Tess wants to ask you some questions,' Sally prompted gently. 'You said that would be all right, didn't you, Penny?'

A slow nod was the only acknowledgement of that. Nervously, Tess decided she had better just get on with it.

'Penny, did you know a man called Tom Reece? I think he might—'

A slight shake of the head from Sally. One question at a

time, Dr Kirkwood had said, Tess reminded herself. Take it slow, keep it simple.

'Penny, did you ever meet a man called Tom Reece?'

Penny scrutinized her visitor but said nothing.

'Doctor Tom Reece? Doctor Tom.'

'Doctor Tom.' Penny nodded. 'He visited sometimes. Then my father didn't like him and he didn't come again.'

'But your father used to like him?'

Penny nodded. 'When I was really young. Then we didn't see him for a while and then one day, he called round to see my father and my father told him to go away. Actually, he told him to fuck off.' She laughed and for a moment the blank look disappeared from her gaze.

'Do you know why?' Tess asked.

The light in the eyes died and Penny shook her head. 'Dad was telling a lot of people to fuck off at that time. I thought it was just the way things were. Mum had gone, he was angry. I suppose that was it.'

'And after that? Did they make friends again? Did your dad talk about him?' Too many questions, she chided herself. Tess tried again. 'Did he come back again?'

'I don't know. He might have done. I didn't see my dad for a while. I went to live with my mother. Then she . . .' Penny's face contorted with remembered pain.

'Then you left,' Sally intervened gently. 'Then you left your mum's place, remember?'

'Then I left,' Penny agreed, 'but my dad had found another child. He didn't need me. Do you know what it's like not to be needed? Not to be wanted?'

Tess glanced across at Sally, not sure how she should respond to that one.

'Tess wants to know about Doctor Tom,' Sally said gently. 'If he made it up with your dad?'

'He came to see him about his new kid,' Penny said bitterly. 'The one he liked better than he liked me.'

She's talking about Naomi, Tess thought. 'I'm sure he didn't,' she said softly. 'He was still your dad, not anyone else's.'

Penny shook her head. She had blonde curls that were greying now at the temples and streaked here and there with silver. She must have been really beautiful, Tess thought. But now there was nothing behind the eyes and her skin was pasty and puffy. Tess wondered if she ever went outside, into the gardens, or if the medication caused the sallow skin, the dryness round the mouth and eyes.

'Sometimes parents say things they don't mean. Sometimes they do things wrong but they don't mean to hurt by it.'

'He meant it.' The light was back in the eyes, but it was driven by anger now, by an inner rage that took Tess aback.

'And did Doctor Tom try and help you?' she asked.

The question was a shot in the dark, just a random something sent out there to deflect the rage but she realized at once that she'd struck a chord of some kind.

Penny smiled and the rage died in her eyes to be replaced by something sly and cunning that, Tess thought, was even more disturbing. 'He knew what I'd done,' Penny said. 'He told my dad. That's why my father liked the other girl more. He knew what I'd done.'

'What you'd done?' Tess was totally confused now. 'What had you done, Penny? What did Doctor Tom know?'

But the moment had gone, Penny's attention shifted from Tess to the view beyond the windows and Sally shook her head. 'Tess is going now,' she said quietly but Penny didn't respond.

Tess got up and followed Sally to the nurses' station where Dr Kirkwood was waiting. She tore the sheet from her notebook and handed it to Tess. 'Sorry it isn't more, but if you've got your number?'

'Sure.' She felt in her pocket and then remembered that everything had been left at the reception desk. Sally, she noticed, was standing so she could still see Penny. 'I'll leave my card with both my numbers, home and work, at reception.'

'Do that,' Sally told her. 'Penny might well have more to say later on. Sometimes she has to have time to process things then little details emerge, you know?'

'Thanks,' Tess said but Sally was already moving away.

'Penny, are you all right? Penny, calm down sweetheart. I'm just here.'

Penny Jackson had got up from her seat and was staring back at Tess, a look of pure hatred on her face.

'You'd best go,' Dr Kirkwood told her and Tess took no urging. One of the nurses left her station to join Sally in the sunroom as Tess hurried away. Behind her, Penny Jackson had begun to scream.

'Are you OK?' Dr Kirkwood asked as Tess collected her things and found a card to leave for Sally.

'Yes, I'm fine. Just a bit . . . shaky, I guess.'

'It can be frightening. You have to remember that for Penny reality is fractured. Small fragments may coalesce from time to time, other fragments . . . it's like her world is made of broken glass and even the pieces left intact are sharp edged.'

'Will she get better?'

'Probably not.'

'Did I . . . Did my coming here make things worse?'

'Again, probably not. We have no way of knowing. You might have joined a few of the pieces together or you may have broken some apart but there's no way of knowing for now if that's a good or a bad thing either way. Sally will let you know if she says anything more.'

'Does Doctor Reece ever come here?'

'Very occasionally. His specialty is young adults and we don't deal with young adults here, not unless it's a major emergency and there are no beds elsewhere.'

'And has he ever come to see Penny?'

'Not as far as I know. But I can check and let you know.' She frowned. 'Doctor Reece is a good man, you know. A compassionate man and an excellent doctor.'

'I know,' Tess said. 'People keep telling me that.'

She was aware of Dr Kirkwood watching her as she left and she wondered how long it would be before she called Dr Reece to tell him of Tess's visit.

'Did you learn anything?' Field asked.

'Not really, no. She's in a bad way. Reece was someone Joe Jackson knew. She said they were friends when she was very small, then her father turned against him and told him to "fuck off". That seems to have been around the time that Naomi Blake was in counselling, but her thoughts and memories are so all over the place I don't know if we can rely on anything.

I'm just worried that asking questions will have made her worse.'

'I'm sure the doctors would have refused to let you see her if they thought that.'

'I get the impression the doctors don't know what will help and what won't. There were moments when, I don't know, it was possible to almost see the woman she'd been, but then . . .' Tess shook her head. 'It's a horrible place. I don't mean the building or the doctors just everything else.'

'Anything else to report?'

'Only that everywhere I go people tell me how wonderful a human being Tom Reece is. And maybe they're right. Maybe we're chasing shadows. Maybe Joe Jackson just had a personal gripe. Maybe he was as nuts as his daughter is.'

She left Field and returned to the little office filled with box files and cold cases. Only Alfie was there. He got up quietly and fetched her a coffee.

'Bad?'

'Bad. Alfie, did you know Joe Jackson's kid?'

'Penny? Yes, slightly. She was just an ordinary little girl so far as I could tell. Then her mam had an affair and left and for a while she stayed with him. Then her mam came and fetched her. I think she must have been about thirteen, fourteen at the time. I remember Joe wasn't coping with all the teenage girl stuff.'

'Teenage girls can be shit,' she agreed. 'I should know, I was one. And did that work out? She seems really resentful of the mother.'

'Well, I imagine that must have cut both ways. Penny started a relationship with the bloke her mother had run off with – or he started one with Penny. Whichever way it was.'

'But she was only—'

'A kid. Yes. Her mam kicked her out and sent her back to her dad. She tried to rekindle the relationship, apparently, but then her lover disappeared on her and we know why now.'

'That was Robert Williams. Joe Jackson killed him.'

'And Penny never forgave him apparently.'

'When do you think she knew?'

'I always wondered if she suspected long before her father died. It was all too convenient. Anyway, lover boy disappeared and I think Joe expected everything to return to normal just because he wished it so.'

'Was he really that arrogant?'

'Oh, he could be. Damned good investigator and he knew it. I sometimes wonder about people who are right often enough that no one believes they can do wrong. They believe their own press and it makes them . . . wrong in the head somehow.'

Tess nodded. Like Tom Reece, she thought. A man everyone seemed to hero-worship.

FORTY-THREE

Patrick had gone back with Daniel to his house mid-afternoon. It was not unusual for him to do so and then spend an hour or so working on the large dining table. Usually, they had the same essays to write or at least the same subjects to wrangle into sense-making reports, and comparing notes, sharing the reading and helping one another to plan had become part of their routine.

Daniel's aunt usually provided snacks and the old house with its tiled hall and half-panelled walls and ticking clocks was, Patrick thought, a very peaceful place.

He and Daniel had worked for about an hour when Daniel's aunt brought coffee and biscuits through. 'How's it going?' she asked.

'Could be better.'

'You'll get there. Your uncle will be late so it'll just be me you and Grandad for dinner. Patrick, you're welcome to stay.'

'Thanks, but it's my turn to cook tonight. Dad won't be home till after six.'

'Are you sure you'll be all right walking back alone? I don't like to think . . .'

'I'll be fine,' Patrick said. 'It's only a few minutes away and I'll keep to the main road.'

'Well, humour me and let Daniel know when you've arrived.' She managed a tight smile.

'I will,' Patrick promised.

'Sorry about that. She's not wanted me out of her sight,' Daniel said when his aunt left.

'It's OK. It's nice that she's bothered. She hardly knows me really.'

'It took her a long time to get over it when Mum and Dad died and I think it just worries her, you know? Like there's a killer round every corner.'

Maybe there is, Patrick thought. 'Was it a long time ago?' He'd refrained from asking Daniel about his parents, but now the opening had been made it seemed like the right thing to do.

'I was twelve,' Daniel said. 'They went away for a couple of days and never came back. Dad lost control of his car and it went off the road and into a river. It was pretty . . . bad. I couldn't believe they'd gone. I thought they'd just . . . it was like they were just a bit late home and we were all waiting for them.'

'I'm sorry,' Patrick said.

'My uncle said I should have counselling but I think it was them that needed it really. Auntie Vi just went to pieces and Grandad was just in bits.'

'Did you see anyone?'

'Yeah,' Daniel smiled. 'You remember that Doctor Reece that came into the lecture. I saw him for a bit. It seemed really weird seeing him somewhere else. It was ages ago, but it still made me feel kind of awkward.'

Daniel sipped his coffee. And Patrick said, 'He was in the hotel that day we went to see Sam and Ginny?'

'Was he? I didn't notice.'

'I asked him about it when he came to the lecture.'

Daniel laughed. 'I wondered what you were talking to him about. What did he say?'

'That I had a good visual memory.'

'Well he was right about that one. Why did you ask him?'

Patrick shrugged. 'I just did,' he said, not feeling easy about suggesting that he'd noticed Dr Reece watching him at other times. 'Did you like him?'

'I suppose. I saw him for a bit and then another person for a bit. It didn't help, not really. They wanted me to talk and I wanted to shut it all out. I could cope with it if I didn't think about it.'

Patrick nodded. He was really not sure about the way therapy was supposed to work. How you could let something heal if you were constantly prodding at it? But what did he know?

He drank his coffee. 'I'd best be going,' he said.

Daniel nodded. 'OK, see you tomorrow. Be careful on the way home.' The last was said with a grin and an eye roll in the direction his aunt had gone, but Patrick sensed that Daniel's aunt Vi was not the only one feeling vulnerable.

FORTY-FOUR

Naomi and Alec had just returned from the shops around mid-morning when Gregory and Nathan arrived. She had been restless and upset since Trinder's visit the previous day and she had talked at length to Gregory on the phone about it. He had promised that he and Nathan would gather what information they could.

She had been hoping, she realized, for something that would rescind Trinder's accusations, but one look at Nathan's face told her that she was out of luck.

'On the face of it,' Gregory told them when they had settled in the flat and Napoleon had been fussed, 'he's above any kind of suspicion. He's a model in his professional conduct, a good husband and father, well thought of in his local community and active with a half dozen charity boards.'

'But?'

'But . . .' Gregory said. He consulted his notes.

'Two daughters aged nineteen and seventeen. Married to Sheila Reece nee Colbrook, she's an NHS manager, responsible for locating and organizing beds across the regional health authority. Youngest daughter, Hester is still at sixth form college and the older one, Rhea, is studying music, in the first year of her degree course. He doesn't have so much as a speeding ticket. Neither does she for that matter. Clean record at work too.

There have been a couple of minor complaints made about him in all the years of professional practice and both were dismissed.'

'What were they?' Naomi asked.

'One was ten years ago, when he was still working for CAMHS, a parent complained that the referral he made for their daughter was not to the most appropriate practitioner. It seems he decided the girl was anorexic and referred accordingly; the parents were in denial about the diagnosis. They made a formal complaint.

'The second was a little more serious. A complaint was made regarding unfair dismissal. A colleague complained that Reece had a personal dislike of him and had started a vendetta. It went to tribunal and no evidence was presented, the case was dismissed.'

'And what happened to the complainant?'

'His name was Doctor Theo Dalby and he died in a drowning accident six months after the tribunal. No evidence was presented because he didn't turn up at the tribunal, apparently.'

'Pressure applied?' Alec suggested.

'No way of knowing. For the most part no one has a bad word to say for him.'

'Was the death suspicious?'

'Apparently he'd been depressed for quite some time. He was found floating in the canal. But his regular route home was along the towpath. He'd been drinking in the local pub and his blood alcohol level was over the limit for driving and a little suspect for walking along a canal towpath on a freezing and icy night. It's moot but the verdict was accidental.'

'And he's not appeared on the suspect list anywhere else?'

'No, but he was definitely in the area when three of the murders were committed.' Nathan said. 'The night Keith Allen died, Reece was at a hotel ten miles away, attending a conference.'

'Alibi?'

'For what? He was never a suspect. No link was made.'

'When Martia Richter died, he was certainly in the same city for the day before and two after. Guest lectures at the university and at a presentation of some kind at the Mechanics Institute. He seems to have stayed on for another day. His wife was with him on that occasion but—'

'Too long ago to establish any kind of timeline,' Alec said.

'And what was the third?' Naomi wanted to know.

'He was in London the weekend Trey Baxter was killed and he may have come into contact with the friend whose flat the body was left in.'

'Contact? How. Why wasn't that noted?'

'Because he was just one of god knows how many people in London for the weekend,' Nathan said. 'And one of the many people who had vague contact with the friend, Andrea Johnson. Her boyfriend attended one of the lectures Reece gave that week as part of a programme of career events run by the University of London. It's incredibly tenuous.'

'And we know this because?'

'Because the boyfriend was, albeit very briefly, a suspect. He had to provide a timeline. Reece's lecture was on that timeline.'

'And how many people attended the lecture?' Naomi asked. 'Nathan's right. It's all circumstantial. Is this what Joe had? All Joe had? That and a "feeling"?'

'Maybe, maybe not. Reece was still in the area when the murders happened.'

'And the chances are any of us could be in an area when a murder happened. Murders happen; you travel around enough it's entirely possible there could be coincidence of events. That you could *happen* to be in three separate cities when there *happen* to be violent deaths.'

'In Gregory's case, it would probably be more than coincidence,' Nathan said. 'And yes, of course it's open to confirmation bias. We – and Joe Jackson – are just looking at the facts that fit a possible presumption as opposed to those that negate it. He could have been hundreds of miles away when the other deaths happened and been in dozens of places when murders *didn't* happen. Coincidence sometimes *is* just two things happening to happen.'

'But you don't believe that,' Alec stated.

'I'm open to possibilities,' Nathan said. 'I think we have to take a hard look at our doctor, see what he gets up to.'

'You mean you've already set up surveillance,' Naomi demanded.

'I'm here, so is Gregory.'

'Which means nothing. Have you?'

'It won't hurt,' Nathan said. 'And there's another reason for watching him. He seems to be taking an interest in you and more particularly, he seems to be taking an interest in Patrick.'

'What?'

Nathan related how on three separate occasions, Reece seemed to have sought their young friend out.

'Could be coincidence again,' Naomi said slowly. 'The first time he could have just happened into that hotel. Then he might just happen to have been standing on the promenade. People do . . .'

'Even you don't sound convinced. The promenade is the opposite direction from home, from the university, from any of his usual routes. And then he was across the road from the flats when Patrick and Daniel Goldman helped to move their friend Sam into his new room. Patrick noticed him heading for the towpath when they came out. When Patrick spoke to him when he came out of his lecture he asked about you. Patrick mentioned seeing him in the hotel and at the promenade.'

'He what?' Alec demanded.

'He asked about Naomi. Said he'd just made the connection that the woman on the beach with the guide dog was an ex-patient of his and an ex-colleague of Joe Jackson's. He said he remembered you and wanted Patrick to say hello.'

'When was this?'

'A couple of days ago. Patrick had no reason to suspect him of anything but he doesn't like him and Patrick's instincts are good, you know that.'

Naomi was shaken. 'Watch him,' she said. 'And make sure Patrick keeps out of Reece's way.'

'Suddenly he goes from good guy to suspect?'

'Anyone goes from good guy to suspect if they even look like they're threatening Patrick or Harry.'

'So we watch and we see what happens,' Nathan said.

'And you two keep yourselves safe,' Gregory instructed. 'Lock the doors and let us know where you plan to be if you go out. So far, he knows nothing about us, we're ahead of the game. Let's keep it that way.'

FORTY-FIVE

It had taken Tess a while to get on to Reg Fincher's notes and in the end she and Nat had split the load and settled down to sift. Fortunately either Reg or the solicitor had been pretty organized. Financial and accounting stuff had been separated out as had deeds to the bungalow, various bits and pieces of legal documents – including Reg Fincher's will. He had no living relatives, it seemed and apart from a few small bequests to friends, he had ordered that everything he owned be sold and the proceeds divided between a couple of children's charities.

'That's sad,' Nat said when she read it out. 'Do you think he ever married? Ever wanted to be?'

Tess shrugged, something suddenly striking her about the crime scene at Fincher's bungalow. 'His walking stick was missing,' she said. 'I'm sure of it.'

'Walking stick?'

'He walked with a limp. Apparently he was born with a deformed foot. It was a big, heavy thing. Hawthorn, I think, kind of knobbly.'

Nat looked puzzled. 'You think the killer might have taken it? You want me to call it through, see if it's at the crime scene?'

Tess nodded. 'Do that. I might just have missed it.'

While Nat was put on hold, Tess picked up the first in her pile of notes. It appeared to be a transcript of a lecture that Fincher had delivered. She scanned at first and then found herself smiling. She could hear Reg Fincher's voice in her head as she read the notes. She had liked him, Tess realized. He would be an interesting man to have talked to.

In the Middle Ages, Fincher wrote, *people were allowed, even encouraged to buy Indulgences. These were like portable forgiveness vouchers, issued by the church and sold by priests and monks and if you bought enough of these*

Indulgences then you could go off and kill someone or commit rape or theft or what have you and you'd be forgiven, even without confession through the intervention of a priest because you'd already pre-paid for all that. They were especially favoured by the rich, as you can imagine. I often imagine them buying a whole book load of these things and tearing out the sheets when they'd used them up. You can imagine it, can't you? 'I've used up my coupon for murder, so I need to drop by the abbey and pick up a few more of those before I go off on the next crusade . . .'

Sounds flippant put that way, doesn't it, but Indulgences were a reality in Medieval life and they probably performed several very important roles. One of course was purely financial. A lot of money flooded into the church off the back of these sales in the same way that if you were rich enough you could pay for a chapel to be built and a monk to pray for you in perpetuity. In another sense, it was a practical solution to a difficult moral dilemma. Killing was wrong. There was a commandment about it and everything. The church told you that murder was wrong and yet then, as now, church and state sometimes demanded that you had another set of moral obligations, the fulfilment of which would lead you to commit murder, sometimes on the most grandiose of scales. If you were a soldier, a commander, a crusader, even someone just sending men off to fight, you were implicated in murder, church- or state-sanctioned though that might be.

And if you imagine the chaos of a battlefield, the idea that a priest could go round to each and every one and hear confession and provide absolution, well, that was a difficulty. So, you pre-paid, as it were. You armed yourself for what you were about to do. Armour? Check. Sword? Check. Indulgence? Check.

Of course, I'm putting a modern spin on something from a different age and a different culture, but the moral dilemma remains. In our secular society we sanction death by state in a variety of ways. Soldiers are seen as heroes by many – as indeed they always were. Though of course that rather depends on which side you are on. I remember an anecdote told to me by an elderly lady who had spent the Second World War in Silesia. She had been maybe ten miles from the death camps but her memory of the war was of running wild in the woods and of her older brother coming home in his new SS uniform. All she could think about at the time, she told me, was how shiny his boots were. I remember asking her what she thought about him now and she just shrugged and said, 'Reg, he was my brother. What should I think?'

What should she think? As it happened, she emigrated here after the war and married, briefly. The man she married had been a soldier in that same conflict. She loved him. He loved her. Her brother had been killed in the war and her strongest memory of him was always as a young man in his shiny boots.

Why am I telling you this? Because human beings are complex and contradictory. Because my friend, Martia, grew old in a country with which her family had been at war. Her children and grandchildren were born here, raised here, taught that the side on which her brother fought had been wrong. And she agreed with that. But he was Still. Her. Brother.

Tess stared at the page. Martia. Was he talking about Martia Richter?

Nat was still gripping the phone to her ear. Still on hold.

'Nat, was Martia Richter married? Did she have kids?'

Nat, phone still at her ear, reached over for one of the folders on the desk behind her. She scanned the cover page, where such information as next of kin would be recorded. 'No, she lived here since 1953, came over with her sister who married a George Barker. It was one of their children, Sally, married name Styles, who found her. Why?'

So Fincher had conflated the two women to make a better story, Tess thought. But that wasn't the point, was it. 'Because I think Reg Fincher knew her,' she said.

FORTY-SIX

' I got curious about Patrick's friend, Daniel Goldman,' Nathan told Naomi. 'So I did a bit of digging.'

'Curious? Why, Daniel's a nice kid. His family seem like nice people. He lives with his aunt and uncle, I think.'

'And grandfather,' Nathan said. 'And there's nothing to worry about. I just have a natural curiosity, you know.'

'You have a dangerous level of curiosity. But what nudged it this time?'

'Gregory and I were just looking for patterns. Victims, friends of victims – you must have done similar searches when you were in the police?'

Naomi nodded. True, she thought. You looked at everyone and their dog to see if there might be possible connections, however tenuous.

'We could find nothing between the dead girl, Leanne, and Tom Reece or any of the other victims. But there is a link between Reece and Daniel. It's the same kind of link that you have with him. Daniel's parents died in a tragic accident when he was twelve and he was sent for bereavement counselling. Eventually, his therapy came via a local charity. St Hugo's. It provides help and care to bereaved kids and Tom Reece referred him.'

'So . . .'

'So, when Daniel and Patrick helped their friend Sam to move, Patrick saw Reece talking to Daniel's uncle. They seemed on friendly terms.'

'So your curiosity was sparked and you looked further.'

'And I found a link of my own. Though it's tenuous and goes way back to before I was born, really.'

'Gustav Clay,' Naomi guessed.

'Gustav Clay. My guardian and Daniel's grandfather were almost certainly known to one another. Clay was involved in the intelligence game from just after the war. So, it seems was Josep

Goldman. He settled here just after the war. He was only a young man at the time, came here first just as the Second World War started and he joined up to fight with the allies. His family was all but wiped out by the time the war ended but they'd managed to send him and his sister away and so saved their lives. Anyway, in 1942 he was recruited to SOE and later his career seems to have paralleled Clay's. It's unlikely they didn't meet.'

'And so.'

'And so . . . probably nothing. But if the old man is anything like Clay, then he still has people he can call on if he feels his family are threatened. It's unlikely his family even know what he did. He's a businessman, owned a couple of small shops, then a bit of property. Made sure his kids got the best education they could. He's not particularly active in the Jewish community, strictly secular for the most part. His older son is a doctor and his younger, Daniel's guardian, is a lawyer. But you talk to anyone . . . to anyone who might know about the old man and they reckon he still wields a lot of influence and not just in high places.'

'That's so conventional it sounds like a bad joke,' Naomi commented. 'And you think the old man's reputation is enough to give Reece pause? How would he know?'

'I think men like our Doctor Reece also have a dangerous level of curiosity,' Nathan said, returning to her the description she had used for Nathan himself.

'So Daniel is safe. But not Daniel's friends.'

'That's my theory. For what it's worth.'

Naomi nodded. 'So what can we do?'

'We can wait and watch. For now, that's all. Reece may be an innocent man.'

'Bollocks,' Naomi said. 'You don't think that any more than I do.'

'Weight of evidence,' Nathan said. 'Once upon a time that would have mattered to you. You'd have been concerned only with what the law could prove.'

Naomi said nothing to that. He was right, she thought. Now she felt so detached from what conventional resources could establish and act upon. So what did that make her? Naomi wondered.

She left the question hanging. Sometimes, she thought, it was better not to ask.

FORTY-SEVEN

Tess had read on. Reg Fincher had been a keen if erratic keeper of journals and diaries. Sometimes weeks would pass with barely a comment and then he would go through a spate of enthusiasm and write at length almost every day.

She had gathered these chronologically and skimmed through those from the eighties, begun seriously with one from the early nineties and been rewarded more quickly than she could have hoped.

When he first told me he had killed someone, I thought he was joking. He presented it as a hypothetical question. We'd both had a bit too much to drink and it was one of those stupid debates people get into when they drink too much and think too much.

How much good would it take to balance a death is what he asked me.

We'd been talking about rehabilitation. It's an issue close to my heart and close to his too – though I think our reasons are very different. For him, I think, it's more about redemption. Not perhaps in a religious way but in some logical, measured quantifiable form.

The ancient Egyptians depict the weighing of a human soul after death. The soul is weighed against a feather. A pure, sinless soul would not tip the balance but one that was leaded with guilt and sin would. He reminded me of this and I told him I thought he'd need a bloody enormous lead feather if he wanted his soul to come out ahead if he really killed someone.

It was a drunken joke. But he didn't see it that way.

He reminded me that none of us is innocent, that we

*all spend a lifetime seeking to balance the books one way
or another.*

*I asked him what he planned to do. Who he planned to
kill. I thought it would jolt him out of his mood. He's a
pig to be with when he gets morose and worse than that,
he never knows when to give it best and go home.*

*What would you do if you thought I'd killed someone,
he asked me and I told him I didn't know. I assumed I'd
call the police.*

*Assumed, he said. And laughed at me. Said I was always
one for sitting on the fence.*

*No one knows what they'll do until they're faced with
a choice, I told him. It would depend on the circumstances.
A best friend is someone who helps you hide the bodies
– another joke; another bad one, I'm afraid. He didn't
laugh. He just asked me, straight out if I was a good friend,
like it was a test.*

*What have you done, I asked him and he seemed
to shake off the mood. Said he had to get home, he
was consulting all the next day and needed to get some
sleep.*

*I've just come back from Martia's funeral. The family were
devastated as you'd imagine. Tom was there. I hadn't
realized he knew Martia, but of course, they both sat on
the Wallace committee a couple of years back. Two ends
of the advocacy spectrum. Tom so involved with the mental
health of the young and Martia with the treatment of the
old. I know that her one regret was that she never had
children of her own but she said that Gina's were like her
own. Gina looked very frail, this is such a blow, I doubt
she'll survive long now. The loss of husband and now
sister will finish her.*

My God, Tess thought. Fincher knew about Reece. Suspected
at least and here was a link. Both of them to Martia Richter.

She knew that it was nothing concrete, nothing solid, nothing
as Fincher had said himself, but a drunken conversation. It
wasn't proof. But it was something.

'Nat, do we have a current number for Sally Styles? Martia Richter's niece?'

'Well, we have a number and we have what might be a current address, I'm sure we can . . .'

Tess took the form from Nat and began to dial.

'What have you found?' Nat asked.

Tess pushed the journal across the desk for her to read. 'Maybe a tiny chink in the armour,' she said.

FORTY-EIGHT

Sally Styles was a small and greying blonde with soft blue eyes. She was dressed in tailored trousers and a neat white blouse beneath a heather-coloured cardigan. It should, Tess thought, have looked twee, but somehow she just looked understated and right. A woman comfortable with herself.

She was sixty years old, Tess recalled from her notes.

'This is my aunt. It was taken a few months before she was murdered,' Sally told her, handing over a picture that showed a woman who looked like an older version of the one sitting across from Tess. 'She and my mother were incredibly close and aunt Martia was very precious to us all.'

'You look a lot like her.'

Sally nodded. 'There was only two years gap between my mother and my aunt and they were often taken for twins. I was named Sarah after my mother, but the name transmuted into Sally when I was a very little thing and it never reverted. You know how these things are?'

Tess nodded. 'And you found your aunt.'

'I found my aunt and I'm glad it was me. My mother would never have survived the experience. Her heart was bad and as it was I think Martia's death hastened her end. She couldn't believe anyone would do that to such a kind soul. Martia was a good soul. She never did a scrap of harm to anyone.'

Sally paused and looked directly at Tess. 'And are you any closer to finding him?'

'I can't really tell you that. I'm sorry.'

'I'll take that as a yes.' Sally took a deep, unsteady breath. 'I hope he burns for it,' she said bitterly. 'It's what he deserves.'

Tess paused allowing silence to fall between them and then she said, 'I have a couple of names to run by you, ask if you knew either of them.'

'The killer?'

'People who knew your aunt but whose names didn't come up in the previous enquiry. New evidence that's just come to light.'

'And can't you ask them about my aunt? Not that I mind, but wouldn't the more direct approach be—'

'One is dead. One can't be contacted yet.' It was a white lie, but it would do, she thought. It was almost true. She couldn't go up to Tom Reece and ask him anything directly. Not yet. Fields had told her she had to hold fire. All they had was a random entry in a dead man's journal; a record of a conversation Reece could easily deny recalling or suggest had never taken place.

'And their names?'

'Doctor Reginald Fincher and Doctor Tom Reece. Did your aunt mention either of them?'

Sally frowned, searching her memory. 'She may have done. She served on a lot of committees, volunteered for all manner of things. She knew a lot of people. The crematorium was packed out, there were people standing outside in the rain. The funeral director had to prop the doors open so they could hear the service.'

'I think Tom Reece might have been on a committee with her. The Wallace board? Does that ring any bells?'

Sally had begun to shake her head, then she stopped and frowned. 'The Wallace . . . oh.'

'Something?' Tess asked.

'Oh dear. I'm not sure.' For the first time Sally looked less than self-possessed.

'Mrs Styles. Sally. It might seem like a tiny thing but it might be important.'

'Of course. Look, my aunt had some pretty . . . decided views. If she took to you she'd be the most loving and loyal friend you could ever hope for. If she took against you, which she didn't do very often, it was quite a different matter. She'd be cordial and decent, of course. She often had to work with people she didn't really care for, but—'

'But?'

'But it was the day we went out for tea. I told the original investigation about the man she didn't like.'

'I assumed that was a stranger?'

'Well, so did I until you mentioned Wallace. It was what she said. "That damned man from the Wallace. What's he doing here?" Then she glared a bit and carried on the conversation she was having."

'The man from the Wallace. You're sure?'

'Inspector, those last hours with my aunt are engraved on my brain. She was worried, scared even in the days before she died. I said we should go to the police and she said to report what! I didn't realize she actually knew the man she was talking about. She never said she knew him. She just talked about someone that bothered her, disturbed her. If she'd said she knew who he was—'

'I don't know if it would have made a difference,' Tess said. 'It would have still just have been a feeling. I don't think there was anything you could have done.'

Because no one would have believed her, Tess thought to herself. It would have been just the fears of some elderly and – who knows – less than compos mentis woman, making an accusation against a man that most regarded as above suspicion.

'There was nothing you could have done,' she said quietly. 'But maybe we can do something now.'

She shouldn't have said that, Tess thought. But she couldn't help herself. She saw the light in Sally Styles's eyes. The fervour, the desperation for justice – or revenge.

'I'll go through all of my aunts old papers,' she said. 'See if there's anything about the Wallace committee or Tom Reece or, who was the other one, Reginald Fincher.'

'Sally, I have to warn you. This can go no further than the two of us—'

'You think I'd risk saying or doing anything that might prevent that bastard getting what he deserves? I'll speak to no one about this. I can promise you that.'

Tess thanked her and then left. Driving back she wondered if she should also have told Sally Styles to watch her back. Or was that just paranoia on her part?

After the death of Reg Fincher, Tess wasn't so sure.

FORTY-NINE

As often happens with major investigations, everything went quiet for a few days. Tess's colleagues made no progress, just generated more material. And on the other side of the fence, Nathan and Gregory's watching brief brought nothing new.

Tom Reece went to work, spent time with his family, had the occasional drink with friends. Ate out with his wife and talked politics with colleagues in the Student Union café.

Then one night Nathan got a call. There had been a break in Tom Reece's routine.

Nathan parked his car down the road and walked slowly to where Gregory had been keeping watch. Their employee who'd been on duty that evening had handed off just after he'd called Nathan.

'He let himself into the flat. Top floor, entrance via the fire escape,' Gregory told him. 'He's been in there for about an hour.'

They stood in silence, standing in deep shadow on the opposite side of the road a little way down from the flat Reece had entered. Council cuts meant that the lights went out in the side roads just after midnight and Nathan blessed the austerity measures now that made their surveillance job that bit easier.

In another fifteen minutes the lights went out and a figure passed out through the back yard and into the road. Tom Reece drove away.

They waited another fifteen minutes and then crossed the road.

It took only a brief time for Nathan to pick the lock and they stood, listening to the near silence of a sleeping house.

Naomi was still wrapped in her dressing gown but Alec had pulled on some clothes. He padded round the flat in bare feet, making tea and soothing a puzzled Napoleon who didn't expect his people to have visitors at two in the morning.

Nathan passed his smart phone to Alec who flicked through the images he had taken. The flash had washed some of the colours and the images looked pale and thin and lacking contrast but their content was clear enough.

'In a drawer in a sideboard,' Nathan said. 'There's a dozen boxes, some contain a lock of hair. There's a ring, a poetry book. Other bits and pieces. Only other thing that looked out of place was the walking stick by the front door. The door has a half dozen locks on it, but he seems to have been less inclined to add security to the fire escape. There's an old Yale and a padlock. Nothing difficult to deal with.'

'He probably didn't want to draw too much attention to the external door, Naomi guessed. You think these are souvenirs.'

'I'd guess so. I'd also guess that he never touched anything in the flat with bare hands. There was nothing there to tie it to Tom Reece.'

'So, what do we do now? There has to be a way of using this.'

'So, we could make sure the evidence was there, call your friend Tess. Anonymously, of course.'

'We could, but Tom Reece could suggest that anything of his found there was mere chance. That everything in the drawer was picked up by a collector of random objects. No doubt some of these items could be tied to his victims, others seem more random and he could spin the entire thing to make himself look like a potential victim,' Naomi said. 'I doubt there's any evidence of him renting the flat. He could argue, very logically that whoever did rent the flat was probably the killer but there was no way you could imply that was him.'

'We need to think carefully about this,' Gregory agreed. 'But at the same time, we have to share what we know. And I'm all in favour of creating a direct link.'

'By planting what?'

'That's something we need to consider,' Gregory agreed.

'In the meantime we maintain a watch on the man. And we think about our options. Putting the flat out of reach might scare him into backing off, at least. While we gather more evidence. While the police gather more evidence.'

'He may just find himself another bolt hole.'

'And we'll be watching him.'

'For how long? Surveillance takes resources. Do you have those resources?'

'We can carry on for a while,' Nathan told her.

'But not forever. There has to be a better way. Something decisive. For everyone's sake.'

'Agreed, but for tonight, that's all we can offer. Naomi, what evidence would be decisive? We need your expertise here. Yours and Alec's.'

'You're talking DNA, fingerprints, blood. Something forensic that can't have got there by another person bringing it on. Anything other than that and he could attribute it to a random act or a threat or a theft,' Alec said.

'The chances are that it's already there. If he's spent time in that room, he'll have shed hair, maybe touched something without his gloves, maybe even cut himself. There'll be something. But if it's small and insignificant . . . it has to be found. Naturally. As part of a normal investigation.'

'Well, I think we should tip off Tess's team anyway,' Gregory said. 'Put the pressure on by taking away his bolt hole and his stash. It might give them what they need to take a closer look.'

'And it might do nothing except warn Reece that someone is on to him and there are only a limited number of people who might suspect him. Who are we putting in his line of fire?'

'No one, if we're careful.'

'And if our guard drops,' Naomi argued. 'Gregory, this is a patient man. No one can stay on alert forever. We know he's a killer. Tess and her colleagues suspect as much, but it's all about the burden of proof.'

A sense of gloom settled on the four of them and Gregory and Nathan left shortly after.

'So, what now,' Alec said.

'We wait and we think and we try to work out a way of tripping him up and we hope he makes a mistake before he kills again. Just like Joe Jackson was doing.'

FIFTY

For two more days they had watched and waited. The media interest had faded a little, the numbers of journalists around the university decreasing as it became plain the investigation was stalling. The eleventh day review, usual in major cases that had stalled, was approaching fast and as Tess stood at the end of the road, looking at the solitary patrol car and the handful of news people and the forlorn flapping of crime scene tape she felt something close to despair.

The student flats had been reopened, though the floor on which Leanne had died was still unoccupied and the university was talking about taking down the internal walls and turning it into a study hall, filling it with computers and tables. Tess doubted anyone would want to live there but she guessed they might just about get away with converting it.

The police presence would remain for a few more days, but slowly even that would be tailed off and already there were more students around, returning from their flight and attempting to catch up with abandoned studies.

In time this would become an almost legendary event. Old alumni would whisper about it. 'Do you remember when that girl died?' and they would shudder and gossip about an event safely passed and feel that they had been in some way tested by it, even though most of them had stood on the periphery and never known Leanne and her friends.

Leanne's name would be forgotten by most. She would become forever just *'the girl that was murdered'*, the act overtaking the individual on the scale of importance because that was what happened. That was the way memory worked.

'It's a sad business,' a voice said and Tess turned and her stomach flipped. Beside her stood Dr Tom Reece.

He was obviously on his way to teach, he carried a leather satchel over one shoulder and an armful of books.

Tess struggled for an appropriate response, remembering almost belatedly that he should not even be aware that he was a suspect.

'It's always a terrible business,' she managed. 'When one person thinks it's all right to take the life of another.'

'And yet, it happens all the time all over the world. It's such a part of the human condition.'

'Which doesn't mean I don't want to do something about it,' Tess snapped.

'I didn't mean to upset you.' He shuffled his books and held out a hand. 'Tom Reece,' he said. 'I don't think we've actually met. I've been encouraging those affected to seek counselling. We have excellent services here on campus.'

Tess almost recoiled but she steeled herself and took the man's hand. 'So I've heard,' she said. 'In fact, I've been reading about you lately?'

'Oh, one of my books?'

'No, actually, one of Reg Fincher's journals. You were once friends, I understand.'

'Indeed we were.'

He didn't even blink, she thought.

'Reg and I knew each other for years. I heard he had a heart attack?'

'No,' she said. 'It wasn't a heart attack. It wasn't natural causes.'

'Not? – Look, you must come and have a coffee and tell me all about it.'

Tess shook her head. 'The investigation is ongoing,' she said firmly. 'And now, if you'll excuse me, I have to go. It looks like you're due somewhere too.'

'A lecture in about half an hour. Well, goodbye, Inspector. It's good to meet you.'

Tess watched him walk away. You cold bastard, she thought. You fucking cold-hearted bastard.

FIFTY-ONE

'He's shown no sign of going back to the flat,' Gregory said. 'I think we should call it in. Not wait around any longer. Fact is, Nathan, we don't have the manpower or resources to keep this up. Naomi's right. Time is foreclosing on us at a rate of bloody knots.'

Nathan nodded. 'I know,' he agreed. 'OK, how do you want to play this?'

'Anonymous call, make sure it's being acted upon, then we stand our people down. That's all we can do.'

Reluctantly, Nathan nodded. 'We'd better tell Naomi,' he said, 'and then we should ensure that Harry and Patrick are brought up to speed. I've been thinking we might warn the Goldmans?'

'How? Do you know them? From what we know they wouldn't believe anything negative about Reece.'

'I was thinking more of a quiet tip off. Josep Goldman will follow it up if he thinks there's any threat to his family.'

'Or he might just tell Reece about it.'

'Which might not be a bad thing. Reece thinks he's invulnerable. It wouldn't hurt to let him know he's not.'

'And how do we get the police to take notice?'

That question was asked again an hour later of Naomi and Alec.

'Find a way of sending the pictures you have,' Alec said. 'Make sure they go to DCI Field, DI Trinder and to Tess. I suppose you could do the same thing for Reece. His email is easy, it'll most likely be his name followed by the university suffix.'

'And just hope there's only one person with his name,' Naomi cautioned. 'Or someone will be wondering what kind of spam they're getting.'

'I don't see what options we have left. Is Tess getting anywhere?'

'Frustrated,' Naomi said shortly. 'There's all these slightly

cracked open doors and no means of shoving them the rest of
the way.'

'Then we do it,' Nathan said. 'And we see what shakes loose.
If it all comes to nothing then we have to think again. Or
consider other action.'

No one asked him what he meant. There was no need.

At five fifteen that afternoon four email messages arrived. Field
saw his at once and Tess a few minutes later. While they were
comparing notes, DI Trinder discovered that he too had been a
recipient.

'It's Fincher's walking stick,' Tess said, examining the
pictures. 'I know it is.'

Field ordered an unmarked car to the address then set about
getting a warrant to search.

Reece didn't see his message until he checked his work email
from home a couple of hours later.

He considered what to do. Tom Reece had stayed ahead of
everybody's game these past years by not acting on impulse,
by being careful and planning to the tiniest detail.

Who had sent this? Who had seen? What was going on and
had the police been informed?

He had to assume so, unless this was a prelude to blackmail.
That, he decided, would probably be the easier option to deal
with.

'We shall have to see,' he told himself. He went through to
the kitchen where his wife and daughter were chatting together
as they prepared the evening meal. 'Rhea and Steve will be
popping in,' his wife told him.

'That's good. I'd better get some beer. Steve isn't a wine
drinker.'

'Already done. You want to lay the table?'

Tom gathered up knives and forks and went through to the
dining room. He thought about what to do next and decided
that the best course of action was to do nothing. There was
nothing in the flat to tie it to Dr Tom Reece. Nothing except,
perhaps, Reg's stick.

He frowned at that one bit of vanity that had led him to take what he knew had been Fincher's favourite walking stick. One, in fact, that Tom had given to him lord alone remembered how many years ago.

But who would know that?

His mind wandered back to the conversation with DI Tess Fuller. He hadn't even known that Reg Fincher kept a journal. Was she bluffing? The conversation took on a different complexion if she already thought of Tom as a suspect in some way. Was she warning him of that? Why would she?

Was she telling him that she had him in her sights?

No one had come to speak to him about either Reg or the girl so it was more likely that he was just one of many names that might have emerged from Reg's writing.

Should he worry? What would be the point? Should he do anything? What could he do that would not be an obvious mistake. He could hardly go and look to see if the police were raiding his flat. That would be a meaningless and risky strategy and exactly the kind of forced error he had spent his life trying not to make.

No, Tom decided. There was absolutely nothing to be done.

So he dismissed the issue, packed it away for later consideration should that become a necessity and instead focussed his thoughts on preparing for an evening with his family and went back through to the kitchen to fetch the wine and salad and the basket of bread.

FIFTY-TWO

'Developments,' Tess said as she stood on Alec's doorstep the following morning. 'Can I come in?'

'Of course. We've not had breakfast yet. Can we get you something?'

'Tea and toast would be wonderful. I've been up all night. Not gone home yet.'

'Come in, sit down and tell all,' Alec said.

'What makes me suspect you might already know?' Tess said as she flopped down, gratefully, on the sofa.

'You have a suspicious mind,' Naomi said. 'What's gone on?'

Tess filled them both in on the night's events. The warrant arriving just before seven and the search beginning.

'The hair will be easy to match, I suppose. The ring matches the description of the one taken from Rebecca Arnold. There's a poetry book inscribed to Martia Richter on the flyleaf and a walking stick that I know belonged to Reg Fincher. Other stuff too . . . we're still sifting but there were twelve little boxes in that drawer. Thirteen deaths including Reg Fincher.'

'Why was the MO so different?' Naomi asked. 'It makes no sense.'

'It's a question I've been asking all along. It can't be because the killer hoped to disguise this as natural causes. A simple tox screen would have picked up the barbiturate poisoning. A favour to a friend, perhaps.'

'A friend?' Naomi asked.

'I've been reading Reg Fincher's journals. He and Reece were good friends at one time. And Reg suspected that he had killed Martia Richter. And there is nothing in the diaries that a good lawyer wouldn't throw out in ten seconds flat. The CPS would never wear it.'

She closed her eyes and rubbed them with her palms.

'Tea and toast,' Alec said and set the mug and plate down on the small table beside the sofa. 'There has to be something you can do.'

'Field is bringing him in for interview, but—'

'That's something, at least.'

'I'm beginning to understand what Joe Jackson must have felt like,' Tess said. 'We know he's as guilty as hell. But there's nothing. Nothing to make a definitive connection.'

'You have to keep pushing,' Naomi said. 'If you're right then he may well have killed a dozen times. You have to keep the pressure on.'

'Right now, I have to eat this and then go home and get some sleep,' she said. 'Field is taking it from here. Interviewing Reece and then we shall have to see. CSI are going over that flat with whatever is finer than a fine-toothed comb and we have to hope he got careless.'

'The stick?'

'He'll have handled it with gloves. There's no way of proving he was at Fincher's place. The glasses and bottle and anything he might have touched were wiped down. Unless we get incredibly lucky . . . waiting for him to get careless is like waiting for snow in August.'

FIFTY-THREE

It had been a very civilized affair. A request had been made that Dr Reece come in to answer a few questions and he had duly arrived. He and Field had chatted about the effect the murder had on the students and the campus and then Field had led the conversation around to Reg Fincher's diaries.

Tom Reece had read the extract and then laughed. 'He promised to buy me a lead feather to use as a paperweight,' he said. 'If ever he found one. This was typical of our conversations, Chief Inspector. Time was Reg and I spent a lot of time together. He was good company, the sort of man with whom you could discuss anything under the sun.'

'And when did you last see him?'

Tom Reece thought about it. 'Must have been three years ago. We spoke on the phone more recently. Maybe a half dozen times in the past few months. The last time was around the time he died. That day or the day before. I could check. He called my mobile . . .' Tom Reece produced the phone and checked back through his records. 'The day he died,' he said. 'The time before was about a month ago and before that, about the same. A month, five weeks.'

'And what did you talk about?'

'This last time or the ones before?'

'In general.'

'We might complain about the vagaries of academia. The pressures of research imperatives alongside the teaching hours. About the girls – my girls – and how they were doing. Reg would have made a very good father I think.'

'And this last time?'

'He seemed bored with retirement. A little disillusioned with it all. He had been such a busy man it must have been hard to let all that go. He told me he'd had a visit from the police. Your DI Tess Fuller, I believe. And that they'd talked about some of his old consultations. I got the impression he was pleased that anyone remembered him after all this time. Reg needed to be useful.'

'But you didn't go to see him.'

'Why would I?'

'And that night, you were?'

'At home with my family.'

'All night?'

'All night, yes. My wife will tell you.'

'And when your wife was asleep?'

'Then no doubt so was I. Look, I've come in and answered your questions, but you'll appreciate that I have to go to work. That I have a busy day ahead.'

Field had no option but to concede and let him leave.

Tom's route to work from the police station took him past the end of the road where the police had raided his flat. He slowed as he passed the junction and peered at the marked car that now stood by the back entrance to the house. A scientific support van was parked close by but he could see nothing more and drove on by, not wanting to draw attention to himself.

Truth was, he felt better now. They had nothing but the ramblings of an old man who had chosen to record a random conversation. A silliness of the sort that characterized many a conversation between old friends and particularly, Tom thought, those for whom the academic world of pure ideas was a dominant feature of their lives. He'd had similar conversations with many others in his time.

He arrived on campus and drove around for a while looking for a slot. Tom hated arriving this late in the morning; it was always a devil to park. Finally, he found a space and pulled in. If he hurried, he'd just about be in time for the usual lecture slot – though he'd called ahead and asked a colleague to fill in, just in case he didn't make it.

Walking across the campus he spotted Daniel and Patrick

heading towards class. Neither looked his way and he paused to watch them as they hurried inside, chatting to one another and then to a group of other students heading in the same direction.

Tom's eyes narrowed as he wondered how much the boys knew or had been told about him. There were too many points of connection between Patrick Jones and Naomi Blake as she had been and Tess Fuller for the boy not to be aware of something at least in connection with Tom.

He hurried on, getting to the lecture hall with minutes to spare and thanking his stand in for her time. Assuring her that everything was fine.

And everything was, Tom thought. He had to let go of the past and move on. To dissociate himself from all that had gone before and begin anew. He was no longer the man who had taken the lives of those individuals whose remains had been found in that drawer in that little flat. That man was gone and he felt renewed.

Opportunities beckoned and Tom looked forward, after a decent interval had gone, to embracing them all.

Josep Goldman examined the letter and the images he had received that morning. It was printed on a sheet of plain printer paper, common stuff that could have been bought anywhere on a standard ink jet printer. The envelope was blank, but for his name, similarly printed on the front.

He had studied it at length, letter, envelope, images, statements it contained that Tom Reece, the doctor who had treated his grandson might be implicated in murder.

His son came into the room and sat down in the chair in front of the old man's desk. 'The police questioned him this morning. No lawyer was present and no charges were brought. He's been allowed to go and he arrived at the university a few minutes ago.'

'What do your instincts tell you?' Josep asked.

'That either someone seeks to blacken the name of an honourable man or that he is already blackened and this is the only way whoever sent this has to expose him.'

'And this man, Fincher?'

'Was murdered. He had a visitor that put barbiturate in his whisky. Fincher drank a good deal of the whisky. He fell asleep and did not wake up again.'

'An act of kindness, compared to how the girl died,' Josep said. 'And who sent this letter, do you think?'

'Someone who knows you or knows about you. And someone who knows the danger to Daniel. I think that is all we should be asking.'

Josep nodded. 'I agree,' he said. 'We consider ourselves warned.'

FIFTY-FOUR

The raid on the flat a mile away from the university made it on to the lunchtime news. Field delivered a press conference, looking tired and drawn. He apologized for his appearance and explained that they had been up all night.

'Crafty bugger,' Alec commented. 'Get the media and public sympathy on your side.'

He appealed for anyone who knew the tenant of the flat or who might have witnessed him coming and going to come forward.

The bulletin ended with interviews with one of the other tenants. A young woman who was clearly horrified that someone in her building was being connected to the university killing.

'He lived upstairs from me. All this time and he was just upstairs. I can't believe it.'

'I doubt he actually *lived* upstairs,' Alec said.

'I think it's a nicety that will be lost on her,' Naomi observed. She sounded depressed.

'Something will happen,' Alec told her. 'There are enough people working on this, on both sides of the law.'

'And is that what we might have to resort to?' Naomi demanded. 'We'll have to put a contract out on him?'

'We're not exactly going to be doing that. I'm not going to say, "Gregory, go out and kill him" and neither are you. Tess and her team will get him. Just because Jackson failed doesn't mean it can't be done.'

Naomi didn't bother to reply. She hoped he was right. She hoped it would all be resolved in a way that satisfied the requirements of legality and order. She wondered what Joe Jackson would have done and decided, on balance, that she would rather not know.

Patrick wandered out of the Arts building and across the concourse. He spotted Tom Reece as he crossed in the other direction, bag over his shoulder and books under his arm.

Tom saw him at almost the same moment.

'Good afternoon, Patrick. Everything OK?'

'It's good, yes.'

'Good. I hear there's been a bit of excitement. A police raid on a flat in Kingstone Road. They reckon it belongs to the killer.'

Patrick studied him carefully wondering what response was expected of him. 'I heard about that,' he said at last. He remembered what Naomi and Gregory had been telling him about Tom Reece and he wondered how much Doctor Reece suspected he knew.

'You'll have to find another place now,' Patrick said.

'I'm not sure what you mean. Patrick, have you been listening to gossip?'

'No, I don't think so. Gossip is speculation. It's what might not be true.'

'And are you accusing me of something?'

Patrick sighed. He was getting in too deep and he knew it. He was playing a game that he recognized had no solution or conclusion. He was indulging someone who enjoyed his own power and the helplessness of others and, it belatedly occurred to him, he was prodding a killer with a stick and that was probably not the best idea he'd ever had.

'Forget it,' he said. 'No one is going to believe you did anything wrong anyway. You're home free, aren't you, whatever.'

Tom Reece smiled. 'You are an interesting young man,' he said. 'A talented young man. And I don't frighten you, do I?'

Patrick considered. 'You scare me,' he said. 'But there are other things that scare me more.'

A flicker of something that could have been anger, could have been disbelief crossed Tom's face. 'It's easy to say the words,' he said. 'Far less easy to cope with the aftermath. To know what you've brought down upon those you love.'

'Like you'll bring down on your family?' Patrick said. 'Like they'll suffer when they find out what you've done?'

Tom Reece turned on his heel and walked away. Patrick watched him go, considering the ramifications of the conversation they'd just had. He'd been foolish, he thought, or perhaps he'd just been true to himself. Patrick knew he wasn't much good at behaving in the ways convention and good sense told him he should.

In the end, he felt he had only one option left. He took out his phone and called Gregory's number.

Nathan was with him when Gregory received the call. He ended the call and relayed what Patrick had said to Nathan.

'So, that's decided then,' Nathan said.

'I don't think we should tell anyone else exactly what Reece said,' Gregory observed.

'Or what Patrick said to us. No,' Nathan agreed. 'Some things are better kept quiet, don't you think?'

Gregory nodded. 'You think Patrick can handle it?'

'Patrick is . . . flexible,' Nathan said, not sure if that was a good thing.

FIFTY-FIVE

Tess had become a regular visitor in the past couple of weeks, popping in regularly to apprise them of any progress. Increasingly, it had been a lack thereof and Naomi could hear in her voice tonight just how frustrated she was.

'This is now a massive, countrywide investigation,' she said. 'Five forces, god alone knows how many individual investigators, thirteen deaths, if you include Fincher's—'

'Any reason you wouldn't?'

'Only the feeling that if he'd spoken out he might have stopped all this.'

'I doubt that,' Naomi said. 'Who would have believed him? You said yourself that the CPS would have chucked out the journal as hearsay. What else did you have?'

'The possibility that someone would have looked deeper, joined a few of the dots, maybe just warned Reece off . . . I don't know. As it is, we've still not moved off square one in terms of proof. All we've got is more bodies, more grieving families.'

'Do the families know their people were part of a serial?'

'God, no!' Tess sounded horrified. 'Each case is being dealt with separately. The teams are cooperating but treating the reopened investigations as though they were single events. We don't want this getting out. The media would crucify every last one of us.'

'It will come out. Eventually,' Alec counselled.

'Maybe. Maybe not. I'm trying not to think of it.'

'Do you think Joe Jackson suspected the scale of this?' Naomi asked.

'How could he? But no, I get the feeling he knew it was bigger than he could see. I doubt anyone could have anticipated this.'

'Maybe you'll get part of your wish,' Naomi said. 'Maybe he will be scared off after this. Maybe this is at least an ending even if you can't arrest the man and see him tried.'

'Not much of a compensation,' Tess said wearily 'and, frankly, I don't believe he can stop. He'll come back. He'll just change his MO, hide his tracks better, pick on someone no one will miss or simply choose to dispose of the body instead of laying it out like some grotesque kind of tableau and we'll never know that he's killed again.

'People like him don't stop. Why should they when people like us do fuck all about it.'

'Something will break,' Naomi said.

'Maybe,' Tess agreed but Naomi could tell she didn't believe it.

FIFTY-SIX

For the past three weeks or so the police investigation seemed to have gone quiet and Tom Reece had stopped even thinking about what had passed. The days had reverted to familiar rhythms of teaching and consultations and precious family time and when he had driven past his old flat a few days before, it looked as though even the crime scene tape had disappeared. It would not be long, he thought, before the 'to let' signs went up.

Everything moved on; whatever the drama it eventually diminished and people forgot or at least put the memories aside.

That, Tom thought, was how the human race survived.

The university campus was a confusing, hotchpotch place. It had grown organically as old buildings had been bought up and converted and new builds physically connected existing structures but didn't always have a common entrance. It wasn't unusual, therefore, to see someone peering at a campus map with a look of utter confusion written upon their faces.

The young man stood on a street corner doing exactly that and looking up and down the road as though trying to get his bearings. Tom Reece, drawing close to where he'd parked his car, shifted the books in his arms and regarded the stranger with amused curiosity.

'Are you lost?' he asked as he estimated he must have done a dozen times that year. 'It's a confusing place and the map, frankly, isn't a lot of help.'

'No, it's not and yes I am. I'm trying to get to here.' The young man pointed at the applied arts building. 'I thought I'd be able to cut through but . . .'

Tom Reece was shaking his head. 'No, the map makes it look like you can. Actually, you have to go down that road there, to the left and then—'

But he never got past the 'then'. His attention focussed on the man with the map and the approaching assailant near silent in soft shoes, Tom Reece had been caught utterly unaware. The blow came out of nowhere, accurate and hard and Tom Reece, killer, planner, man who prided himself on the control he had over life and death, his own and others, was gone before his body hit the ground.

His killer paused for the few seconds it took for Nathan to kneel beside the body, satisfy himself that death had occurred and strip Tom Reece of his watch and wallet and mobile phone.

Then Gregory strode away, back the way he had come and Nathan took the route that Tom Reece had suggested just before he had died. Turning left towards the main campus before getting into his car and driving away.

There were no CCTV cameras in the street where Reece had parked his car. They had chosen it with care, knowing that and also taking the gamble that on Thursday afternoons, when Reece only had a late class and would therefore find it hard to park closer to his department, would choose, as he had many times before, to leave his car in this little street a few hundred yards from any major thoroughfare.

It had taken two weeks for the plan to come to fruition but now, Nathan thought as he drove away, it was done.

FIFTY-SEVEN

Patrick was at Daniel's place. They had finished the work they had assigned to that afternoon and were now channel-hopping on the television and chatting about nothing in particular but pausing when a news report featured a familiar name. They had heard the news about his death earlier that day, but it seemed there was little fresh to report.

'It's sad about Doctor Reece,' Daniel said. 'I thought he was all right really?'

Patrick nodded. 'Tough on his family,' he said. 'I saw them on the news at lunchtime.'

They had looked devastated. His widow at a press conference appealing for witnesses. Wondering who might have attacked her husband in what police were treating as a random mugging. He had been hit over the head and robbed. His wallet and mobile phone missing. His watch also gone.

'My husband was a good man, a kind man, who always put others first. His patients thought highly of him and when he moved into teaching his students loved him. Whoever did this has . . .'

She had broken down after that, turned to be comforted by the two young women who stood on either side of her.

Patrick felt sorry for the family. He knew how hard it could be to lose the people you love, which was why he could not stand by when someone threatened those that Patrick cared about. Why he had made that call to Gregory and why Gregory and Nathan had taken matters into their own hands. Patrick now had to live with the knowledge that he had, in a very direct sense, caused Tom Reece's death. Been responsible at a distance. Patrick probed at that thought. Presently, it was like a loose tooth or a missing filling; you knew you should leave it alone, but it was there and it was irresistible, even if it caused a momentary pain.

He could live with what he had done, Patrick had realized. He could not have lived with the risk of doing nothing. Of waiting for Tom Reece to decide that enough time had passed, that police interest in him had died down, that he was ready to take yet another life and that life would be someone close to Patrick Jones.

Yes, Patrick thought, he could live with his actions, accommodate them and eventually put them into a box alongside all of the other painful experiences in his life and leave them there.

Daniel's uncle came in and sat down on the sofa. 'Are you actually watching anything or just wasting the batteries?'

Daniel handed him the remote. 'Not really. There's nothing on.'

'How many channels?'

Patrick glanced at his watch. 'I'd better get home,' he said. 'You want a lift?'

'No, thanks. It's only a few minutes away.'

Ephraim nodded. 'Go carefully,' he said.

'I will.' *But I'll be fine*, Patrick thought, and the strange thing was when he glanced back at Daniel and his uncle now arguing contentedly about what to watch was that he thought that Ephraim knew that too.

EPILOGUE

Dance class night. Harry followed Naomi and Napoleon up the dusty wooden stairs and into the ballroom. Long ago this building had been a tailor's shop and this upper floor had housed the cutting rooms. Cleared out of the benches and storage it was a perfect space, with its smooth, worn wooden boards, polished by beeswax and years of leather shod feet. It echoed now to the clip of heels and the shuffle-slide of dance shoes as their classmate's practised steps.

Naomi parked Napoleon in his favourite corner and changed from her street shoes. 'How's Patrick?' she asked. 'I've not heard from him in a few days.'

'Overwhelmed with coursework and reading a stack of old books Bob lent him. He's been at Daniel's place most days between classes and when he's home he's either in his room or spread out across the living room floor. He's fine, though. I think he's finally settling into his course and he's chosen his module options for next year.'

'That's good,' said Naomi nodding. 'I worried that all this would have unsettled him.'

'I think it has,' Harry said. 'I think he's anchoring himself in the things he *can* control. His coursework, the projects Bob is giving him.'

'I heard from Nathan,' Naomi said. 'Gregory's gone off somewhere and he's back at the cottage in Yorkshire. He says he plans to redecorate, make it into a proper home.'

'Good, I think that's what our Nathan needs right now. A base, some normality, something that's his. And Alec has a new job, too. All change, it seems.'

Naomi nodded. From Monday Alec would be working three days a week for a local company that provided discreet security for high-end event planners. She couldn't quite see her husband enjoying the society weddings and stately home music events that were the company's speciality, but . . . Alec seemed happy about it all.

'And what about you?' she teased as the teacher called on them to prepare for a 'warm up waltz'. 'Harry the accountant? Any changes planned there?'

Harry laughed. 'As Patrick keeps telling me, accountancy is just my job. Harry Jones is far more than that.'

He placed a hand on Naomi's back and took her hand and Naomi surrendered to the music. The people she cared about were safe and happy and she was dancing with a much loved friend. What more could anyone possibly want?